Look for More Titles by Cassandra Chandler

Cygnian 7
NUAR
KRAL
LAR
DORN
BRON
TARN
ROM

The Department of Homeworld Security
Gray Card
Resident Alien
Business or Pleasure
Tied up in Customs
Entry Visa
Duration of Stay
Duel Citizenship
Invasive Species
Export Duty
COALITION RECKONING
Import Quarantine
Homeworld for the Holidays
Nothing to Declare
Rate of Return
Trade Secrets

—

PARANORMAL ROMANCE NOVELS

The Forbidden Knights
FORBIDDEN INSTINCT

—

PARANORMAL ROMANCE NOVELLAS

Court of the Yuletide Fae
The Yule Cat
The White Stag
The Krampus

Court of the Springtime Fae
Jack Frost
Prince Charming
The Oak King

—

SCIENCE FICTION - HORROR ROMANCE

The Blades of Janus
PACK
PROGENITOR

PARANORMAL - HORROR ROMANCE

The Summer Park Psychics
WANDERING SOUL
WHISPERING HEARTS
LINGERING TOUCH

—

COLLECTIONS

The Department of Homeworld Security
THE DEPARTMENT OF HOMEWORLD SECURITY OMNIBUS 1
THE DEPARTMENT OF HOMEWORLD SECURITY OMNIBUS 2

Courts of the Fae - Duets
WINTER AND SPRING

Wandering Soul

The Summer Park Psychics
Book One

Cassandra Chandler

Copyright Page

Wandering Soul
The Summer Park Psychics, Book One
Copyright © 2015 by Cassandra Chandler
Print ISBN: 978-1-945702-52-5
Digital ISBN: 978-1-945702-51-8

First eBook edition: July 2015
Second eBook edition: May 2017
First print edition: July 2015
Second print edition: May 2017
10 9 8 7 6

cassandra-chandler.com
P.O. Box 91
Mission, Kansas 66201

Dedication

For those who don't give up on love.

*Don't miss out on any of
the eerie romance in Summer Park.
Subscribe to Cassandra Chandler's newsletter at
cassandra-chandler.com now!*

Chapter One

Flames fell from the rafters as Dante and Edgar staggered toward the door, Mary's limp form held between them. Dante blinked his watering eyes to clear them of smoke. Each breath burned its way into his lungs. A timber crashed to the ground close enough to singe the hairs on the back of his neck.

Only a few more steps and Mary would be safe.

When they stumbled onto the cobblestone street, Dante gasped in the chill, damp air. The evening breeze cooled the left side of his face. If he could have torn off the mask that covered the right side without horrifying Edgar, he would have. The scarred skin beneath was slick with perspiration.

They did not stop until they had carried Mary to the other side of the street, where she would be safe from the horses of the Fire Brigade. Edgar took her weight so Dante could remove his jacket. Dante laid it on the pavement to provide a comfortable place for Mary to rest, then helped Edgar sit with her.

"Mary? Mary!" Edgar cradled her head in his lap, growing more hysterical by the moment.

"She needs you to be calm," Dante said, lightly touching Mary's throat. Her pulse was fast, but strong. Her breathing was not labored.

Dante rose, pulling off his vest. He ran to a nearby rain barrel and submerged the dark fabric till it was soaked through. He wrung it out and brought it back to Edgar, then knelt at Mary's side.

"Take it," Dante said. "She will be fine. You both will."

Edgar took the sodden vest and used it to dab Mary's forehead. His face was pinched with concern. Dante did not have time for further reassurances.

He slid his mother's wedding ring from his little finger. The metal was warm, gold gleaming in the light of the fire.

He passed the ring to Edgar and said, "Sell this to start your lives together. Consider it a dowry."

Edgar grabbed Dante's arm as he started to rise, but quickly pulled away. Dante did not miss how Edgar paled as he stared at Dante's mask. Giselle's lies had wormed their way even into Edgar's mind.

"You cannot be considering going back in there," Edgar said. "Leave it to the Fire Brigade."

"Klaus and Giselle are still inside."

"You would risk your life for them? They tormented you."

"That does not mean they deserve this fate." There was

no time for Dante to explain. "I do not wish to die, but I could not live with myself if I did not try to save them."

Edgar's mouth pulled down in a grim line. "What do I tell Mary?"

Apparently, Edgar held little faith that Dante would survive. Dante looked down at Mary and dusted a lock of hair from her forehead. She looked so frail and young.

With a sudden certainty, he knew he would never see her again. Even if he survived, he would not return. Mary considered Dante family. She would want them all to stay together, though she and Edgar and even their children would be judged and shunned for their association with Dante, as his own mother had been. He would not allow that to happen.

"Tell her I want her to be happy."

As Dante stood, Edgar handed back his vest.

"Take this. It might help."

Dante gratefully accepted the wet garment. "Take care of each other. Love each other."

Edgar nodded briefly, then lowered his gaze to Mary once more. Dante turned to face the theatre. The fire had spread since they escaped. Smoke rose thickly from the building, blacking out the stars. There was no time to waste.

Though the main door had not yet succumbed to the fire, it was worse than he had imagined inside. Rafters were falling throughout the building, distant crashes mingling with roaring flames that licked across the ceiling and poured down the walls.

He crouched low to keep his head beneath the smoke as he made his way to the office where Klaus and Giselle spent most of their time poring over ledgers for the failing theatre. Nearing the room, he saw Klaus lying on the floor. Dante leapt over a timber to reach his brother's still form, praying he was not too late.

"Klaus…" Dante's throat seized, the loss overwhelming him. Klaus stared at the ceiling with glassy eyes that reflected the inferno surrounding them.

Dante had only known they were brothers for a week, yet the pain of Klaus's loss brought Dante to his knees. He would never know why his brother hated him so much. Or why their father had waited until the very moment of his death to tell Dante they were kin. He would never understand why Heinrich had abandoned him. He could only guess it was due to his disfigurement.

The last moments of their father's life played through Dante's mind once more. Heinrich's revelation that he was Dante's father. The pained expression that swept across his face as he clutched his chest and fell from the catwalk where they had been speaking. The memory was so vivid, he could almost feel Heinrich's grip going lax as he tried to hold on.

His most cherished dream, being part of a family, had literally slipped through his fingers. It had driven him somewhat mad at the time. He had even thought he had seen an apparition floating near him, a glowing angel whose gaze held a sadness and longing that matched his own.

Dante gently closed Klaus's eyes. He could indulge in self-pity later, if he survived. Giselle was still in the theatre. There was a chance to save his brother's wife. Dante was not sure she would deign to let him touch her, even if it was to carry her from a burning building.

He found Giselle not far from Klaus, a timber resting on her back where it had struck her down. She seemed to sneer at Dante, her lips curled up from her teeth. The lockbox for the theatre's proceeds was clutched against her chest, scuff marks on the floor showing where she had dragged it back toward herself after falling.

How could someone be so filled with greed, even in the face of death? Dante left Giselle and the lockbox where he found them.

He headed for the side door that led to the carriage house, hoping the fire had not yet consumed that part of the building. Above the crackling flames, he could hear men shouting and the cries of frightened horses. The Fire Brigade must have arrived.

He started back the way he had come, only to find a wall of fire. The ceiling groaned in agony, moments from collapsing. Flames surrounded him. At every turn, smoke and heat assaulted his senses.

He was going to die, and for nothing. He had not been able to save Klaus or Giselle. His home was being consumed around him. Everything was turning to ash. Tiny particles made their way through the now dry vest he held to his mouth.

Dante spun in circles, looking for a way out—any way out—but there was none.

If his mother had known he would die this way, perhaps she would have given him a different name. Adding to that dark irony, the only part of his person not roasting in the blaze was the scarred skin beneath the mask covering the right half of his face. It seemed the porcelain protected him from more than the shrieks of startled people. If he had breath to spare, he might have laughed.

Until one of the rafters came crashing toward him.

He curled into a ball, though he knew it was futile. Instinct overpowered reason. Clenching his eyes shut, he waited for the impact, the searing heat and pain it was sure to bring.

Instead, he felt someone's arms wrap around him, their chest pressed against his back as if they were trying to shield him from his fate. The heat that had been baking him vanished. He opened his eyes to see the rafter resting on the floor, somehow occupying the same space as his feet. Flames whose heat he could not feel rose from the wood.

His body was glowing with a soft golden light. He had

seen this light the day Heinrich died, emanating from the apparition. Dante's benefactor gripped him more tightly, pressing her body against his.

He glanced over his shoulder to see the apparition's face. He could not quite make out her features through the light she exuded, but he knew the deep chestnut of her eyes.

He had died then, and this was the angel sent to take his soul to the afterlife. He would gladly go with her. Perhaps he would see Heinrich again.

She placed her hand on his shoulder, and said, "Trust me."

Dante did not think he could speak. Instead, he nodded. She helped him rise, then shifted to stand before him, keeping her arms around his chest the entire time. She squeezed him tightly enough that his sore lungs protested.

How could he still feel discomfort when he had moved beyond his body? But more pleasant sensations quickly followed.

She pressed her face against his chest, her cheek smooth upon his skin where his shirt had fallen open. Her hair was as golden as the light surrounding her, stray strands tickling Dante's chin. She clung to him as if her life depended upon it.

The thought unsettled him somewhat, as did her next words.

"Hold on tight."

Dante had no idea what to expect. He wrapped his arms around her, marveling at the slightness of her form. He had never dared to hold another person so closely. He felt her body tense, her grip on him tightening even more, and then a great force whipped him from his feet.

The building around them disappeared, replaced with a frozen void. The contrast from the recent heat of the theatre would have robbed him of breath, except he found that he could neither inhale nor exhale. Even the light of the angel vanished, though he still felt her arms around him. He clung to her desperately.

Light returned along with a sudden sensation of thousands of needles pricking him over his entire body. His knees folded beneath him, and he dropped to the floor.

"Dante? Dante, are you all right?"

He could not speak, his body trembling violently from the icy darkness she had pulled him through. Was this what death felt like?

"I'm so sorry," the angel said. "I didn't think it would be this bad."

She cast a dark cloak over him and joined Dante on the floor, molding her body against his back. She was warm, and as she rubbed his arms and chest, some of the chill receded. The pins-and-needles sensation slowly left his skin, and his breath began to even.

"Stay with me."

The warmth of the room seeped into him and his

tremors subsided. He felt the strength return to his limbs, yet was reluctant to rise. With how tightly the angel held him, he wondered if she would even let him should he try. He was content to further collect himself, resting in her arms.

The afterlife was not what he had expected. It looked surprisingly like a private box in a theatre. Two chairs rested in the center of the room, facing a closed curtain of rich purple. Beyond, Dante heard voices and music paired in the unmistakable cadence of a performance.

His afterlife was to be in a theatre? He had hoped for something a bit more varied from his mortal existence.

"Please stay with me," the angel said, still rubbing Dante's arms and chest.

He gently clasped the angel's wrist to halt her efforts to warm him. Though his teeth still chattered slightly, he managed, "I assure you, I have no plans to go elsewhere."

She did not speak, but wrapped her arms around his shoulders, holding him close. Dante could not stop his smile. She was certainly affectionate, this angel of his.

Though he was loathe to leave her embrace, he did not want to spend eternity on the floor. He pushed himself up so he was sitting.

Questions began queueing up in his mind. About the afterlife, the angel, even the play beyond the curtain. He felt her rise to her knees, and turned to make the first of many inquiries, but his voice caught in his throat at his first true sight of her.

Her hair was a halo of gold floating around her face in soft waves. Her eyes were a rich shade of brown and so full of warmth that the last of Dante's chill fled at once. Her lips were pink and full, slightly parted as she gazed at him. Though she no longer glowed, her flawless skin was lightly sun-kissed.

Dante could see a great deal of it. The dress she wore had no sleeves and nothing covered her chest down to the top of her bosom. The black fabric ended just above her knees and was pulled so tightly around her figure that it left little to the imagination.

Well, perhaps that was not entirely accurate. Shocking thoughts filled his mind from the way she leaned toward him, seemingly oblivious to the view that provided. She was kneeling right at his side, and for a moment, Dante wondered what would happen if he closed the small distance between them.

She would most likely scream. At the very least push him away. He snapped his gaze to hers, pushing the fevered thoughts from his mind.

"How do you feel?" she asked.

"I scarcely know where to begin."

"Are you hurt?"

While the prickling sensation that had greeted him upon his arrival had hardly been pleasant, Dante found himself feeling quite well. "I do not believe so. For the most part, I am confused."

"That's understandable," she said. "I'll explain everything as soon as I can. But right now, we have to go."

Perhaps this was merely a way station and his journey had not yet ended. It made sense to take him to a familiar place, a theatre, while shepherding him to the next stage of his existence.

The angel rose and offered him her hand. He took it in his as he stood, though he had recovered enough to stand on his own. He could not resist the chance to touch her again.

"Where is it that we are going?"

She smiled softly. "Home."

Chapter Two

Summer Park, Florida—2015

Closing night for the play had brought in a full house. The performers were pouring everything they had into their lines, the crew backstage following their prompts with laser focus. Elsa could still feel the pull of it, all those artists in the act of creation, the emotions of the audience heightening the energy in the theatre.

She had used that energy to bring Dante back with her to her time. She couldn't believe it had worked, even with him standing right in front of her.

She kept a tight grip on his hand, his skin rough from crafting sets for the theatre. He'd been cold when he first arrived, but now she could feel the warmth of his body. Elsa leaned into it, staring up at him.

His eyes were a shade of hazel she'd never encountered before, the color seeming to shift as she watched. She could only see one of his eyebrows, gracefully echoing the shape of his eyes. His face was a perfect balance of strong lines and elegant angles. There was a slight cleft in his chin, and his nose was straight, neatly bisected by the porcelain mask that covered the right side of his face.

One of the actors on stage shouted a line loudly enough to snap Elsa out of her reverie. The play would be over soon, and they needed to leave before the audience filled the hallways of the theatre.

Elsa had consulted on the modern adaptation of *The Phantom of the Opera* now being performed outside her private box. If anyone saw her walking out of the theatre with a man dressed as a more classic version of the character, they would have questions she didn't want to answer.

She glanced at the door, and a flash of gold shining against the dark charcoal of the carpet caught her eye. She released Dante's hand and stooped down to pick up her ring. Well, not really *her* ring.

"This is yours." She placed the ring in Dante's palm.

"My mother's ring. How is it that you possess this?"

"It's a very long story, and we really do need to leave."

Elsa walked to the door and opened it a crack. She peered down the hallway in both directions. It was empty. When she turned back to him, he was sliding his mother's ring onto his pinky finger.

From Dante's perspective, he'd only been without the ring for a few minutes. Elsa had been wearing it for years.

Ironically, she, the time traveler, didn't have time to think about that at the moment. She bent down again to pick up the velvet cloak pooled at his feet. Standing on her tiptoes, she threw it around his shoulders, then fastened it at his neck.

The cloak was much shorter on him, but it would cover his face well enough. It was the mask she needed to hide. He frowned as she lifted the hood into place, tilting his head away from her so his face was even more hidden.

"People will ask questions if they see your mask," she said, resting her hands on his shoulders for a moment. They were firm and warm, even through the layers of fabric. She pulled her hands away before she did something stupid, like lean in and kiss him. "I hope you understand."

"I understand all too well."

She threaded her arm through his elbow, then led him from the box and through the hallways of the theatre. She kept her pace as brisk as she could without being too conspicuous, hoping he wouldn't see anything too modern.

Elsa had funded the production in part so she had a say in what theatre they used. She had selected this one for its Victorian-inspired décor. Dark carpeting covered the floor, and ornate moldings offset floral designs painted on the walls. The light fixtures were made to look like candles, even down to the flame-shaped light bulbs.

They walked down the stairs to the lobby without encountering anyone. She let out a breath of relief and guided Dante toward the side exit.

The night air was muggy after the chill of the air-conditioning inside. A trash bin in the alley added a faint smell of garbage to the humidity. It wasn't the best first impression for Dante of the modern world, but the front exit wasn't an option. She couldn't risk him seeing cars driving by. She had things to explain first.

They walked around to the back of the theatre, where she had instructed the driver she'd hired for the night to wait. He was standing dutifully by the rear door of the limo, which he opened when he saw them.

She nodded at the driver, then slid into the back seat, pulling Dante in after her. Once the door was closed, she gave Dante the back bench seat to himself and took the one closest to the driver. She wanted to be sure the partition separating the front and back compartments of the limo remained closed. With what she and Dante had to discuss, Elsa didn't want anyone listening in.

"This is a carriage," he said.

"Yes. I'm a little surprised you realized that."

"It has a seating compartment set on four wheels, though they appear quite thick and heavy. I confess it more closely resembles a train car than any carriage I have seen, but there are no tracks for it to ride upon."

She had planned to expose him to the modern world slowly, to give him time to adjust. She knew he had a keen intellect, but she hadn't known how observant he was.

They pulled away from the curb and he placed his hands on either side of the seat. Elsa had traveled to enough times before cars were invented to know it was second nature for those used to the jostling rides of a horse-drawn carriage. In the dim light, she could see Dante's head move from side to side as he looked around the compartment.

"A horseless carriage," he said.

"Another astute observation."

"Not so. It is apparent that we are moving, yet the coachman had not time to harness horses to the carriage. Also, there were no horses in the alley."

She smiled, wishing she could see Dante's expression. She could almost hear the hint of a smile in his voice, as if he was joking with her.

"Have you seen a horseless carriage before?"

"Designs only. But promising work on many aspects of the invention is under way in several countries. I am sure we are on the brink of a great advancement. That is to say, those we have left behind."

Elsa wasn't sure what he meant by that. Was it possible he had already figured out that she had brought him to another time?

She was counting on him being able to adapt, but this seemed a little fast. Then again, she'd only really observed Dante during the biggest ups and downs of his life, moments when his emotions had been strong enough to leave an imprint on the ring he wore.

Even after a century had passed, she felt the energy of

those moments stirring in his ring when she bought it. She had been able to use their pull to travel back in time and witness his life.

As powerful as that pull had always been, it was nothing compared to being in Dante's actual physical presence. His touch was intoxicating. Addictive.

Elsa needed to keep her distance. She was supposed to be helping him. Dante would be relying on her to guide him through his new life, his new world. It was her job to protect him, and the weight of that responsibility was only just settling on her shoulders.

For a floundering moment, she wondered if she was completely out of her depth.

"I do not know whether to feel obliged to you or fearful," he said.

"I prefer neither. I'm here to help you, Dante."

"You know my name. I am afraid you have me at a disadvantage."

"I'm Elsa. Elsa Sinclair."

"Dante Lucerne," he said.

"I know."

After a brief silence, he said, "May I ask you some questions, Miss Sinclair?"

"Please, call me Elsa."

"Very well, Elsa."

Hearing him say her name sent a shiver down her spine. She rubbed her arms to tame the goose bumps running wild along her skin.

"Please, take this." He took off the cloak and handed it to her.

"Thanks." She folded the cloak on her lap.

She could see him better now, though not as well as she would like. He was staring at her, and her stomach started doing flip-flops. Riding backward in the limo turned the sensation from pleasant to nauseating. At this rate, she'd wind up getting sick on the side of the road.

"I'm sorry, I can't ride backward like this."

She crossed to the other side of the limo, sitting as close to the window opposite him as she could. She put the cloak on the seat between them as a reminder to stop touching him. She wanted to reassure herself that he was okay, that he was really here with her.

"Are you all right?" he asked.

"It's just a little motion sickness."

"I can hardly feel that we are moving, yet we seem to be passing the lamps at quite a speed."

He was reacting well to the things he'd already figured out. Elsa hoped he would react as well to what she was about to tell him next. It was one thing to make the leap from horse-drawn carriages to cars. It was quite another to hear someone talk about time travel.

The nausea returned full-force as she recalled the last time she'd told someone about her ability. She shoved the memory ruthlessly into the back of her mind. This wouldn't end that way. Dante would understand.

She let herself put her hand on his arm, drawing his attention from the view out the window. His skin was so warm.

"I understand this is confusing. Please trust me. I think eventually you'll be very happy here. It just might take some getting used to."

"I imagine so," he said.

"I have something that will help."

Elsa glanced around the seat, searching for the book she'd brought along on the development of automobiles. Since they'd be starting off in a car and he had seen carriages, she thought it was a good way to ease him into believing that she'd taken him forward in time.

The limo's interior was too dark to see properly, so she reached up and switched on the overhead light. Electricity might have been a better place to start.

"What on earth is this?" Dante reached up and cautiously pressed his fingers against the glass.

Elsa was stunned for a moment by the wonder unfolding on his face. The corners of his lips lifted slightly in an almost-smile. He gently traced his long fingers over the surface of the light fixture.

When he turned back to her, his eyes were a roiling blue-green. Elsa's heart seemed to stop. She couldn't catch her breath.

His smile faded, and Dante sat back against his seat,

turning his face away from her. "I apologize. I did not mean to startle you. Perhaps you should extinguish the light."

"I wasn't startled."

"There is no need to preserve my feelings in this matter." The smile he gave her then was rueful. "I assure you, I am quite accustomed to this reaction."

"What reaction?"

"I know that my appearance is…troublesome."

Only in that it made Elsa want to do things that she really shouldn't be thinking about. She couldn't suppress a short laugh.

Dante angled his face a bit toward her, watching her from the corner of his eye. If only he knew how ridiculous that was.

"There is nothing about you that troubles me." Except perhaps that he felt the need to wear his mask at all.

His gaze softened, but he didn't say anything in response. She knew better than to push on this issue so soon. In his time, the mask had been necessary. Elsa would do everything she could to make him feel comfortable enough to show his face to the world. She would start by taking his mind off the matter.

"And the answer to your question is, that is an incandescent light bulb." She dropped her voice to a whisper, remembering the driver. The barrier between the front and back of the limo might be closed, but Elsa was still paranoid. She leaned closer to Dante. "I think those were pretty close to development in 1881 as well, but we'll cover those later."

She saw the book she'd been looking for tucked between the seat and the side of the limo next to him, and reached across to grab it. At that moment, the limo hit a pothole, throwing her off-balance. She might have fallen off the seat, but Dante reached out and grabbed her, pulling her against him.

Elsa's hands landed on his broad shoulders, her breasts pressed against his chest. She thought that time might have stopped entirely, Dante was holding so still. He wasn't even breathing.

He was warm, or maybe she was cold. She couldn't tell. All Elsa knew was that she wanted to be closer, wanted more of them to touch. Parts of her body that she had neglected for years responded to him.

Finally, he asked, "Are you all right?"

"Yes, of course," she said, laughing a little as she pried herself off of him. "Sorry about that. I was just trying to reach this."

She stretched past him and picked up the book. Her heart was still thundering from the contact. It was making her lightheaded.

"Please, look through this." She handed him the book, then leaned back in her seat.

"Carriage schematics?" he asked, leafing through the

first pages.

"Just keep going."

Dante skimmed through page after page. "This is quite extraordinary," he said. The more he read, the more creases appeared in his brow. He also began to frown. Elsa hadn't expected that.

"What is it?"

"This is possible," he said.

"Absolutely."

"That is not what I mean."

He closed the book and set it on top of the cloak, his gaze roving over the limo's interior. His hands followed, touching the glass of the windows, the stitching of the seats, the hard plastics and treated wood. He even lifted Elsa's cloak, rubbing the fabric between his thumb and forefinger.

"Talk to me. What's bothering you?"

"The things in this book, though extremely advanced, are within the realm of possibility. There is a logical progression, an evolution of technology, as it were, that cannot be denied. But it is impossible that I should be witnessing them."

"Not everything that is possible can be explained." Her heart picked up again and, for a change, it wasn't because of his closeness.

Dante stared at her for a very long time. She could practically see the thoughts churning in his mind like the waters of a stormy sea.

"Miss Sinclair," he said. "Where exactly am I?"

Elsa glanced to the front of the limo to make sure the partition was still closed. It did little to reassure her. She scooted closer to him and leaned in close.

"You're in America," she said, her voice as low as she could manage. That part wasn't so hard to share. "Florida, precisely."

"Florida…"

Dante looked out the window, though at this time of night, nothing was visible except a dark horizon and stars overhead muted by the tinted glass. Elsa could see his mask reflected back at her. It was surreal.

She had been working for years on bringing him to her time and still had trouble believing he was here. How hard must it be for Dante?

He picked up the book, holding it up as he faced her again. "That does not explain this."

Elsa took the book from him and opened it to the imprint page. She traced down the printing information until she reached the copyright date. Her hands trembled as she lifted it for Dante to see.

It was right there for him in black and white, but apparently he needed to hear the words to believe them. In a hushed voice, he said, "Copyright 2015."

Chapter Three

"You cannot be suggesting that the year is two thousand and fifteen."

Dante might have laughed, if not for the way Elsa clutched his arm, her gaze darting to the front of the cabin. She shifted toward him in her seat, till there was no space left between them. His breath quickened as he felt the softness of her breast pressing against his arm.

"Please keep your voice down," she whispered in his ear. Her entire body trembled.

He lowered his voice to match hers. "Are we in danger?"

She stared at the front of the cabin, though all he saw was a solid wall. A solid wall in a vehicle more advanced than any from his time. Was he actually considering that what she said might be true?

"Not exactly," she said. "But it's important that no one finds out about where you're from. I mean, *when* you're from."

He found neither her tone nor her demeanor reassuring. "I take it that I am not supposed to be here?"

"You *are* supposed to be here, Dante." She turned to

him at last, all traces of her uncertainty vanishing. She took his hand in hers once more. "I wouldn't have been able to bring you forward if it wasn't meant to be."

The tremor in her slight frame ceased, as if punctuating her words. Dante was certain she absolutely believed this to be true. But could he believe the rest of it?

His mind was still full of the images from the book she had shown him. Automobiles of all manner were described and pictured within, a variety so great and complex, it was staggering in its implications. If he dared to trust its contents, cars were common. Even a century seemed not long enough for such advancements to have taken place.

If he believed what the book contained, what his own senses told him, what of the rest of it? It would mean that Elsa had somehow transported him through time. She had pulled him from a fire that would certainly have killed him and carried him through that icy void of darkness. And now they were in America and the year was two thousand and fifteen.

"This is a bit difficult to believe."

Elsa let out a short laugh. "I'm having a little trouble with it, myself. I wasn't sure I'd be able to get you here. I'm so glad it worked."

"Given the alternative, I find myself in agreement."

She paled and turned her face away from him. "I couldn't..." Her voice came out low and stilted. "I couldn't let you die like that."

"I was not the only one who perished in the fire."

"You were the only one I could save. I'm sorry I couldn't do more. I'm sorry about the others."

Dante's throat constricted as he thought of Klaus and Heinrich, even Giselle. He turned his face so that his mask was toward Elsa and closed his eyes, shielding him from her view while he collected himself. He felt her touch his shoulder, her skin cold through the thin fabric of his shirt.

She slid her hand behind his back and pulled him closer. Though it seemed he was taking liberties, he could not resist her offer of comfort. He wrapped his arms around her, resting his head in the nape of her neck.

"This is a new start for you. A new world. I'm right here with you and will help you through it."

A new world. Yet he was still himself. Being in a different time did not alter his appearance. He doubted people had changed so much.

And yet, there was Elsa. He had yet to see fear or revulsion or pity in her gaze when she looked upon him. She did not shun his touch or avoid touching him, as if she thought his scars were catching.

"I am forever in your debt," Dante said.

Apparently, that was not the best turn of phrase. Elsa stiffened, slowly releasing her hold on Dante as she slid toward the other side of the carriage. She smiled politely, but it held sadness instead of warmth. Somehow, his words had pushed her away.

"You aren't in my debt. You never will be."

"I apologize. I merely meant—"

"It's okay. I just don't want you to feel like you owe me anything." Elsa brushed her fingers against the ceiling of the compartment, extinguishing the light.

How could he not feel indebted to her after she had saved his life? And she seemed to be taking a great risk by bringing him to her time. The journey had been harrowing enough for Dante. He could not imagine it had been any more pleasant for Elsa.

"We're here." She lifted the cloak and turned to him. "I hate to ask this of you, but could you wear this until we're inside?"

"Of course." He fastened the cloak around his neck, then pulled up the hood. She handed him the book, chewing fretfully on her lower lip as she stared past him out the window.

The carriage—*automobile*—turned onto a narrow lane lined with palms. The trees' dark silhouettes blotted out the stars in fingerlike patterns that spread only from the very tops of their trunks. Dante felt the vehicle stop, and glanced through the window to see a large mansion.

Bright lights flowed out from the latticed windows, painting stripes of green on the otherwise darkened lawn. The walls were stone, the design reminiscent of many buildings Dante had seen in London in his time. He was a bit disappointed at the familiarity of its appearance.

The coachman—no, driver—came around to open the door and stepped aside as Dante exited the automobile. Dante turned back to help Elsa emerge into the balmy night. She thanked the driver, then threaded her arm through Dante's as they walked the stone path to her doorstep.

She opened the door and ushered Dante into a large foyer. Two rooms flanked them—a dining room and a library, from what he could see. A large staircase wrapped around the wall to their left, ending in a landing on the next floor.

A long hallway straight ahead ended in a dark room, its black and white tile flooring only visible from the light of a beautiful crystal chandelier above. Dante could hear the sound of running water and dishes banging against the sides of a sink from the unlit room.

"Winston," Elsa hissed.

Dante was uncertain who Winston might be, but from Elsa's deportment, he assumed the man was in some sort of trouble.

She shook her head and sighed, then turned to Dante. "I'll take your cloak."

Before he could act, she reached up and unfastened the cloak. Her hands slid along his arms, following the descent of the fabric. Having more of his wits about him, and with the benefit of the bright lights above, the effect of her proximity was much more immediate.

His heart quickened, his skin tingling where her hands had paused just above his wrists. He could well imagine those delicate hands removing more of his clothing in a similar fashion. Dante tried to think of something else, anything besides the sweet smell of roses that surrounded her.

He cleared his throat, and said, "Thank you."

Elsa stared up at him, her eyes wide as if she was feeling something akin to wonder. His imagination must be running wild again, projecting his own emotions onto her.

Her lips parted slightly, and he had a strange impulse to run his thumb along their satin surface. Her chest stilled as his gaze strayed to her décolletage. The black fabric of her dress accentuated the golden tint of her skin, which gleamed with a pearl-like cast. Dante was certain if he kissed her neck, she would taste of honey.

She finally stepped back, folding the cloak over her arm. "I should hang this up."

A flush rose to his cheeks. At least she could only perceive half of it. He willed his body back under control, holding the book about automobiles before him to hide his state. Dante was relieved when she walked away, and used the opportunity to take a deep breath and calm himself.

Where were these errant thoughts coming from? He had long since given up on having a physical relationship with a woman. But Elsa was awakening longings and desires he had no right to direct toward her.

"Winston!"

Elsa called out sharply enough that Dante started. There was a commanding edge to her tone that he had not heard before. She hung the cloak in a closet near the front door, then returned across the foyer, her heels clicking on the floor.

A man stooped with age appeared in the darkened doorway. "I thought I heard you come in."

Elsa crossed her arms and let out a sigh. Winston shuffled toward them, one hand tracing the wood paneling along the stairs.

"Now, don't be starting with that." A thick cockney accent slurred his words. "If I decide to wait up for you to be home safe, that's my business."

"And if you're so tired in the morning that you burn the toast, that's mine." There remained an edge to her tone, but she was smiling playfully now.

"I can always make more toast, and the squirrels won't fault me for the mistake."

She laughed and stepped forward, uncrossing her arms so she could hug the old man. If he was a servant, she was certainly not treating him as such. She kissed his cheek, bringing a rosy flush to Winston's face.

"I suppose you've forgiven me, then?" He patted her arms and laughed as well. "But what's this? Smells like you stood too close to a campfire." He started sniffing the air, then said, "Elsa, what on earth have you brought home with you?"

"Not what, Winston. *Who.*"

Winston stared blankly at the door, seeming to look right through Dante. Only then did Dante realize that Winston's pale gray eyes had the unfocused stare of the blind.

"I believe I am the one who requires forgiveness," Dante said. "I am in a bit of disarray."

Winston stiffened when Dante spoke, his arm tightening around Elsa.

"Winston, this is Dante. He's the guest we've been preparing for."

"Oh. Well, then." Winston scowled in Dante's direction. "You've got an accent on you there. I can't quite place it."

"Dante was born in London and raised abroad. And that is the end of the interrogation for tonight." She kissed Winston's cheek again, softening the scowl on his face.

Apparently it was not merely with Dante that Elsa was affectionate. He struggled to suppress a strange surge of jealousy.

She had rescued Dante in London, but how did she know of his other travels? He added that to the list of questions he must eventually ask.

"We'll just get cleaned up and then go to bed," Elsa said. "I mean, he'll be in his room, of course."

She corrected herself so quickly that she stumbled over

the words. Her gaze darted toward Dante briefly, and her face turned bright red, the flush spreading down her neck and chest.

Winston's mouth twitched into a grin. It must be for Winston's benefit that she had reacted that way. Winston could not see Dante, and might consider the worst—Elsa bringing a man home in the middle of the night.

Winston patted her arm. "I'll bring up a pot of chamomile tea after a bit."

"Only if it's no trouble," she said.

"How's this trouble? It's my job." Winston laughed and waved his hand behind him as he headed down the hall, leaving them alone once more.

Elsa's smile was more subdued when she turned back to Dante. It was just as riveting.

"Come on. I'll show you your room."

She led him to the stairs, the light gleaming off her bare shoulders where her hair fell aside. He was too distracted to notice the flash of black fur that darted in front of him until the very last minute.

"Leo!" Elsa stopped abruptly.

Dante was only able to avoid stepping on it by throwing off his own footing. The book went tumbling onto the stairs.

Elsa ducked beneath his arm, catching enough of his weight that he did not fall. His shirt was still open more than was proper, and her palm landed directly upon his chest. The chill of her skin took his breath away.

"You are so cold."

"Am I? I didn't notice."

Dante grasped her hand, lifting it to his lips to breathe upon. After a moment, he pressed it back against his chest to warm it further. He watched her reaction carefully, looking for signs of revulsion. Instead, her eyes darkened like smoldering embers.

Once more, his body responded to her closeness, only this time, he did not know if he had the strength to pull himself away.

What would she do if he lowered his lips to hers? If he tilted his face to the right, she would not even have to gaze upon his mask.

His mask.

Picturing it felt like being doused in an icy stream. What was he thinking? She was beautiful, intelligent, kind and obviously well off. All of time was at her disposal. She could have her pick of lovers. Why would she ever choose him?

Dante stepped away, releasing his hold on Elsa's hand. A delicate crease appeared between her brows, but only for a moment.

"There is a cat in your house," Dante said.

"Yes. That's Leonardo."

She clicked her fingers at the sleek black cat licking its paw at the top of the stairs. It looked up as she said its name, sitting straight and gazing down upon them. Its eyelids lowered after a moment, and the little creature sighed as if they were beneath its notice.

"Leonardo, mind your manners." Elsa walked up the stairs and picked up the cat, then began scratching under its chin and along its neck. It purred loudly as she cuddled it to her chest. "You'll have to forgive Leonardo. He likes to try to trip people. Winston treats it like some kind of game, but I worry."

Dante thought of suggesting she keep the cat outside, but something in the way she was holding it made him think better of that. He stooped to pick up the book he had dropped. As he rose, he inspected it for damage and was relieved to find none. He followed Elsa up the stairs, watching her carry Leonardo along with her as she led Dante down a hallway that continued from the landing.

"I'll be close in case you need anything." She stopped at the first door on their right. It was carved of a deep walnut that matched the rest of the house. "My room is right here."

She gestured to the partly open door with the cat. Leonardo twisted in her grasp, then slipped to the floor. Dante watched it dart inside the room, his curiosity roused at the thought of seeing where Elsa slept.

The light that spilled forth from the hall revealed a canopy bed set against the far wall, covered with pale golden fabrics. A row of windows with gauzelike curtains stood behind it. Stacks of books occupied every surface, even creeping along the floor around the bed.

"I like to read too," Elsa said.

The way she shrugged her shoulder brought Dante's attention back to her sleeveless dress. He looked away quickly to quell any fantasies the sight might provoke, but his gaze landed upon her bed. The golden sheets would accent her skin perfectly.

He turned around, hoping that would be more effective. It seemed since this flame had been lit, it was difficult to control.

"You're just next door." She took a few steps farther down the hall before stopping in front of another intricately carved door.

This was an even better distraction. She opened the door, then reached into the room to turn on a light. She stepped aside so he could enter first. Dante wondered what sort of new wonders awaited him.

He was glad his back was to her, so she could not see the shock that was no doubt on his face as he peered inside.

A dark four-poster bed took up most of the far wall, which was covered by heavy curtains. He could only surmise there were windows behind them, though they were completely concealed by the thick red fabric. The bed was similarly smothered in red and gold.

Dante had used those colors in his room in the

basement of Heinrich's theatre, taking worn curtains from the stage to make his bedding and add some semblance of warmth to the cold stone walls. The place had still felt like a dungeon, though it was better than trying to live in the rooms above with the others.

He pulled himself from his morose thoughts and surveyed the rest of the room. There was a settee to his right, along with a heavy wooden desk. Intricate scrollwork adorned its sides, as well as the chair before it. An armoire in a matching style dominated the left wall, dwarfing the open door that led to a dark room beyond.

He stepped over the threshold, feeling like a ghost. If anything, the furnishings were more old-fashioned than those to which he was accustomed. He turned to see a dormant fireplace set in a wall of bookshelves, completely filled with volumes of a similar design to the one in his hand.

Dante swallowed hard and spun in a slow circle. His skin prickled from the familiar nuances of the place. If he did not know better, he would have thought that all of what had come before was a dream, and he had simply found his way to some aristocrat's home.

The thought made him shiver. He did not want to be reminded of where he had come from. He wanted a fresh start. Dante could well imagine waking in that bed, the night pressing on his confused mind and planting doubts of his sanity.

Time travel? A beautiful woman whose touch stoked desire deeper than any he had ever imagined? It was difficult enough for him to believe while fully awake.

He would simply need to avoid sleep...

"What do you think?" Elsa asked, a vulnerable cast to her smile.

"It is not what I expected."

"What did you expect?"

Dante searched his mind for something that would not make him seem ungrateful. He truly appreciated everything she had done, despite the eerie ambiance of the room. He noticed a small carved ship sitting atop the desk near the settee, and said the first thing that came to mind.

"Hammocks."

"Hammocks?"

"They are quite efficient, really. I had thought perhaps their use would have expanded over time." He smiled at her, hoping she would realize he was making light of his circumstance.

Elsa gave him a puzzled grin, but she laughed, the sound like music. "We can see about installing some. But I wanted it to feel like home for you, at least at first. To help you adjust."

"I appreciate you going to such efforts."

"This is the best part." She took the book from him and placed it in the single empty spot on the bookshelf. Her gaze roved over the orderly rows. When she found what she was looking for, she pulled out another volume. "Here's a good place to start."

She handed him the book, the broadest smile yet gracing her lips. He reluctantly looked at the cover of the book, wanting to stare at that smile until he could call it to mind at will in perfect detail.

On the solid green cover of the book, gold letters were etched on a dark brown square.

"This is a book about plumbing." Dante read the title again. He could hardly think she believed he would be more interested in this than her smile.

"That is book one of a history of plumbing all the way up to the present. I commissioned this encyclopedia set for you." She gestured at the wall once more, then stared at the books with reverence. "By the time you've read all of these, you should understand more than most people about modern technology, including me."

"You commissioned them?"

She turned back to him with that radiant smile. "I knew you'd have questions that I wouldn't be able to answer. And plumbing is a good place to start, since you'll probably be wanting a shower soon."

He looked down at his shirt, stained with his sweat and soot from the fire. He had not realized how dreadful his appearance was until that moment.

"Of course. I apologize."

"For what?" Elsa's smile dimmed and she shook her

head, as if she could not see anything wrong with him.

Dante's heart began pounding. That was what truly mesmerized him about this woman, even more than what she could do, what she had done for him. From the very beginning, she had looked upon Dante in the same manner that she might any other man. Elsa barely even seemed to notice his mask.

"Is something wrong, Dante?"

"No." He smiled at her and shook his head. "Nothing is wrong at all."

Chapter Four

After showing Dante around his bathroom, Elsa indulged in a shower of her own. Spanish mosaics in vibrant reds, blues and yellows brightened the walls of the room. Beneath a wide window in an alcove, a huge bathtub beckoned, but she could feel the exhaustion of her journey catching up with her.

She still lingered for a while, sitting on the edge of the tub and enjoying the fresh scent of roses from her soaps as she dried her hair. She knew her obsession with decadent bathrooms was strange, but hiding in them so often as a child had left its mark on her.

She shook her head, refusing to let bad memories intrude on this space. She had much better things to think about. Like Dante.

He was in her time, in her home. He was right next door.

Elsa couldn't believe her plan had worked. The play was the perfect boost to bring Dante back with her. She had traveled through time using art before, but never as it was being made, using the very moment the powerful emotions that charged the piece were being experienced.

She had never felt anything like it.

Everything was coming together just as she'd hoped. Well, except that she couldn't seem to keep her hands off of him. And it was only getting worse.

While she showered, she kept thinking of Dante doing the same. She shivered again at the thought of his pale skin slick with soap, imagining his hands roving over his body, following rivulets of hot water.

"What is wrong with me?" she muttered, drying her hair more vigorously as she stood and walked to her bedroom.

It made sense that she'd be fantasizing about the naked man in the shower next door, since her baths were the most sensual thing she'd experienced in the past three years. Aside from writing her novels.

The mental list of things she needed to tell Dante grew. She was writing a novel about him. For him, really. Before she told him that, she needed to work up the courage to explain the stories that had stemmed from his life, even though they bore little resemblance to it.

Elsa threw on the first pajamas her fingers encountered in the drawer of her armoire—a matching tank top and pants in a soft shade of pink—then ruffled her hair once more with the towel. The room was starting to spin a little, and Elsa knew she didn't have long before she would have to pay the price of ferrying Dante to her time. She still folded the towel before hanging it up to dry on the rack in her bathroom.

When she brought back Leonardo, she had passed out for a few hours. She hadn't meant to bring the cat with her, but when he could somehow see her and had followed her into a busy street, she'd grabbed him out of the way of a horse to keep him from being trampled. She hadn't been thinking at the moment, just reacting. And then they were both back in her time, sitting in front of the painting she had used to travel.

That painting only held one moment with enough emotional resonance for Elsa to connect with. Dante's ring, on the other hand, held dozens of moments she'd been able to view. And that was after the many times she had visited his mother, which was yet another awkward thing Elsa had to tell him.

If she hadn't stumbled onto the first of his mother's paintings, Elsa wouldn't have discovered Dante. She wouldn't have been able to save him from the fire or bring him to her time. And she was certain she was meant to bring him forward.

Like Leonardo, Dante had seen her while she was traveling. It was the day his father, Heinrich, had died. Her heart had nearly broken at how distraught Dante was, and she had longed to be able to do something to help. When his gaze locked on hers, she knew she could.

Passing out for a while was nothing. Elsa would have done anything to save him. She just needed to get him settled before it happened. She leaned against the bathroom door until the dizziness subsided, then went to his room.

Winston was there when she arrived, setting up tea and some cookies at the small table near the fireplace. Leonardo had followed him in and was curled on the settee, flicking his tail back and forth.

"Thanks for the tea, Winston." She wrapped one arm around him and hugged him tight.

"You're quite welcome." He leaned into her a bit. "What's this? You're cold as ice."

Elsa ran her hands up and down her arms. Now that he mentioned it, she was a bit cold. Pushing the thought away, she said, "My hair is wet."

"That'll cool you off. A spot of tea will fix you right up, as soon as that friend of yours is ready to join you."

"He's a good man, Winston. Give him a chance."

Winston made a harrumphing noise and started pouring the tea.

Elsa realized she hadn't shown Dante his wardrobe. Most of the clothes inside the armoire were in the style of his time, again, to help him gradually adjust. But she'd bought him some comfortable pajama pants, not knowing what he usually slept in.

Her imagination started up again, and she pushed away the thought of Dante naked between his sheets. She needed to rein this in. She also needed to leave before he came out of the bathroom.

The dizziness returned with a vengeance, the walls spinning around her like she was at the center of a carousel. Elsa gripped the door to the armoire until the room stopped moving.

Only a little longer, and Dante would be safely in bed. Then she could collapse in hers. She could make it.

She grabbed a pair of pajama bottoms from the armoire's drawer and tossed them on the bed where he would see them. She could wait in the hall until he was dressed, and then…

Then the world tilted and the floor rushed up at her. She heard Winston yelling her name as if he was far away.

This was not part of the plan. Dante needed her. There were still things she had to tell him. Elsa felt as if she was swimming against a strong current. She slipped further away from Winston's voice, sinking into darkness.

Chapter Five

Dante had never been so clean in his life. His shower was nothing less than luxurious. Elsa had left typeset notes on thin rectangular tiles placed throughout the bathroom explaining the purpose and use of the various items in amusing detail.

The tiles themselves were even more intriguing than their content. They looked like small pieces of paper that had been encased in a smooth, transparent material that left them impervious to water. He would certainly ask her about them as soon as he had a chance.

His mask rested on the back of the sink. Dante picked it up and turned it over in his hands, not wanting to put it on quite yet. He wasn't sure why. The lighting in the room was bright, much brighter than he was used to. He set down his mask and placed his hands on either side of the cool surface of the sink.

Morbid curiosity. That was all this was. He should not indulge it. And yet, he knew he would.

Dante ran his hand over the fogged surface of the mirror and looked at himself.

If anything, the lighting made the scars look worse. He

could see each bright red welt rising from the surface of his skin in greater detail, the shadows highlighting his disfigurement like some sadistic bas-relief. His mother had never told him what happened, though she bore similar marks on her hands.

Why had Elsa brought him here? What had she seen in him that could possibly overpower this?

He would wake up soon, and find this all to have been a dream. Or perhaps his mind had finally snapped from the persecution and oppressive loneliness he suffered. He wasn't sure which was the better alternative. At least if he was mad, he could stay in this wonderful delusion.

"Help! Help!"

He jumped at the sound of Winston's frantic voice. Dante ran to the door and flung it open to find the old man huddled on the floor over Elsa's prone form. There was a pair of pants at the foot of the bed, barely more than leggings, but Dante pulled them on as he approached.

"What happened?"

"I don't know! One minute we were talking, then I heard her sort of sigh and then thump to the floor. I was afraid to move her. I can't see how bad it is."

"Calm yourself," Dante said.

"Calm nothing! How is she? Is she hurt?"

Dante turned his attention to Elsa. She was pale, her lips bloodless and her brow furrowed. Her breathing was quick and labored. He gently touched her shoulder. Her skin was much cooler than it had been earlier in the evening. He could not rouse her.

Dante's heart seemed to wish to crawl out of his body, but his throat would not accommodate it.

"It's bad, isn't it?" Winston said.

"I do not know. Could it be a fainting spell?"

"Fainting spell?" Winston sputtered. "I'll give you a fainting spell. She's cold as ice. Come on. Let's get her to the bed."

Winston rose, leaving Dante to carry Elsa. He slid his arms beneath her and lifted her from the floor, his heart still in his throat. Winston hobbled to the bed, then turned down the covers.

As Dante set Elsa upon the bed, Winston said, "I'm calling Garrett."

"Garrett?"

"He's a doctor. Lives right next door. You get in there and keep her warm." Winston started for the door at a pace that was possibly too quick to be safe.

"I beg your pardon?" Dante said.

"You heard me. Get in there and pull the covers up and keep her warm till I can get us help."

Dante looked down at Elsa's still form, his mouth suddenly dry. "I am uncertain if—"

Winston turned sharply at the door. "Listen, you! Elsa trusts you enough to have you live with her, so I'll trust you too. Now get in there before I knock your teeth in!"

Dante nodded foolishly, too flustered to recall Winston's blindness for a moment. "Of course."

"And if I find out you tried something with her while I'm gone, I'll really give you a walloping." Winston disappeared through the doorway before Dante could say any more.

Elsa shuddered, a crease appearing at the center of her forehead. Could he really be contemplating following Winston's instruction? Perhaps the covers would be sufficient. Dante pulled them up to her chin, tucking them in around her shoulders. Her brow smoothed somewhat, and she sighed his name.

Dante froze, uncertain if he had heard correctly. It could have been his imagination, fueled by the extraordinary events of the evening. Regardless, it gave him the courage to lift the covers and slide into the bed behind her.

He slid one arm under her neck and the other over her waist, pulling her as close as he dared. Her body fit snugly against his.

She was terribly cold. Dante reached up to brush a few strands of hair away from her face. He was intent upon her to the point that he nearly cried out when some small thing leapt upon his back.

Elsa's cat crept over him as if he was no more than a pillow. It sniffed at her lips, then crawled under the covers and curled up against her chest, purring loudly. At least it could lend its warmth to her.

Winston entered the room, murmuring to himself. Dante craned his head over his shoulder and saw that Winston was carrying a great burden of blankets.

"Allow me to help you," Dante said. He started to rise, but Winston stopped Dante with a look so piercing, he wondered for a moment if Winston's blindness was a charade.

"Don't you dare. You just keep her warm."

Winston dropped the blankets on the foot of the bed, then started spreading them atop the pair. Dante adjusted them so they were covering Elsa, yet not burying her cat so deeply that it would be smothered. She seemed rather fond of it.

Winston paused for a moment, then threw the final blanket over them. "I hear Garrett's car. I'll be right back."

As he left, Dante's stomach lurched. His mask was in the other room. Winston was blind. There was no harm in him being near Dante without his mask. But this Garrett fellow... Who knew how he'd react?

The man was a doctor, so hopefully Dante's face would not send him screaming from the room. The lighting was dim, and Dante's right side was toward the pillows. There was that, at least. But what would Dr. Garrett think of finding Dante in bed with Elsa, barely dressed as they were?

He was spared from his racing thoughts as Winston entered the room again, followed by a man so tall his head nearly brushed the top of the doorframe. He was blond, his skin richly bronzed by the sun, and he had the flawless features of a leading man. A perfect match for Elsa.

He was dressed in a thin gray shirt with sleeves that did not reach his elbows. His pants were similar to the ones Dante currently wore. Perhaps this was the fashion of the tropics.

"You must be Dante," Garrett said, surprising Dante with a genial smile.

"And you must be Dr. Garrett."

"Dr. Wolfstrom, actually, but I'd prefer you call me Garrett."

Despite Dante's misgivings, he found himself liking the man. Garrett's smile came easily, and his tone lacked any hint of condescension. There was a lilt to his voice, an accent Dante did not recognize.

Dante started to move away from Elsa, but Garrett motioned for him to stay.

"Winston said she's cold, and body heat's all we have at the moment." Garrett glanced at the empty fireplace, then crossed to the opposite side of the bed. "There's not much call for furnaces in Florida. If it's all the same, I'd rather you stay where you are."

"Of course," Dante said.

Garrett set his black doctor's bag down near the pillows and pulled out what looked like a stethoscope. Dante's theory was confirmed as Garrett clipped its listening tubes onto his ears, then crawled across the bed toward Elsa and placed the chestpiece above her heart.

Garrett listened for a moment before shifting the device to check a few other places. Finally, he opened each of her eyes, shining a tiny light into them.

Dante angled his head more toward the pillows. Garrett must be able to see Dante's face, but Garrett's gaze never strayed to his, and Garrett made no mention of it. He seemed barely aware of Dante's presence until handing Dante the smallest thermometer he had ever seen.

"Put this under her arm, if you would." Garrett smiled, and said, "I like to do things old-school."

Dante nodded as if that statement did not confuse him, then lifted Elsa's arm gingerly to place the thermometer. He fought the flush trying to creep up his neck as the scent of roses flooded his senses. Elsa melted against his body as if they were meant to fit together. He reminded himself to remain focused on assisting her and not think of how right it felt to have her in his arms.

"How is she?" Winston's worried voice cut through Dante's thoughts.

Garrett shook his head and said, "It looks to me like she's just passed out."

"Passed out?" Winston said. "That's not like her."

"This isn't the first time." Garrett scratched Leonardo's head as the cat purred even louder. Garrett winked at Dante and said, "She slept right through our second date. I came over to pick her up for dinner and she passed out before we made it to the car. She was fine in a couple of hours, but it damn near broke my heart."

Dante felt as if the floor had dropped out from under him. An invitation to dinner was unmistakably courting behavior. And Elsa had accepted.

Garrett and Elsa were involved. It made sense. He was a doctor, handsome and charismatic. Why Garrett had not trounced Dante for being in bed with Elsa was the mystery.

"I apologize." Dante thought to rise, but he was trapped. If he sat up, Garrett would see his face fully before Dante had a chance to cover himself.

"Don't worry about it," Garrett said. His smile broadened and he slapped Dante on the arm. "That ended years ago. This little guy stole her right out from under me."

Garrett scratched Leonardo's head once more, then pulled the thermometer from beneath Elsa's arm. His brow furrowed slightly as he examined it, but then he shook his head and slid to the side of the bed. He placed his tools back in his bag, which he sat on the bedside table.

"Her temperature is a little low, but not dangerously so. We'll keep an eye on that. Winston, did you turn off the AC?"

"Yes sir," Winston said, shuffling toward the fireplace.

"Ugh, don't call me 'sir'. You know I can't stand that."

Garrett walked over to Winston and put his hands on the older man's shoulders and squeezed, then patted him on the back. Dante's heart warmed toward them both. The whole group treated each other as family. It was a beautiful thing to behold.

"I keep forgetting." Winston chuckled roughly.

"I'll keep reminding you. Now sit down before I wind up with two patients. I've got this."

Dante risked lifting his head to watch as Garrett built up a raging fire. The doctor seemed as confident with menial tasks as with his examination of Elsa. Again, Dante found himself liking Garrett.

Winston sat at the small table before the fire, his face drawn with worry. "She never mentioned fainting spells. What could have brought it on?"

"Any number of things," Garrett said, adjusting the blazing logs a final time before rising and putting the poker back in place. "Overexertion is at the top of my list of suspects."

"She does like to do that," Winston said. "She went to that play again tonight."

Garrett laughed. "Of course she did, Winston. It's Saturday."

"Is it?" Dante asked. He immediately regretted letting the question slip from his lips.

Garrett glanced at Dante without flinching. He felt his cheeks heat, but held Garrett's gaze. Dante had never felt more exposed in his life. Garrett looked at the scars on Dante's face briefly, then turned back to Winston. That was all.

"I'll stay at least through the night," Garrett said. "But I'm sure she'll be fine after she gets some rest."

"Thank goodness," Winston said. He was still wringing his hands.

"Do you think you could make us some coffee?"

"Of course. It's the least I can do." Winston stood, the ghost of a smile crossing his face, and headed out the door.

Garrett walked back to the bed and sat opposite Dante. "I didn't want to say this in front of Winston, but she actually warned me that something like this might happen again. How she knew is the mystery. The last time was just after Leonardo came to live with her." He laughed, and said, "Maybe it's the excitement of new roommates."

"I do not wish to be a burden to her." Dante could scarcely think that Elsa's bringing him here was unrelated to her collapse.

"Come on," Garrett said, the easy smile returning to his face as he leaned against the headboard. "If we weren't burdens for Elsa, what would she do with her time?"

Elsa shivered, and Dante pulled her closer without even thinking. He could not believe how soft she felt against him. He did not miss the shadow that crossed Garrett's face before the man looked away.

"What is she to you?" Dante asked. He hadn't meant to

give voice to his thought.

"We're friends."

"Friends."

"Good friends." Garrett shrugged, his smile becoming a bit strained. "We've known each other for years. We tried dating at first, but it didn't work out."

"I cannot imagine why." Dante tried to keep any bitterness from his tone. A handsome man like Garrett would surely find his company in high demand.

"I worked in the ER when we met. My hours were crazy back then. I'm mostly retired now, but I think that ship has sailed."

The look Garrett gave Dante was one he'd never seen before. At least, not directed at him. Something akin to anger flashed across Garrett's gaze, followed quickly by resignation.

"I am sorry." Dante understood little of what Garrett had said, but it seemed appropriate to apologize.

Garrett shrugged, his smile returning. He crossed his legs before him on the bed and folded his hands over his chest.

"My theory's that she doesn't like blonds." Garrett winked at Dante and continued. "Jazz tried to set her up with an artist from the gallery a while back, but Elsa didn't take the bait. Jazz said Elsa didn't even realize it was a blind date. Which is probably good, because if Elsa knew, she would've killed Jazz."

Dante took a moment as his mind pored over Garrett's words. *Setting Elsa up* with someone in conjunction with speaking of dates helped his understanding. However, the idea of a *blind* date puzzled him. He dismissed the idea of actual blindfolds and presumed they merely had not met previously. This Jazz person was making the introduction.

"I am unfamiliar with that name. Where is he from?"

"*She* is from Kansas City." Garrett's smile faded, one eyebrow rising on his forehead. "Elsa didn't tell you about Jazz?"

Dante scrambled to provide an explanation that would not rouse Garrett's suspicions, determined to keep Elsa's secret safe.

"We have not known each other for terribly long. I am eager to learn more about her friends."

"I bet," Garrett said, a smirk deepening the dimples on either side of his face. "Jazz is Elsa's best friend from college. They met at some arty school up in Virginia. Her real name is Ling, but since she's from Kansas City, people called her Jazz. It really suits her, so it stuck."

"Does it have something to do with the cattle trade?"

"What?"

"The word *jazz*. I am unfamiliar with it."

Garrett stared at Dante, his jaw slack. Dante must have made some dire mistake, given away his ignorance of this time. His fears were realized when Garrett said, "Where the hell did Elsa find you that you don't know what jazz is?"

Not wanting to lie to the man, Dante came up with a palatable truth. "I fear where I am from is quite behind the times."

Garrett laughed. "Well, my friend, you are in for a treat. Jazz is only the best form of music ever invented. I know all the best jazz bars around. Once Elsa's back on her feet, you and I can hit the town and paint it red."

Dante wondered if any of the books in the encyclopedia set covered the common vernacular. He could tell there was quite a bit he needed to catch up on. But it was clear that Garrett meant his words as a sincere invitation. He was not concerned to be seen with Dante in public. Garrett did not even know that Dante had the good manners to wear a mask.

His throat constricted at the thought. Could people truly have changed so much that he could walk the streets without hearing gasps or screams?

"Thank you," Dante said.

"For an excuse to go to the clubs? I'm looking forward to it already."

The conversation was strangely intimate. It was hard not to feel comfortable in Garrett's company. Dante could not recall ever having such a discussion with another. He had been lured into similar conversations briefly, but those had always taken cruel turns.

Garrett seemed genuine, accepting. Already, by

bringing Dante to her home, Elsa had given him an opportunity he had never encountered before. Friendship. He was not used to being with someone who treated him as an equal. His closest experiences had been mentoring Mary and being mentored by Heinrich.

Grief pierced Dante's heart at the memory of his father, sharp and deep. The weight of Klaus's loss pushed the knife in further.

Without his mask, Dante could not hide his distress. He was more exposed than he had ever been. Vulnerable. Visible. It was too much.

"Might I trouble you to bring me my mask?" Dante's voice took on a rough sound, like waves breaking on a rocky shore.

"Your mask?"

"It is just beyond in the other room. When Winston cried out, there was no time for me to put it on."

"Sure."

Garrett rose from the bed, and Dante took the moment of semi-privacy to close his eyes and try to regain his composure. He took a deep breath, but that merely filled his lungs with the sweet fragrance of Elsa's hair. While it brought to mind more pleasant thoughts, they did nothing to help calm him.

The light was still on in the bathroom. Garrett picked up Dante's mask, slowly turning it over in his hands. He took a few steps toward the bed, but paused in the doorway. His gaze never left the mask.

"What the hell?" Garrett said, lifting the mask. "Did Elsa put you up to this?"

"I beg your pardon?"

"This mask. It feels like porcelain. And the design is just too much. There is a line, man."

"I fear I am still at a loss."

Garrett shook his head and said, "I don't know what you guys have going, but this is a little messed up."

Garrett's lip twitched up, as if Dante's mask offended him. The irony of the idea nearly made Dante laugh aloud, until Garrett looked up at them, the same expression of distaste on his features. He walked around the bed, then set the mask on the bedside table nearest Dante.

"Look, if you guys want to dress up and play *Phantom of the Opera*, that's your business. But I think it's a little weird and more than a little unhealthy. Tell me you at least have some more practical masks you use out in public."

"That is the only mask I possess."

In fact, it was *all* Dante possessed, aside from his mother's ring and the clothes he'd been wearing when Elsa brought him to this time. Dante was used to having little, though this brought the matter to extremes.

"Well, if you ever want something more comfortable, come see me." Garrett pointed over his shoulder. "I'm just next door."

Dante could not fathom what had upset Garrett so, but

it was troublesome enough to end their conversation. Strangely, even after such a short time, Dante missed talking with him. Garrett sat by the fire, a grim set to his lips as he stared at Dante. Exhausted as he was, he doubted he would sleep under Garrett's watchful gaze.

Chapter Six

Gravity was crushing every molecule of Elsa's body. The mattress couldn't possibly keep supporting her. She envisioned it collapsing as she sank into the earth.

Panic chewed at the edges of her mind. She pushed it away by focusing all of her energy on waking up. Gradually, the weight lifted until she felt strong enough to force open her eyelids.

Dante was lying on the settee, a book splayed open in his hand as he slept. Most of his face was concealed behind his mask. With each gentle rise and fall of his chest, Elsa's panic was replaced with wonder. She might have thought she was dreaming, except for the bone-deep exhaustion. She was too tired to be asleep.

He had pulled the settee right next to the bed, close enough for her to reach out and touch him—if she could lift her arm. He was wearing black slacks and one of the white linen shirts from his wardrobe. His shirt had fallen open a bit, revealing his pale skin.

She noticed he wasn't wearing any shoes or socks. A warm feeling spread through her at seeing him dressed so casually in her home. He looked comfortable, like he belonged. Several dozen books from the encyclopedia set were stacked around him, forming a miniature city.

Dante must have sensed her watching him, because his eyes slowly opened, an earthy jade today.

"Elsa?"

She shivered at the velvet sound of his voice.

"Has your chill returned?" He put his book next to him as he rose from the settee. He sat next to her on the bed, then lifted one of her hands in his and pressed it against his left cheek for a moment. He didn't release her hand when he lowered it from his face. "You seem warm enough. How do you feel?"

When Elsa tried to speak, her throat was dry and raw. She half expected sand to come out instead.

"I'm fine," she croaked.

Dante frowned. "Let me get you some water."

She wanted to stay in that perfect moment for a while longer, to tell him not to go, but her mouth wouldn't cooperate. Instead, she tried to gauge how much time had passed.

Light peeked around the edges of the curtains, so it was at least morning. She was still in Dante's room. Other than the relocated settee and stacks of books around it, nothing had changed.

Dante set the glass of water on the bedside table. Without hesitating, he wrapped his arms around her and pulled her against his chest. Elsa's heart started pounding.

She was vividly aware of every place their bodies touched.

All too soon, he released her, having propped her up against some pillows. He sat next to her on the bed, then brought the glass of water to her lips.

Being coddled was strange and seemed inappropriate. She was supposed to be helping him, not the other way around. Her arms trembled as she reached for the glass. She wasn't sure if it was from fatigue or his proximity.

"Please, allow me to assist," he said.

She didn't have the strength to argue. Instead, she nodded, then drank half the glass with his help. Finally able to speak again, she said, "I'm sorry I slept late."

"You may sleep as long as you like. I am merely relieved to see you so much better."

Better than what? Her brain felt like it was made of cotton. She struggled to put words together in a way that made sense. The last thing she remembered was being in his room and laying out some pajamas for him. She must have passed out.

"I was just tired. I didn't mean to leave you alone so long."

"Winston and Leonardo have been excellent company. And Garrett has been visiting twice a day."

"Garrett?"

A surge of adrenaline scattered the fog in her mind. Garrett had been there while she slept? How had Dante explained his presence? What had he told Garrett?

Action seemed imperative. Elsa leaned forward, but Dante gripped her shoulders, then gently pushed her back against the pillows. It was a good thing too, because the room was starting to spin again.

"You must not let yourself get overexcited."

"How long was I asleep?"

"A little over two days."

"Two days?" she nearly shouted. Her mind reeled. How could she have left him alone for two days? And right after bringing him to her time. He must have been so lost. "I'm sorry."

"It is I who must apologize. Bringing me here appears to have taxed you greatly."

"You didn't tell them, did you?" The question slipped out before she could stop herself, but once it was spoken, she couldn't think of anything except his answer.

"I have kept your confidences. You can trust me."

If only she could. But trust was something that had died in her long ago.

Winston arrived before she could say anything else. His eyes had dark shadows under them, and his shoulders were slumped.

"Any change?" Winston asked, shuffling toward them.

"Indeed." Dante stood, pushing stacks of books out of Winston's way to clear a path to the bed.

"Good morning, Winston," Elsa said.

Winston's eyes widened and a broad smile spread

across his face. "Oh thank God."

He stumbled over to her, hands outstretched. Elsa grasped them, leading Winston toward her so he could sit on the bed at her side.

"Are you all right?" Winston asked.

"I think so."

Winston leaned forward and pulled her into a hug. "I was so worried."

"Um, Winston, could you not squeeze me so hard?"

"Oh dear." He pulled back. "I didn't hurt you, did I?"

"No, I just need to use…" She glanced over at Dante, trying not to blush.

"Yeah, I bet you do. Sleeping for days. A grown woman!" Winston stood, but didn't let go of Elsa's hands. "I'll help you up."

Dante was lingering nearby, and said, "Perhaps you would allow me?"

"That's a good idea." Winston turned to Dante and said, "You get her comfortable while I make lunch. She must be famished!"

Winston patted Elsa's hand, then hobbled out of the room. Before she could argue, Dante stepped forward and lifted her from the bed. He did it with practiced ease, and she wondered if he had been the one to carry her to bed in the first place.

The image brought on another shiver, which she tried to ignore. It wasn't easy, feeling his chest pressed against her side. The scent of sandalwood enveloped her.

"Are you certain that you are not cold?" he asked as he headed toward the bathroom.

"I'm fine. Why do you keep asking about that?"

He tilted his head away, but she could see the red flush creeping over his skin even with his mask.

"You were quite cold the night I arrived," he said. He stopped at the door to the bathroom, then set her on her feet. "Are you certain you can manage on your own?"

"I'll be fine."

From the way his jaw tightened, he seemed to disagree. "I shall be close. If you need anything, you have only to call for me."

He spoke with such intensity, almost protectiveness. But again, that was backward. Elsa was supposed to be in that role. Before she could take care of anyone else, though, she really needed to take care of herself.

"Thanks." She slipped through the door.

She rushed through her most basic bodily needs, eager to get back to him. When she opened the door to the bedroom again, Dante was standing by the armoire, tracing the carvings with his fingertips. He paused when he saw her.

Determined to show him she was fine, Elsa started toward him, but after two steps she wasn't sure which way was up again. It didn't matter, because he was there to catch her. He gathered her against his chest as if it was the most natural thing in the world.

Her heart felt strangely full. Leaning into him, she felt warmth suffuse her body. No one had ever carried her so tenderly before.

She couldn't let herself enjoy it. If she did, it would be that much more painful when she finally had to let him go.

"Are you all right?"

"Yes, I'm just still a bit dizzy. And I'm not used to being carried around."

"Until you are recovered, perhaps you should strive to become accustomed to it." Dante said, heading to the door. Her stomach did a happy little flip. "I presume there is a kitchen elsewhere in the house?"

She had to clear her throat to reply. "Downstairs."

He nodded, but paused at the open doorway. In a soft voice, he said, "I have not left this room since you brought me here."

"Not once in two days?"

"That would have meant leaving your side and I could not bring myself to do so." He drew in a quick breath, as if trying to pull the words back into his mouth. "That is to say…"

"Thank you."

The smile he gave her was gentle, and he held her a little closer to his chest. She wondered if he was even aware of it. He took another deep breath, his arms stiffening around her, then stepped over the threshold. He paused again on the other side and let out a brief laugh. Elsa felt his arms relax, and he bowed his head as if relieved.

"I half expected to be transported back to my time."

"I would bring you back again."

"I—" Whatever he'd been about to say, he seemed to think better of it. "I appreciate that."

"I don't think it'll be necessary, though. Leonardo's been with me for years now."

Elsa had never told anyone about Leonardo. The only person she had ever spoken with about her power... Well, it was best not to think about that.

The conversation felt even stranger with Dante carrying her. As much as she loved being close to him, the idea of needing someone to take care of her was unnerving. She was literally burdening him.

Her weakness would pass. She was certain of it. And then she could be the one taking care of him. She just had to make sure she didn't enjoy herself too much in the meantime. With a sinking feeling, she realized she could get used to feeling his arms around her all too quickly.

Dante glanced at his feet while walking to the stairs, as if checking to make sure Leonardo wasn't trying to run between them. That was probably a good idea.

"You brought the cat from another time?" he asked.

"Yes. It was an accident, though."

"How so?"

They'd reached the bottom of the stairs, which meant Winston was much too close for them to be talking about time travel.

Lowering her voice, she said, "Could I tell you about it later? I'd rather not discuss this around Winston."

"Of course."

Dante carried her down the hallway to the kitchen. A plate of sandwiches was already on the table, and Winston was standing near the stove, the kettle just beginning to whistle.

"Is that an electric range?" Dante asked, an edge of excitement to his voice.

"Yes, it is." Elsa hadn't thought this through. Dante was going to have questions. Strange questions that she'd have trouble answering in front of Winston.

As if on cue, Winston chuckled and said, "You don't have stoves in your hometown, either?"

Dante must have faced this sort of thing during the days that Elsa was sleeping. She wondered how he had managed.

"I have never seen a stove of this variety," he said, glancing down at her. She smiled, hoping that his other conversations had gone as well.

"I think I'm strong enough to sit up." She nodded toward the table. Dante crossed the room and gingerly set her in a chair. "Thanks."

Within moments of Elsa having a lap, Leonardo ran

into the room and jumped onto it. He purred loudly, hitting her in the face with his tail as he pranced around on her legs. Winston turned toward them, carrying a tray with the teapot and three cups.

"Allow me," Dante said, taking the tray and setting it on the table. He poured the tea and added milk and sugar to each of the cups, then handed one to Elsa and one to Winston before sitting down himself.

The moment was completely surreal. She was having tea with Winston and a man who, three days ago, had been in the late 1800s.

"I called Garrett to let him know you're awake," Winston said. "He left strict orders that you're not to overdo and to keep getting plenty of rest."

"I think I can manage that." She took a bite of her sandwich and found that she was absolutely starving. She tried to pace herself in front of Dante, but wondered if the stack of food in front of her would be enough.

"Can you now?" Winston snorted, then turned to Dante. "This is on you, Dante. Turn your back on her for a minute, and she'll be doing all kinds of things she oughtn't. Laundry and dishes."

"I assure you, Elsa's well-being is the very highest of my priorities," Dante said. His words sent a thrill through Elsa, and she felt herself blushing.

Winston made a "hmph" sound, but he was smiling. "Garrett will be by this evening. I'll make a special dinner."

"I would be happy to assist," Dante said.

"Your job is to look after Elsa." Winston laughed and said, "Trust me, I have the easier task."

Elsa was too tired to be offended. Plus, she was enjoying the conversation too much, watching Dante and Winston smile as they talked to one another.

They finished eating and, exhausted though she was, she couldn't stand the thought of going back to bed. There was so much she wanted to show Dante, so much to tell him.

"Let me show you around the house," she said.

"I would like that a great deal." Dante pushed his chair back from the table and stood. He began gathering up dishes, but Winston reached out and swatted at his hands, landing a few pretty good thwacks.

"You're as bad as she is. That's for me to do. Go on now."

Dante looked like he might object, but was distracted as Elsa nudged Leonardo from her lap, then tried to stand and fell right back in her chair. Her legs wouldn't support her.

"Allow me." Dante swooped her up again.

She couldn't resist leaning against his chest. His arms were strong around her, lifting her with ease. She had never enjoyed someone's touch so much.

"Where shall we begin?"

Elsa had been staring again. He was polite enough not

to mention it, so neither did she. She had to get herself under control.

"How about the library?"

Some rooms hadn't changed much in a century. Her library was full of books and the dining room held a table and chairs. They spent a long time in the entertainment room, talking about movies and television shows and the technology that brought entertainment so effortlessly into people's homes. Dante seemed willing to stand there holding Elsa while she explained everything, but she insisted he at least set her on the couch for that part of the tour.

He was particularly interested in how the remotes worked and asked for a demonstration. His eyes widened in wonder as the first images appeared on the screen. She convinced him to wait to actually start watching something until after they'd gone through the rest of the house. She was eager to show him the studio and the gardens outside, wondering if he'd love them as much as she did.

She steeled her resolve before he picked her up this time. She would not lean into him, no matter how strong his chest felt. She would not melt into his arms, even though they gave her the first glimmer of what it might be to feel safe.

The French double doors that led into the converted solarium were just down the hall. She waited for Dante to pause in front of the doors before saying, "I saved the best for last. This is the studio."

It was more than a studio, though. It was her sanctuary, her most holy ground. She reached down and opened the doors, watching Dante's face as he took in the room for the first time.

It was her deepest dream that the two of them would eventually spend many hours here together, whether working on a shared project or on their own. The openness of the room might be too much for Dante at first after spending so much time in the basement of his father's theatre. She didn't want to push him too far too fast.

The exterior walls and the ceiling of the studio were made up of windows. In the bright afternoon sun, every inch of the room was illuminated with natural light. Flowers and greenery pressed against the steamy glass on the far wall.

Dante walked to the center of the room, spinning in a slow circle. His gaze rested first on the easels in the painting corner, then passed to the workbenches where sculpting tools were set up. Against the interior wall, there was a sewing corner with a dress form and shelves filled with fabrics, paints, clays and every kind of tool for creativity that Elsa could think of. Her writing desk was nestled against the wall of windows.

"Do you like it?" she asked, unable to contain her curiosity.

A soft smile played at his lips, and his eyes were wide

with wonder. "In the past few days, I have managed to convince myself that I had not died and moved to the afterlife." His voice was low and reverent. "In this room, I find myself questioning that once again, for I can hardly conceive of a more lovely paradise than this."

Elsa's heart seemed to explode in her chest. Visions of them spending time together in this room played out in her mind like a kaleidoscope. They would leave the second set of doors open to the patio to enjoy the breeze and have tea outside when they needed to let their creative energies replenish.

She imagined them walking through the garden, arm in arm. They would pause beneath the climbing roses. Dante would take the opportunity to lean down to kiss her...

She shook her head to clear it of the last part of her fantasy. He was relying on her to introduce him to this new world. She couldn't—wouldn't—let herself cloud his experiences with her own selfish desires. Besides, if she let herself fall in love with him, she would ruin any chance they had of being friends. She wanted him in her life forever. Passion had a way of burning out, leaving only ash and destruction behind.

"Are you all right?" He frowned down at her, his brow furrowed. His eyes were almost gray against the robin's-egg blue of the afternoon sky behind him.

She forced herself to smile and shook her head. "I'm fine."

Dante didn't seem appeased. He carried her to the nearest chair, at her writing desk, and finally set her down.

"If you would please indulge me," Dante said. "It would not do for you to have a relapse of your earlier condition. Neither Winston nor Garrett would forgive me if I let that happen while you were in my care."

He knelt in front of her so she didn't have to crane her neck to look up at him.

"I'm supposed to be taking care of you," she said.

"You have already done more for me than anyone in my life."

"I don't think that's true."

"My life has not been filled with kindness, apart from the blessing of my mother." There was no bitterness to his tone, only a sad resignation.

"What about Heinrich?" Elsa realized her mistake just as the words slipped from her lips, but it was too late. She couldn't take them back.

Dante paused for a beat too long. Suspicion clouded his eyes. "What do you know of Heinrich?"

Elsa knew more about Heinrich than Dante could imagine. She'd only stumbled across Dante because of her fascination with his parents. She had never seen two people more in love.

It took years and a considerable amount of money, but Elsa had collected all the art that she knew touched their lives just in the hopes of seeing a couple who were kind to one another rather than violent. It was so drastically different from her parents and all the men that came after her father.

How could she possibly explain all that without driving Dante away? She figured she didn't have to worry about him leaving. Dante had nowhere to go. He was trapped with her.

She was too familiar with what that felt like. She vowed once more to help him establish himself in her world, to achieve independence. Knowledge was easy to provide for him. A legal identity was another matter.

He stood and took a step back, but she grabbed his hands and said, "There's more I need to tell you."

What would he say if she bared her soul to him and told him everything? The only other time she'd confided with someone, things had gone horribly wrong, and Dante had much more reason to be upset. Elsa had never felt like a voyeur before, but she'd also never spoken to anyone she observed during her travels. Her entire body was trembling, reminding her that the wounds she had suffered as a child weren't just to her heart.

"You should rest," Dante said. "We can discuss this later."

She let out a huge sigh, grateful for the temporary reprieve. She still felt like she might be sick, but it was passing. Closing her eyes, she rested her forehead against the backs of his hands.

"Perhaps I should call Garrett," Dante said.

"No, I want you." Elsa's face tingled with embarrassment. "I mean, I want us to be alone so I can answer your questions. About this time, not... Not how I brought you here."

She glanced up at him, hoping she had covered for letting that slip out. He regarded her silently for a few moments.

"If you are certain you are well enough." His voice softened. "I would like that as well."

Chapter Seven

If Elsa had not explained herself, Dante would have thought he misheard. As it was, the haste with which she spoke, coupled with the way she clung to him, conveyed her desire more clearly than any words. She wanted him near her, though he still had not determined why.

"There's a lounge chair outside." She gestured to the thick foliage beyond the windows. "Maybe we could sit in the garden for a bit?"

An urge that he could not suppress overcame him, and he reached forward, scooping her up into his arms again. She gasped, but smiled as she wrapped her arms around his neck. He was growing accustomed to having her next to him, feeling her embrace. He found himself smiling back at her.

The fact that she seemed not only to not mind his proximity, but perhaps even enjoy it was one of the most novel things of all about this new world. Dante doubted anything in his previous life could have been as satisfying as Elsa's soft exhalation as she leaned against his chest. Her tremors subsided as he held her.

Another double set of doors led to the garden, much

like the ones between the house and solarium. A key rested in the lock of the right-hand door. Elsa reached down to turn it, then pressed the handle. The door swung open onto a stone patio surrounded by lush green plants adorned with brightly colored flowers.

The studio seemed like Heaven, with resources to dabble in so many of the creative arts. But if the studio was paradise, then surely this was the Garden of Eden. Dante stepped out into the bright afternoon light.

Warm gray bricks spread out in a path before him that opened up into a circle like a stone sun. He could see several paths trailing out from that center, with vivid greens and beautiful flowers embracing them. Everywhere he turned, Dante saw color. Beautiful, glorious color. All spectacularly illuminated by the sun.

He lifted his face to the cerulean sky, watching clouds as thick as cotton drift lazily across the horizon. Emerald grass stretched out beyond the garden, ending in copses of bizarrely shaped trees.

Even while traveling with the circus with his mother, Dante had never left the cities where they performed. He'd never been to the country, had never even dared to venture to a park. But here, there was quite literally an entirely new vista.

"It's beautiful, isn't it?" Elsa said, drawing his attention back to her.

He wondered how even that magnificent view could

have distracted him from the beautiful woman in his arms. The light caught every strand of her hair, making it shine more brightly than any gold he had ever seen. Her eyes were honey-brown in the sun. The color had returned to her lips, a rich heliotrope.

Once more, he had the urge to gently trace his thumb across her lips. They parted as he stared at her, and the desire flared, quickly spreading to other parts of his body. His hands were busy holding Elsa. Perhaps he could brush her lips with his own...

She cleared her throat and said, "The chairs are right over there."

"Of course." Dante's voice came out a bit breathless.

He walked into the sunburst pattern of stone. Just across from the patio doors, several chairs flanked a table with an enormous umbrella sprouting from its center. He gently placed her in the lounge chair and then set about adjusting the umbrella to make sure that she was protected from the afternoon sun. When he was satisfied, he sat in a chair opposite her, hoping to marshal his thoughts with the help of some distance.

"If you sit in the sun, you'll burn." She reached to the nearest chair and weakly pulled it toward her in the shade. "Come sit next to me."

His theory that she enjoyed being close to him was gaining strength by the moment. Dante sought to test it further, watching her expression as he pushed the chair nearer, turning it so they would face each other. As he sat, her smile deepened, her eyes crinkling up at the corners.

She enjoyed his company. He still had no idea as to why. She had all of time from which to choose companions. Why him?

She drew him from his musings. "How is the encyclopedia set working for you?"

"Quite well, thank you. The knowledge within them is beyond remarkable." This was an excellent topic. Focusing on his learning would distract him from the fullness of her lips, the thin fabric of the revealing shirt she wore.

"What's your favorite thing you've read about so far?"

"It is difficult to choose."

"Well, what stands out to you?"

Dante looked over the grounds, soaking in the rich scent of earth and the heat from the patio stones. The sensations relaxed him as he tried to formulate his thoughts.

"I read the books covering transportation. I could scarcely believe the section on airplanes, though the physics behind them was clearly explained. However, there was nothing regarding…"

Elsa's face had paled, her forehead pinched above the delicate slope of her nose. Though he would feel better once he understood how she had brought him here, he could not bring himself to strain her further.

"Forgive me. We were not to speak of this."

"No, it's okay." She began chewing on her lower lip—an unconscious habit he'd noticed the night before when she was worried. "You won't find time travel in those books."

Dante kept his voice as gentle as he could. He did not wish to frighten her away now that she seemed willing to broach the topic. "I take it the occurrence is uncommon?"

"I'm the only person alive that I know of who can do it."

"But you keep your ability secret, so how can you be sure?"

"If anyone else can do it, they're smart to keep it to themselves."

He reflected on her words, the vehemence and utter hopelessness with which she spoke. As advanced as this time was, the instinct to persecute others was deeply ingrained in the human psyche. Dante was well acquainted with this. Nothing would inspire fear in people's hearts faster than something they did not understand.

"You have not even told your friends?"

"No one else can know. Please."

"I will keep your secrets."

She let out a deep sigh, her smile returning. "Thank you."

She shifted the conversation back to the encyclopedia set and how well he was assimilating the information.

Apparently, the subject of time travel was closed once more.

Dante barely minded. He settled back in his chair to enjoy the conversation and the beautiful view. His gaze did not stray from Elsa.

Chapter Eight

The shadow of the umbrella slowly drifted across the patio while Elsa and Dante talked. She watched him rearrange it several times to keep them in the shade. The third time, she said, "It must be getting close to tea time. We should go help Winston."

"I will assist him," Dante said. "You need to rest."

"I can at least come along."

"The sun and fresh air seem to be doing you good. We should make use of them while we can."

"If we're out too much longer, we'll have to light the citronella candles and turn on the box fan in the studio to keep the mosquitoes away."

"I promise, I will only be a moment."

She smiled and nodded, even though she didn't like the idea of him leaving her behind. Who knew what kind of questions Winston would ask. It made her heart beat faster to contemplate, but she knew she would have to trust Dante not to tell people her secret.

They were still in the honeymoon period of their relationship, getting to know each other. Eventually, the novelty would wear off and they would need more time to themselves. Time with others. She couldn't be with him constantly. But she could enjoy their time together now.

The afternoon had passed with a dreamlike quality. They didn't just talk about what he was learning, but about art and creativity itself. He was turning out to be even more amazing than she had expected. Considerate, kind, intelligent, artistic. He was everything she wanted and couldn't let herself have.

Dante stood, but paused before he left. His lips parted as if he was about to say something, but instead, he gently lifted Elsa's hand and kissed her knuckles so softly she barely felt his lips.

Fire flooded her body. His warm breath on her skin was like a spark set to kindling longing for a flame. Dante released her hand as he stood, and she had to stifle the urge to reach out to him. He bowed, then walked briskly through the studio doors, as if he was as eager to return as she was to see him again.

Elsa couldn't take her eyes off of him as he left. His broad shoulders perfectly offset his tapered waist. His legs were long, his backside... She should not be thinking about his backside. Or any side of him. Not while drooling, anyway.

Closing her eyes, she leaned back in the lounge chair, taking deep, steady breaths. She had not brought Dante to her time so that they could have a relationship. Well, other than a lasting friendship she hoped they'd develop. He needed to be free to do as he wished with whomever he wished.

There were plenty of women in her time that would be just as flattered by his attentions. He needed to know he had a choice. He needed to be completely independent if there was ever a chance for something more between him and Elsa. Otherwise, she would never know if what he felt was love or gratitude.

He had already said he felt indebted to her, and a sense of obligation would be the worst of all. Her heart bunched up in her chest, reality crushing her dreams underfoot like an empty tin can.

Dante would never be independent. He had no identification, and Elsa had no idea how to get him any. It was the one part of her plan she hadn't been able to figure out. Ironically, she had run out of time.

She could sense that the moments in his life that she could connect with through the ring were almost used up. She couldn't visit the same moment twice. When she had seen he was about to die, she had to bring him back right then.

She didn't know what to do. Even broaching the topic would raise questions about who Dante was, where he had come from, and most importantly, how he had arrived. If the wrong person found out, they would both wind up in a lab.

If he decided he wanted reconstructive surgery when

she told him about it, who knew what his bloodwork would show. Elsa had already tested the waters with Garrett to see if Dante sounded like a good candidate, but even if she paid the bill, Dante would still need identification before anyone would operate on him.

There were too many variables, too many things she couldn't control. She closed her eyes, pushing all the thoughts away. He was here, now. He was safe. She would keep him that way.

Imagining them as a couple was a dangerous dream to have in the first place. She knew firsthand the harsh realities of how relationships could change people—bring out the worst in them. She needed to keep that reality as a shield, to protect herself from wanting too much, from hoping for more.

She could dream up as many "happily ever after" endings involving Dante as she wanted. But he was a real human being, with human failings. A human temper.

"Elsa! Are you okay?"

Elsa jumped at the unexpected voice coming from the side of the house. She glanced over at the path to see Rachel running toward her.

This was a nightmare. Rachel was Elsa's chattiest friend. As Jazz's assistant in the gallery, Rachel's outgoing nature was useful. When trying to keep something private, she was the last person Elsa would want to involve.

The white of Rachel's jeans was blinding in the late

afternoon sun. A matching white purse was slung over her shoulder, and she wore a pale blue blouse that was almost the same color as her eyes. With the addition of her perfect features and supermodel height, she was absolutely stunning.

"Garrett said you were sick. Are you sick?" She pulled Dante's chair closer to Elsa and sat.

"I've felt better." Elsa smiled and pulled herself up higher in the lounge chair. Rachel grabbed Elsa's hand and squeezed it, her enthusiastic grip chasing away the last lingering sense of Dante's gentle touch.

The sooner Elsa could get Rachel to go home, the better. Dante would be back any moment, and if Rachel saw him, the questions would be nonstop. Elsa didn't have the answers ready yet.

"Is there anything I can do for you? What do you need?"

Rachel was in full manic mode, her exuberance seeming to suck up all the energy in the area. Normally, her awe of pretty much everything was endearing. At the moment, it was sapping Elsa of what little strength she had recovered.

"I think what I need most right now is rest." She hoped Rachel would get the message and leave.

Elsa should have known better.

"Let me keep you company, then. I haven't seen you in so long."

That much was true. Rachel had been conspicuously absent for a couple of months. Now that she had brought this to Elsa's attention, her curiosity was piqued.

"Why is that?"

"I'm not supposed to say." Rachel looked at the ground, her expression as sad as if she was five and had just dropped her ice cream cone. Then a smile spread across her face, her mood switching so quickly it made Elsa dizzy. "But I can trust you to keep a secret."

If only she knew...

Rachel scooted her chair even closer to Elsa, beaming. Whatever this new secret was, Rachel was over the moon about it.

"I met someone."

"I should have guessed." Elsa smiled and asked, "And who is this new love of yours?"

"I'm not supposed to say." Rachel's gaze once more trailed off toward the ground. This sad look vanished even faster than the first. "He's an artist! He has a new exhibit opening at the gallery soon."

"You know Jazz doesn't like it when you date the artists displaying at her gallery."

"Yes, but all the best artists display there. No one can discover the next hot trend like Jazz can. His career will be spectacular with her help."

"Just remember your own career. You can learn a lot more from Jazz than from one of her clients."

"How can you be so unromantic when you've written a dozen bestselling romance novels?"

Rachel dropped Elsa's hand and leaned back, pouting. Elsa knew men were often devastated by that look. Luckily, she was immune. Arching an eyebrow, she scowled until Rachel looked away.

Rachel's tone was a bit petulant when she said, "I wouldn't have gotten involved with him if I didn't think it was serious."

"Rachel, you always think it's serious. Remember when you dated that bicycle delivery guy for a week and started picking out china patterns?"

"Hello, I'm an interior designer. Anyway, that was different. That guy was totally wrong for me. This one is an artist. An artist!"

Elsa sighed. From the breathy way Rachel said the word, it was obvious he wasn't just an artist. He was what Rachel thought of as *an artist*. Which meant he was probably one of the most sensitive, moody, temperamental men that Elsa would ever have the misfortune to meet. She'd met artists Rachel dated before and hadn't liked any of them. She especially disliked how they treated Rachel.

Torn between encouraging Rachel to leave and making sure she wasn't getting into yet another bad relationship, Elsa said, "Maybe we can have lunch next week and talk about it."

"Oh no. I don't think I can get away with that."

"What do you mean?"

"Well, he's a very private person. No one's supposed to know that we're dating. In fact, he doesn't know that I'm here visiting you." Rachel gave an impish grin. "He thinks I'm running an errand for Jazz. And technically, I am. I just decided to take a little detour on my way to the contractor."

Elsa's stomach gave a sudden sideways lurch, the hair on her arms standing on end like a live wire had passed too close to her skin. "He doesn't want you talking to your friends?"

"He's kind of figured out that I have a little bit of trouble keeping things to myself." She shrugged her slender shoulders as if that made it all right.

"Rachel, that's part of who you are," Elsa said. "Has he ever thought of just not telling you things he doesn't want other people to know?"

"Hey!"

"Well? This guy can't expect to keep you in a cage so you don't ever talk to anyone. You're a people person. If this guy can't appreciate you for who you are, he's not right for you."

"You don't even know him."

"The people who really love you figure out how to let you be you while maintaining the relationship."

At that moment, Dante emerged from the studio doors, carrying a tray with a pitcher of iced tea, two glasses and some cookies.

"I trust you will enjoy…" His voice trailed off as he saw Rachel sitting at Elsa's side.

Elsa couldn't help but wonder what Rachel looked like to him. She was petite, her flaxen hair hanging around her face in waves that seemed as wild as her spirit, yet somehow not at all disheveled. And she had the blue eyes that were supposed to go with blonde hair, along with the creamy complexion and rosy cheeks.

Rachel also knew how to dress, and Elsa realized with a shock of embarrassment that Dante had only seen her in pajamas since that first night at the theatre. She reached up and straightened her tank top self-consciously. Rachel was so much better at being blonde than Elsa was.

Rachel seldom used her looks purposefully, but when she did, it was devastating. She knew just how to pout, just how to veil her eyes, and just how to swish her hips to get any man's complete attention whenever she wanted it. It had never bothered Elsa before, but now, with Dante staring at both of them at the same time, she felt completely outclassed.

Not that it should matter to her. What did matter was Rachel's inevitable reaction to Dante.

Rachel turned around slowly in her chair, her gaze scanning his clothes, his face and his mask. Even the way he stood set him apart from other men. No one's posture was that good anymore.

"Oh my God," Rachel said. "You're finally writing the book!"

Rachel let out a squeal that was closer to a shriek, clapping her hands as she leapt up from her chair and practically skipped across the patio. Dante frowned as she ran in circles around him, like an over-excited terrier.

Elsa started to swing her legs over the side of her seat, but Dante quickly crossed to her, Rachel trailing behind. He set his tray on the table, then lifted Elsa's legs back onto the lounge chair. "Elsa, you know you are supposed to be resting."

Elsa could hear the strain in his voice.

Rachel let out another squeal. "Oh my God. Where did you find this guy? He's perfect!"

"Rachel..." Elsa warned.

But the momentum of Rachel's excitement would not be denied. Dante turned to face Rachel, blocking her path to Elsa almost protectively. Elsa felt a flutter in her stomach at the thought.

"Is he from the theatre?" Rachel asked. "From the play you've been going to every weekend? I bet that's it."

"Rachel!"

Elsa's tone must have snapped Rachel a bit back to reality. She finally tore her eyes away from Dante and glanced at Elsa.

Elsa took a deep breath before speaking. "This is Dante. He's a friend who will be staying with me for a while. And

I'm sure he doesn't like being ogled like that."

"Then he shouldn't be so gorgeous!" Rachel said, smiling as she sat back down in one of the chairs at the table.

Dante looked like he'd been slapped. He took in a sharp breath, every vertebra perfectly stacked atop each other, but didn't say anything.

He probably thought Rachel was teasing him, playing a cruel joke, like Giselle often had. But flirting came as naturally to Rachel as breathing, and she really did have a point. Dante was absolutely gorgeous. Elsa's heart sank a little, as she added that to the list of things he needed to realize before she would consider him independent.

"Are you an actor from the play Elsa funded? Are you helping her with her book?"

Elsa stifled a groan. She was going to tell Dante about all of this, but not now. Not like this. Elsa was desperate to make Rachel stop.

"Rachel, please. Leave him be."

"I am here to help Elsa in whatever way I can," Dante said, his voice smooth, but with a cold evenness that Elsa had only heard him use with people from his time. People who had tormented him.

"Wow, you even sound like him."

"Like who?"

Rachel laughed, oblivious to the chaos she was spawning. "The Phantom of the Opera."

Chapter Nine

"You are the second person to speak of this apparition. However, I am at a loss." Dante had not questioned Garrett on the matter, hoping to avoid a topic that seemed quite uncomfortable for him.

"You've never heard of the Phantom of the Opera?" Rachel smiled and lifted one slender shoulder toward her head, inclining it as she gazed at him. "I get it. You're a method actor. Since you're supposed to be the Phantom, you wouldn't know about the character."

"I am afraid I do not follow your meaning."

"Sure." Rachel nodded in an exaggerated manner. "Is Dante your real name or a stage name?"

"It is the name my mother gave me."

The way the woman gawked at him and her coquettish gestures reminded Dante of the actresses in Heinrich's theatre. He would not serve himself up for her amusement.

"It's a great name." Rachel turned to Elsa. "You should totally use that in your book."

"You are a writer, then?" Dante angled his face so that only his mask was toward Elsa, hoping to hide his expression until he had gained better mastery over his emotions. Rachel was Elsa's friend, and Dante did not want Elsa to think him impolite.

"I was going to tell you," she said.

Rachel interjected once more. "I can't wait to read that book! Especially with you going all out and hiring someone to play the part of the Phantom in your house!"

Playing a part. Was this why Elsa had chosen him to be her companion? Was she truly writing a book about him? His life did not seem interesting enough to warrant such attention. Dread mingled with curiosity within him.

"Perhaps you could assist me with my role."

"Sure!" Rachel said.

He sat next to Elsa. "Tell me of this Phantom, as if I knew nothing at all."

"Oh how fun!" Rachel clapped her hands together. "Well, the original story was written like over a hundred years ago, but a ton of other versions have come out since then. Basically, the Phantom is this mad genius who runs around in catacombs or something under an opera house in Paris. He only surfaces to create his music, but he mostly winds up killing people."

"I beg your pardon?" Dante was uncertain if he had heard her correctly. Aside from his living in the basement of Heinrich's theatre, there was nothing in what she said that bore the slightest resemblance to Dante's life, for which he was extremely grateful.

"He's really good at inventions," she said. "He makes

all kinds of traps and stuff and uses them to kill anyone who gets in his way."

Dante's heart sank as Rachel's story took on a familiar note. Giselle had seemed to delight in spinning tales about him. She painted him as a deformed monster that lurked in the basement of the theatre, coveting her and using the mechanisms he designed for the theatre's productions to ill effect.

"So," Dante said. "He is a villain."

"I guess he is in most of the stories, but people still sympathize with him. He's an outcast, and everybody wants to be accepted. See, his face was all messed up when he was born, and he was raised in a freak show."

Dante felt his jaw drop. He quickly checked his mask to ensure it was in place. "They believe his disfigurement justified him in murder?"

"Well, not exactly," Rachel said. "But anyway, don't worry. Elsa hates all the horror movie versions of the story. I'm sure in her book, you get to be the good guy."

"Indeed."

Dante glanced briefly toward Elsa. Her face was pale, her eyebrows pinched above her nose. Through parted lips, she pulled in breath after breath, as if drowning. When their eyes met, she leaned forward, clutching his arm.

"I'm sorry…"

Her words hit him like a blow. There was no denial. She was an author writing a book about him. Bringing him to her time was the same as commissioning the encyclopedia set. She had brought him forth for her research.

"Is there more?" he asked.

Elsa's eyes glittered as if she fought back tears. She pulled away from him and, angry as he was, he missed her touch.

Rachel continued, though she spoke a bit haltingly. Perhaps she finally sensed that something was wrong. "There's the love story, of course."

Dante's gaze snapped to Rachel. "Love story?"

"Yeah, that's my favorite part. I've seen movies and plays and read books all based on the same story, and I still wonder whether the young protégé will choose the mentor or the childhood sweetheart." Rachel leaned forward and patted his knee. "I always cheer for you."

"Cheer for…"

Dante shook his head, appalled as he realized what Rachel meant. Mary had been of age when they met, but he was not the sort to take such a young bride. He had been careful to always play the role of mentor with her, though she was the only person in his life who did not seem profoundly disturbed by his appearance.

He looked to Elsa. "I was twice her age."

"Giselle," Elsa said, as if that explained it all.

Truthfully, it did. Giselle's exaggerations at work once more. The thought that Elsa was trying to tell yet another tale surrounding his life made his stomach churn.

"Does he ever break character?" Rachel asked.

Elsa let out a long sigh. "Rachel, I really do need to rest. Could we maybe visit some other time?"

"Sure, now that I know you're okay." Rachel leaned over to give Elsa a quick hug, and said, "You guys are really taking this method acting seriously."

Elsa stared pointedly at Dante. "I've been working on this book for a long time. I want to get it right."

Rachel stood and slung her purse over her shoulder. With a broad grin, she said, "I bet you do. It's no wonder you're so tired with a hottie like this helping you with your 'research'. I'm sure he's being very thorough."

"Rachel!" Elsa gasped, her face reddening instantly.

Dante caught the insinuation and said, "I beg your pardon?" at the same time.

Rachel just laughed. "As much as I'm looking forward to reading the book, you should really let Elsa get some sleep."

She hurried off around the side of the house, waving once over her shoulder. After a long silence, Dante heard what must be the engine of Rachel's car starting. It faded into the distance.

He stood and walked to the greenery at the edge of the patio. Taking a moment to gather his thoughts, he gently traced the white petals of a gardenia with his fingertips.

"I'm sorry," Elsa said at last. "I didn't want you to find

out that way."

"Find out what, Elsa?" He could not bring himself to look at her. "That you have brought me to your time merely to assist your efforts to spin more tales around my life? Or that history remembers me as a monster?"

"Giselle's stories took on a life of their own. They merged with other tales, traveling from one person to the next over decades and turned into urban legends. *The Phantom of the Opera* is not your story. That's why I'm writing this book. To tell your story. I'm writing it for you. I'll destroy it right now if you tell me to."

Dante did turn toward her then. He had to see the truth in her eyes. When he spoke, each word was clipped, demanding.

"Why am I here?"

Elsa swung her feet to the ground and stood before he could stop her. She seemed steady enough that he left the distance between them. He did not trust himself to keep seeking answers if he was distracted by her touch.

"Because I couldn't let you die."

Dante could not help but think she must have had some other motive behind her actions. She had paid such a toll to bring him here. What would she expect of him in return?

She took several quick breaths, as if she was preparing to leap over some hurdle. When she spoke, the words rushed from her lips in a flood.

"I use my ability to go to other times and places to do research for the books I write. I was researching something else when I found you."

"And decided to write this book of which Rachel spoke."

"Yes."

Elsa winced when the word left her lips, as if speaking it pained her. Despite his misgivings, Dante wanted to comfort her, but he would not allow himself to do so.

"If I hadn't made that choice, I would never have discovered that I could save you," she said.

"What do you mean?"

"I was researching the book and I saw Mary and Edgar after the fire." Elsa's voice quieted, though the tension never left her slight frame. "When Edgar gave Mary the ring."

Dante felt as though the ground shuddered beneath him. He had been confident that Mary would be all right. Knowing beyond doubt that she and Edgar had a chance to lead a happy life together removed a weight from Dante's heart he hadn't known he carried.

"Was she well?"

"Physically, she was fine. But she was so upset." Elsa's gaze became unfocused, as if she was seeing something far away. "She kept saying that they didn't find your body. She refused to give up hope that you were still alive. And when I heard her say that, I knew. I knew I could save you.

I had to."

Elsa looked at him then, and the raw despair that flooded her features staggered him.

"I would have done anything to save you."

She took a hesitant step toward him, but her legs gave way. He was not close enough to catch her before her knees struck the stone of the patio. She caught herself with her hands, but her arms trembled from holding her weight. Dante ran to her side, then knelt next to her. He drew her against his chest.

"Are you all right?"

"Yes." Elsa shook her head. "I'm just tired of being so...tired." She took a deep breath and leaned against him.

Whatever else he believed, he knew that she had risked herself to bring him here. She was still paying the toll of that journey. He lifted her from the ground and carried her into the studio.

"I can walk."

"I believe we have both seen that is not the case."

The nearest chair was at the desk nestled against the wall of windows just inside the door. Dante set Elsa upon it as gently as he could. He knelt before her, turning over her hands to inspect her injuries. The soft skin of her palms had been roughly lacerated from the stonework of the patio.

"It's nothing."

Dante brushed the grit and pebbles from her hands as

delicately as he could. "I am sorry that you fell."

"It wasn't your fault."

"I am not so certain of that. You would not be in this state if you had not brought me here, whatever your reasons. And I am grateful to be here."

"I knew this was going to upset you. That's part of why I was putting off telling you. I don't deal well with conflict."

She had that unfocused look about her again, and Dante wondered what horrible specters of the past she was seeing. He could not leave her there to face them alone.

"I am not of the opinion that ignorance is bliss, but rather, it is dangerous. If I am to adapt to this new world, there are things I need to know. Not the least of which is how others will react to my presence, given the legends that may be associated with me. I would rather you preserve my safety than my feelings."

Elsa nodded. "I'll do my best, but please try to understand, I'm not used to talking about any of this. It's hard for me to share."

"You have been alone with this for a very long time." When Elsa tried to look away, Dante dared to cup her cheek with his hand, his thumb gently stroking the softness of her skin. "I will keep this in mind, so long as you also remember that, no matter what else happens, you are no longer alone."

Her eyes filled with tears. She blinked them away,

smiling at Dante, though there were lines of strain at the corners of her lips.

"It'll be hard to forget, since you insist on carrying me everywhere." She lifted her hand to cover his and pressed her cheek into his palm. She tightened her grip for a moment, then pulled his hand away.

He knew she was making light of the situation, and he let her. There were weights she carried deep within her soul. The more time he spent with her, the more obvious they became.

Though he could not bring himself to smile, he did lift her from her chair, preparing to carry her to a more comfortable spot for her to rest. For the first time, she did not melt against him, but instead reached for something on her desk.

"Wait."

Dante lowered her back into her chair and watched as she picked up a strange box. It was shaped somewhat like a book, but had cords coming out of it, which she promptly removed.

"Is that a computer?"

Despite what had just passed between them and the uncertainty he still felt, a surge of excitement flowed through him. He had read of computers and was eager to witness one in use.

"Yes, it is." She picked it up and held it to her chest, then leaned forward as if she intended to stand.

"Elsa, please," Dante said, using a tone more stern than he had ever dared with another. Her eyes widened slightly, but she paused and allowed him to pick her up once more.

Her skin was warm, her body soft against him. Even now, he ached to pull her closer. How could it be that holding her in his arms felt so natural, so right? The scent of roses came to him from her hair. Dante felt a sudden urge to bury his face in it, perhaps trail his fingers down her neck before placing a kiss on the graceful slope of her shoulder.

His voice came out unexpectedly low, with a rough tenor, when he managed to speak. "Where am I to take you?"

Elsa's lips parted, her eyelids lowering briefly. For a moment, Dante wondered if her thoughts, her desire, had mirrored his own. But then, she cleared her throat, and said, "The entertainment room, please."

When they arrived, he gently deposited her on the couch, though he was loathe to let her slip from his embrace.

"The movies you want are in that cabinet there." She pointed to a shelf next to the large television.

"I must first tend to your injuries."

"I'm fine, really."

"Then it should not take long."

Another bathroom adjoined the room. Inside, as expected, he found clean washcloths, which he ran under cold water. An unbidden memory played through his mind, of dousing his vest during the fire. Had it only been days ago? Or decades?

It was too much to consider. At the moment, he needed to focus on Elsa. He wrung out the washcloths and took a towel from the rack above the sink, then returned to her side.

She shifted away from him as he sat next to her on the couch. At first, he thought she was trying to put distance between them, but the sight of her soft smile, the rosy flush creeping up her neck convinced him it was actually an invitation.

The doubts that plagued him faded in the light of her offer, and he found himself sliding even closer to her. He gently dabbed at her hands with the wet cloth. When he had satisfied himself that her wounds were clean, he placed her hands together with the cool cloth held between to help soothe them.

He wondered if he dared to lift the hem of her pants to inspect her knees. Though she seemed to enjoy his touch, surely there were limits he dare not cross. Regardless, it needed to be done. Dante shifted to sit by her feet, turning so that he could see Elsa's face. He needed to watch her expression.

Her eyes were wide as she watched him slide his hands along the sides of her shapely calves. Her skin was like silk. Her lips slowly parted and her breath became uneven.

When her legs were exposed up to the tops of her knees, she finally glanced at him.

Her eyes were heavy-lidded, smoldering. They burned like embers, and the heat of her gaze raked Dante down to his soul.

As quickly as the look appeared, it vanished, leaving him to wonder if it had been nothing more than a flight of fancy. Returning his focus to his task, he took two more wet cloths and laid one on each of her knees. They bore red marks from her fall, but the skin had not broken.

He lifted her legs carefully, then placed the towel beneath her knees for support. His hands trailed down her calves, a lingering touch that he could not resist. Elsa never shrank back. She never looked away.

He could feel his heart hammering in his chest. She had brought him to her time, her home, to assist with her book. It made a certain sense that she would want to hear from him what his life had been like, but after Rachel's words, he wondered if it was possible that Elsa wanted more. Could she be seeking to create new moments between them to use as inspiration?

If so, Dante was uncertain he would even try to resist.

Chapter Ten

Telling Dante about the legends surrounding him had always been part of Elsa's plan, but not so soon. He needed to adjust, to adapt to his new world and get to know her. He needed to trust her first.

From his perspective, they had only met a few days ago. She was surprised he was still talking to her after what Rachel had told him.

"Shall we begin, then?" Dante was kneeling right next to her, his hands lingering on the backs of her legs. Her skin felt electrified, tingling heat pooling low in her body.

Before she could respond, Winston wandered into the room, an empty glass in his hand. Dante leapt up, then walked several steps away from Elsa. He cast a guilty look at Winston.

"Not interrupting anything, am I?" Winston asked.

"Winston…" Elsa said.

He chuckled. "I heard a car a bit ago and thought you might need another glass for tea."

"The tea!"

Dante gestured for her to stay in place. "If I may—our unexpected visitor has gone. However, I fear it was quite a distraction. I will go and fetch the tea presently and bring it here. That is, if you will both excuse me?"

"Go on, then." Winston snorted. "You don't have to be so formal about it."

"If you would be so kind as to remain here and ensure that Elsa does not try to leave the couch," Dante said. "I would be much obliged."

"Absolutely. She needs to be resting, and I'll see that she does."

"Don't forget to lock the studio doors when you come back in, please," she said.

"I will take care of it. Do not worry."

In the doorway, Winston stepped aside enough for Dante to pass, but reached out and patted his shoulder. Elsa didn't miss the smile that crossed Dante's face at the gesture.

Winston inclined his head as if listening to Dante's retreat, then joined her on the couch, sitting next to her when she scrunched up against the cushions. Winston was practically beaming.

"I like him."

"That's high praise, coming from you. What did he do to get in your good graces so quickly?"

"Why, he's been taking such good care of you, of course. Don't think I don't know. He's been doting on you for days." Winston leaned in and whispered, "And it's about time too."

"Dante's just a friend, Winston."

Winston shrugged. "For now, perhaps. But he's a fine man. You could do a lot worse."

She was well aware of that. In fact, she didn't think it was possible to do any better. Before she knew that she would be bringing him back to her time, she'd dreamed so many times of living with Dante, of loving him. An idealized love. It was hard to keep those dreams at bay. But he wasn't some weird time-travel mail-order groom.

"And how are you, my love?" Winston asked, reaching over to pat her knee. His hand landed on the wet cloth that Dante had so thoughtfully applied. "What's this?"

"It's nothing. I just took a bit of a tumble in the garden."

Winston puffed out a breath. "That's it. I take back all the nice things I said."

Elsa laughed. "It's too late for that. I know how you really feel about him."

"And what about you?"

She took the dry towel from under her knees and set it on the coffee table, then folded the damp washcloths and placed them on top. They weren't wet enough to soak through and damage the wood.

"It's complicated."

"Pfft. I'll let you in on a secret. Life is a lot simpler than you think. And it's also shorter. If you like him, you need to act on it."

"I don't know that he likes me as much." She wished she hadn't let that slip out, but Winston just laughed and patted her knee again.

"He likes you, all right. He's just too well mannered to let on about it. Why else would he stay by your side all this time?"

Elsa could think of dozens of reasons that had nothing to do with Dante liking her. Fear and uncertainty were at the top of the list. And even if he had been starting to warm up to her, that had been halted by Rachel's untimely information dump.

Dante cleared his throat, appearing in the doorway. How long had he been standing there? Elsa turned scarlet thinking about it.

"You!" Winston turned around. He jerked his thumb over his shoulder toward her. "I expect you to take better care of Elsa from now on."

"It was my fault," she said.

"I fear I must disagree." Dante entered the room and set the tray of tea and cookies on the coffee table. He straightened stiffly. "I should have been more vigilant. For that I apologize. Both to Elsa and to you, Winston."

"Well, you just see to it that it doesn't happen again, or you'll get that walloping I promised you the first night you came."

"I do not doubt it, sir."

"Well, then. I'm off to make dinner. You kids have

fun." Winston stood and slowly shuffled down the hallway.

"He threatened to wallop you on your first night here?" That was hardly the welcome she wanted for Dante.

"There were extenuating circumstances."

"I can't imagine what they were. Maybe he was joking."

"I am quite certain he meant every word. It was shortly after your collapse."

"He was probably just upset."

"We both were."

"I didn't mean to scare you."

Dante let out a short chuckle and shook his head. His right side was toward her, and he inclined his body so most of his face was covered with his mask. Elsa couldn't stand when he did that, hiding right in front of her.

"The matter was hardly under your control," Dante said.

"Still, I wanted your first days to be pleasant. That's one of the reasons I was trying to put this off. I want you to be happy here."

"Happiness based on half-truths is seldom lasting."

"Full disclosure, then. Or as close as I can manage."

Elsa held out her hand to seal the agreement. At least, that was what she told herself she was doing. She wasn't just coming up with an excuse to get him closer. The flutter in her chest when he took a step toward her and gently grasped her hand had nothing to do with it.

"I appreciate your efforts."

He let go of her hand, which was just as well since it was already starting to shake. He sat next to her and waited for her to begin. If only she knew where to start.

Going all the way back to the first time she'd time traveled was much too intense. The memories there were dark enough that Elsa never wanted to think of them again. Besides, she didn't want to overwhelm him with too much information. She decided to start with the legend, since Dante was so focused on that at the moment.

"These legends that grew up around you, they have very little to do with who you are or even what Giselle said about you. The story has taken on a life of its own."

"A nefarious one, it would seem."

"There are many versions of the story. Some are frightening, but some are actually quite lovely."

"From what Rachel said, I do not see how that can be so."

Elsa sighed, trying to find the right words. She knew this was a turning point both in their relationship and in Dante's relationship with her time.

"There's something compelling about the notion of an artistic genius working so hard to keep creating his art. It resonates deep within many people's souls."

"Even if he resorts to murder?"

"Not all of the stories say that he did. Some of them say

he was blamed unjustly."

"As Giselle blamed me for Heinrich's death."

"I'm so sorry. I couldn't keep her from saying so in your time. But I can write a different story now. Your story."

"Your book?"

"Our book. I won't write it without you. And I will never show it to another person unless you want me to."

Elsa picked up her laptop. She typed in her password and opened her manuscript folder, then turned the computer around so he could see the screen. He shifted closer as he watched her use the track pad to select the document.

"This is the file with everything I've written so far," she said. "It's only a rough outline and notes, really. Tap it twice, and the file will open. Or you can press the key that says 'delete' and the file is gone. I'll promise you I will never try to write it again."

"You identify so strongly with this character who would do anything for his art, yet you would destroy your work so willingly?"

"You're more important." Elsa hadn't meant to speak with such intensity. She tried to cover it up, but only made things worse. "Besides, for most people, it's not about the art. It's about the longing for love and acceptance. That's something everyone can relate to."

Dante watched her silently for a few moments, then he

said, "At the very least, I should like to read it first."

"If you tap on the track pad here, you can open the document. Read it whenever you want."

"Thank you."

She thought he might get so distracted by the laptop that he would forget about watching the movie, but she wasn't so lucky.

"I believe I am ready to proceed."

Elsa leaned forward to put the laptop on the coffee table. Dante reached out and took it from her, then set it aside for her.

"If you do not mind, I would like to avoid Winston's ire. I do not doubt he would make good on his threat if you were to injure yourself again. Indeed, I should not resist his punishment."

"He shouldn't have said that. Especially not on your first night here."

Dante ran his fingertips over her laptop, an unconscious habit that sent shivers down Elsa's spine. She couldn't keep herself from imagining those long fingers skimming over her skin.

"There is something else you should know about the night I arrived."

"Okay." When Dante didn't continue, Elsa said, "You can tell me anything."

"You were quite cold when you collapsed. Winston and I were gravely concerned. There were few resources with which to warm you. We resorted to what was most readily available."

"I don't see a problem with that." She remembered stacks of blankets on the bed when she woke up.

He turned, his gaze focusing on her with an intensity that made her shift in her seat.

"The primary heat source for that first night was…me."

"You?"

Elsa's mind immediately filled in everything he hadn't said. Her skin prickled as she could almost feel Dante's arms around her, his body pressed against hers, the heat of his chest at her back, his long legs twining with hers. She'd only had time to set out a pair of pajama bottoms for him. He probably hadn't even been wearing a shirt.

"I assure you, I was a complete gentleman," he said. "Garrett and Winston can attest to this, as they were present as well."

Nothing could dampen the pure desire that flooded through her body. All she could think of was Dante next to her. Dante in bed with her. Dante half-naked with her.

"I think I'd like some tea." She reached toward the glass as he did. He was probably trying to help her again, but their hands collided.

A shock ran up her arms from the contact, lighting her up even more. She had the strongest urge to grab his arm and pull him down on top of her. She took deep, even breaths to try to rein in her libido.

No wonder he seemed so comfortable carrying her around and touching her. That contact was nothing compared to spending an entire night in bed together.

How could she ever look at him again without picturing that night? And how could she ever stop herself from wanting more from him than she had any right to ask?

Chapter Eleven

Any hopes Dante had that Elsa's interest in him went beyond the academic drowned in the darkness of her eyes, the way she gasped for breath. She must be revolted at the thought of sleeping next to him.

"I apologize." His voice was colder than he had expected. "I should have confessed this sooner."

"You didn't do anything wrong." She curled her legs up under her and leaned against the arm of the couch. Pulling away.

He was not surprised by her reaction so much as how disappointed he felt. The dream of Elsa desiring him had taken root within his mind despite his misgivings. He could not even offer to leave. Where would he go?

At the very least, he could ease her discomfort by completing this task as quickly as possible.

"Perhaps we should proceed."

"I suppose so."

She pointed at a shelf she had shown Dante earlier that was full of movies. The bottom half of the shelf was a cabinet with closed doors.

"There's a made-for-TV movie version on the far right

inside the cabinet. I think that'll be the best one to start with."

It did not take long for him to follow Elsa's instructions and begin the movie. She had told him to think of it as a theatre in a box. The metaphor was charming, though unnecessary. Dante had already read the texts on video recordings.

Seeing the technology at work was much more exciting. Elsa was inured to it, however. By his reckoning, she was asleep before the second act had even begun. Her head slowly listed to one side, until it was resting on the arm of the couch.

Dante waited until he was certain she was deeply asleep before pausing the movie and shifting her so that she was more comfortable. He gently lowered her arm to her side and covered her with the blanket that was neatly placed over the back of the couch.

It was difficult not to linger, watching her sleep. The rise and fall of her chest and the soft sounds of her breathing soothed him, even in his current state of uncertainty. Perhaps especially so. It reminded him of his first night in this time, when he had held her in his arms as she slept.

Everything had seemed much simpler then, and the absurdity of that nearly caused Dante to laugh aloud. He contained himself, ensuring he did not wake Elsa.

He smoothed down a few errant hairs on the side of her

head and was about to return to his seat, but she sighed in her sleep, brushing her cheek against his hand. He let his thumb trail along her warm skin, then down the line of her jaw.

Her breath distinctly quickened, her lips parting, as if waiting to be kissed. Mesmerized, Dante leaned forward, wondering if her lips would feel as lush as they appeared. He felt her warm breath on his face before he marshaled himself.

He stood abruptly, taking a few steps away from her as he collected himself. What was he thinking? Taking advantage of a sleeping woman… Perhaps this legend was not as far from the truth as he would like.

Dante sat back down on the couch, putting as much distance between them as he could. He took a deep breath and pressed the button that would resume the movie.

So much had happened in such a short amount of time, so much progress made. And he himself had somehow become part of the legends of this world, however tangentially. He could scarcely believe it.

Whatever else she was, Giselle was a master storyteller. She had begun to spin her tales as soon as she joined Heinrich's theatre, leading Dante along and using him to invoke Klaus's jealousy and hasten their marriage.

Dante had often overheard Giselle telling admirers about the reclusive savant who dwelled beneath the theatre and built apparatuses for each production. She painted him as a tortured soul that Heinrich had brought into his home out of the kindness of his heart. She also called Dante a deformed monster who coveted her from the shadows.

A dozen people had seen Heinrich's fall, had watched as Dante clung to his father's arm, trying to pull Heinrich back onto the scaffolding. When Giselle first said that Dante pushed Heinrich to his death, the voices of protest were strong. Gradually, they diminished.

Her story had begun to take root even before the fire. Had it only been two short days ago? And yet, it was a century away.

The memory of Heinrich's death spawned a sharp pain in Dante's chest. Dante clutched one hand above his heart, the other covering his eyes, willing himself back under control.

It would not do for Elsa to awaken and find him so distraught. She might think that it was because of the movie, but no. The more he thought of it, the more the legend made sense. His reputation had died along with his father.

Dante did not need to torture himself with more of the tale. He stopped the movie, switching over to the television. The images were equally overwhelming at first, though in a much different manner. They distracted him from the morose train of his thoughts.

He watched for several minutes, listening to the new vernacular. Television would be an excellent tool for adaptation. Perhaps as important as the books she had commissioned for him.

The laptop sat before him, holding yet another book with knowledge that could assist him. Not a view into this time, but into how Elsa herself saw Dante—what she thought of him.

One moment, it would seem she could not be close enough to him. The next, she would pull away. Dante hoped her manuscript might provide some clarity on the matter.

He picked up the laptop, marveling at how light it was. The screen was mostly dark, a moving display of lights that looked like sentient fireworks flying across its surface in mesmerizing patterns. He watched it for some time before finally tracing his fingertip over the track pad's surface, as Elsa had before.

Immediately, the screen flickered to life, the fireworks replaced with a static view of a monochromatic background with a square in the center asking him for a password.

Elsa had not mentioned a password.

He had avidly read all of the books he could on computers and he understood the premise easily enough. He did not want to wake her to have her open the document for him. Not only was she still exhausted, but he preferred to read this in private.

All he had to do was use what he knew of her.

Admittedly, that was not much. He first tried Leonardo's name, then Winston and Garrett, hunting out the letters and pressing each in turn. None of them worked. Dante thought for some time before typing in *phantom*, but it also did nothing.

Strangely, that reassured him. He glanced over at Elsa's still form, watching her take slow, even breaths. Fortified by that peaceful sight, he turned back to the computer. He had not exhausted the list of names he could try, but, on a whim, decided to enter his own next.

It worked.

Dante sat back, stunned by this revelation. Elsa had selected his name as her password. Not the Phantom's. Dante's name.

He felt as if a weight had been removed from his chest. She had said that he was more important to her than her book. Knowing this, it was easier for him to believe her. And he wanted to believe her.

But more than that, he wanted her to see the man that he was, not the legend he became.

He opened the document, eager to see what she had done with the myths surrounding his life. Skimming through the outline, he found extensive notes that she had marked as backstory. Rather than dealing with the legend, they primarily focused on his parents.

There was a lengthy section regarding his mother and her "bright and loving spirit". Several examples of her kindness were briefly described, most of which Dante was unaware. Elsa wrote about Dante's mother with such warmth.

Her notes also spoke of Heinrich's relationship with Dante's mother in great detail. Dante had no idea his father had been so loving, but again, Elsa had documented several events where Heinrich had made a special and sometimes stunning effort to convey his feelings.

Elsa also set forth the beginning of Klaus's hatred for Dante, the jealousy Klaus had felt at the birth of his younger brother. There were references to what Elsa called "the event", but those sections were strangely obscure.

When Dante reached the section regarding the fire in the theatre, he read the paragraph over at least a dozen times, refusing to believe. Finally, he set the computer away from him on the table and leaned back from the screen. He covered his eyes with his hands and rested his head on the back of the couch, trying not to think on what he had read.

It was some time later that he felt Elsa shift next to him, her hands on his arm.

"Dante, are you all right?"

He took a few slow breaths, not daring to uncover his eyes until he had composed himself somewhat.

"Is this true?"

"Which part?"

"The fire. That Klaus and Giselle set it on purpose."

Saying the words aloud sickened him. Everything Heinrich had worked for, gone. Everything he had wanted to give to his sons, nothing but ash.

"The theatre was bankrupt thanks to Klaus. There was an insurance policy, and Giselle wanted the money."

"But they died." The horror of discovering their bodies returned—the loss and futility. As did the memory of Elsa, pulling Dante from the inferno.

"Things didn't go according to their plan. Klaus was drunk, as usual." Her voice was sharp with a bitterness Dante did not understand. The edge dulled, as she continued. "I'm sorry. I didn't expect you to read this alone."

He finally removed his hands from his face so he could look at her. She was kneeling next to him, one hand on his shoulder and the other upon his arm. Her color had much improved and she seemed better able to support herself. Still, she chewed on her lower lip, strain pinching the skin around her eyes.

"How do you know all of this?"

"I was there. Klaus couldn't work the lock on Heinrich's safe. By the time he and Giselle loaded up the lockbox, the fire had spread. Klaus succumbed to the smoke and Giselle... Well, you saw what happened to her."

"I had no idea they had sunk so low."

"Not even when they accused you of killing Heinrich?"

"You know of that too?"

"Yes."

How should he be surprised anymore? Dante shook his head. "I could understand their confusion. As you said, Klaus was often inebriated, and with Heinrich's death… It all happened so fast. To this day, I blame myself."

Her hand tightened on Dante's arm and she rose on her knees, her face quite close to his. Her brow furrowed and her lips pulled down at the corners. When she spoke, her voice was like steel and her eyes flashed as hot as the fire from which she had pulled him.

"Heinrich's death was not your fault." She paused, fretting her lower lip. When she spoke again, her voice had softened. "He was dead before he fell off the scaffold."

"You were there that night as well."

"You saw me."

"I was not certain what I saw."

"I am." Her grip loosened on his arm. She sat back on her legs, leaning against the couch as if her outburst had drained her. "I think he had a heart attack. There was nothing you could have done to save him. You almost died trying to pull him back onto the scaffold, but he was already gone when he fell. I could see his face."

She shivered, her eyes staring blankly over Dante's shoulder, as if she was viewing the memory instead of the room around them. Dante impulsively reached for her, cradling her face in his hands so that she looked at him instead.

"Think no more upon it, I beg you. It was a horrible moment, and one that is best left behind the both of us."

In his mind, the memory was blurred. Too many emotions warred within him. Heinrich had only just told Dante that he was Dante's father moments before falling from the scaffold. Dante had learned more by reading Elsa's notes than Heinrich had been able to explain.

Knowing that Dante could not have saved his father was an added balm to his soul. He had so many reasons to be grateful to her, though he dared not express his thanks.

Elsa smiled gently at him and nodded. She let out a sigh, gripping his hands and pulling them from her face, though she did not let them go.

"It must have been strange for you to see me."

"Not so very strange," he said, returning her smile briefly. He was unsure whether to continue, but she was being so open with him. Dante wished to reciprocate. "You glowed with the same light as the night you pulled me from the fire. I thought you were an angel come to take Heinrich to Heaven."

"I wondered why you came with me the night of the fire," she said. "I was afraid when I came back for you that you wouldn't trust me. I guess you thought it was safe to trust an angel with your life."

Dante let out a short laugh and shook his head. "In that moment, I thought my life was already forfeit. I did not trust you with my life. I trusted you with my soul."

Chapter Twelve

The next day, the invisible weights bogging down Elsa's energy were gone. The emotional ones were heavier than ever. Making it through dinner with Garrett hadn't been the gauntlet she feared. It had actually been pleasant, and a much-needed boost after what Dante had confessed.

Putting his life in her hands was bad enough, but his soul?

What he said didn't change anything. The bottom line remained. He was depending on her, and she was going to come through for him. She would help him establish himself, hopefully they would become friends, and that would be enough for her.

She dressed as quickly as she could, then headed to Dante's room. He wasn't there or in the kitchen. Elsa went to check the entertainment room and noticed the doors to the studio were open.

When she reached the doorway, she saw Dante leaning over a canvas on the easel in the painting corner. The doors to the patio beyond were wide open, letting in a cool morning breeze.

"Good morning." He smiled brightly when he saw her,

then went to the sink to wash out his brush.

It took Elsa a few moments to recover from that smile, from seeing him in the morning light streaming through the windows, from…everything.

"Good morning," she finally said. "Am I intruding?"

"Not at all. I believe I have finished the piece."

"Finished? Have you been up all night?"

"I was unable to sleep."

"You should have woken me."

"I hardly think so. You need your rest, and I have much to catch up on. When I tired of reading, I came here. I hope that is all right."

He set the brush aside and turned back to her. The sun struck his tousled hair, tiny highlights of lighter brown appearing that she had never noticed before. It was wavier than she'd seen it as well, and his jaw was shadowed from not shaving.

The confidence she'd felt that morning about just being friends vanished. She wanted to touch the rough stubble on his cheek, to curl up next to him as they read together. She wanted to wake up with him beside her every morning and go to sleep in his arms every night.

Elsa shoved down the urgent longing that pressed against her heart. "What did you paint?"

"You are welcome to look. Allow me to help you."

Dante started toward her, but she knew that meant he was planning to carry her. The thought of him holding her was too painful to bear at the moment.

"I'm much better this morning." She briskly walked toward the canvas. His smile faltered, but she tried not to think about that.

Curiosity helped her push aside her melancholy as she neared his work. She wondered what he had chosen as his first subject. The painting surprised her.

Flowers from the garden outside gracefully filled the canvas, captured in breathtaking colors. On one long, green leaf, an emerald lizard sat, staring out at her with inscrutable golden eyes. The brushstrokes were confident and bold, adding movement to an otherwise still scene.

Elsa felt a sense of awe and wonder wash over her like an ocean wave. It lifted her from her body, but set her back down a moment later. The odd sensation happened several times before she realized that his painting was activating her ability, but the only place it could take her was the present moment—the present spot.

She had never felt anything like it. It was beyond contentment, beyond peace. A feeling of home.

Warmth surrounded her. She was being supported by someone, enfolded in that emotion. It wrapped around her like an embrace. Like Dante's arms.

He was holding her up. Her knees had gone weak and she was leaning against his chest. His strong arms were wrapped tightly around her.

The left side of his face was closest to her as she looked

up at him. His eyes were as blue as ocean water over white sands.

"Are you all right?"

"Of course."

"You started to fall again."

"Did I?" She felt her body again like waking from a dream. It had been a long time since her power triggered without her controlling it. "I think I need to sit down."

Dante lifted her from the ground and, as lightly tethered as she was to her body, it felt like a dip on a roller coaster ride. She let out a giggle and was mortified. She definitely needed more sleep.

"Sorry."

Dante's concern softened into a smile that quickly grew. "Whatever for?"

His smile didn't fade as he carried her outside onto the patio and set her on the lounge chair. He pulled another chair close, closer than he'd done the day before, and sat next to her, leaning forward with his elbows resting on his knees.

"Here we are again," she said.

"I can think of nowhere else I would rather be."

Elsa laughed, then realized she agreed. No matter what became of the two of them in the future, right now, the present moment, was absolutely perfect.

"Me too. Your painting is amazing."

"Yes, literally stunning, it would seem." His tone was

teasing, but then grew serious. "Unless you are having some sort of relapse."

"No, not at all. The painting just triggered my ability unexpectedly."

"I do not understand."

"Right. I haven't explained how it works yet." She took a deep breath and dove right in before she could talk herself out of it. "The way I travel is through works of art. If a piece is especially filled with emotion, either by its creator when it was made or by events that happened around it, I can latch on to that energy and travel to those moments."

"My painting caused you to travel through time?" Dante looked perplexed, his eyebrows furrowing.

"No. Well, yes. I'm not explaining this well. Your painting made my powers activate, but there was nowhere and no...*when* for it to take me."

"And so it made you faint?"

"It made me start to travel, but since I was already at the destination, I didn't go anywhere."

"I'm terribly sorry. I did not mean..."

"Don't worry. It was really pleasant, actually. I've never felt anything like that." She laughed again and clasped his hand. "What do you call the piece?"

"I had not considered a name. But I would think *In the Sun* should do nicely. My little friend seemed to be enjoying herself immensely as I worked."

"It's a beautiful painting."

"I am glad you like it."

He lifted Elsa's hand to his lips and pressed a gentle kiss on her knuckles. The gesture had felt completely natural, but it took them both by surprise. Dante's eyes widened and he quickly lowered her hand again, shifting in his chair.

Elsa couldn't think of anything to say to cover the awkwardness of the moment. He cleared his throat and saved her from having to try.

"If you travel through art, how is it you discovered me? I spent my life in the circus and the theatre. There were no great works of art around me."

Apparently, he wanted to act as if that precious kiss hadn't happened. She could do that. Elsa was becoming well-practiced at denial since Dante had arrived.

"It's more about the emotions that are experienced around the pieces than their greatness, both that go into creating them and that surround them."

Dante was still holding her hand, and she lifted it slightly, keeping her grip on his fingers so he knew she wasn't trying to extricate herself. Sunlight glinted from his ring, highlighting the etchings of vines that coated its surface.

"My mother's ring?"

Elsa nodded. "Did you know that Heinrich made it for her?"

"I did not." Dante looked at the ring as if he was seeing it for the first time.

"This ring has seen so many important moments in people's lives." She ran her thumb over its surface reverently. "I've seen them all. Amazing moments. Painful moments."

She tried not to, but she found herself staring at Dante's mask, remembering that horrible moment when he'd been burned. That was the worst moment she had ever witnessed. She wished she could scrub the memory from her brain.

If he saw her looking, he didn't mention it.

"Would you tell me?"

"Some things are better left in the past."

"I thought I made my opinion on that matter clear."

She shook her head. "But this is bad. Really bad."

"It is knowledge I am strong enough to bear. Can you not have faith in me?"

A glimmer of something bright and possible fluttered in Elsa's chest. She realized that she actually could. The feeling flooded her body with warmth, with hope. She wanted to let it soak in soul-deep, but Dante was waiting.

This would be hard to say and harder yet for him to hear. She tried to get her thoughts in order, to figure out the best way to tell him.

"The first time Heinrich told your mother he loved her, he gave her this ring."

"That does not seem so terrible."

"That part wasn't. But they started off in a bad place, even though they loved each other deeply. Heinrich left his wife for your mother."

Dante's smile vanished, his lips tightening. "It troubles me to think that she would have become involved with a married man."

"You never met Heinrich's wife. She was horrible. Klaus was her son, and she was wealthy enough to have easily supported him. But when Heinrich left, she insisted he take Klaus."

"She abandoned him," Dante said. "That is why Klaus hated me."

"There was more to it." Elsa's stomach was in knots as she went on. "Your mother was Klaus's governess and much more of a mother to him than Heinrich's wife had ever been. In all my travels, I've never seen someone as kind as your mother. She was so cheerful, even in the face of terrible circumstances. She started over with nothing twice, sacrificing everything for the people she loved."

Dante was silent for a few moments, then said, "You were observing my mother when you discovered me."

"Both of your parents, actually. I found your mother first. She painted too. Not just sets and banners for the circus, but actual paintings."

"Did any of her paintings survive?" He leaned a bit closer to Elsa.

She smiled, and shifted toward him as well. "There's one in the library. A landscape."

He looked toward the studio doors, as if he was about to run to the library. Instead, he turned back to her.

"The emotions surrounding it must have been strong. I hope they were happy ones."

"For the most part, they were. I didn't know it was possible for someone to love others the way she did." Elsa's own pain rose up, pinching her throat shut. She had to push away the memories to go on. "I think she would like that you're painting. You definitely have a future in it, if that's what you want to do."

"I would scarcely know how to begin."

"I can help with that. Do you remember Garrett talking about Jazz last night at dinner?"

"Are you referring to the music or your friend?"

Dante grinned at her, and the logical thoughts progressing orderly through Elsa's mind scattered like startled birds at the sight of that playful smile.

Finally collecting herself, she said, "My friend."

"With the art gallery."

"I could arrange an introduction."

"Perhaps when I have a few more pieces to show her."

"Just let me know when you're ready. We can have her over for dinner or something."

He smiled and said, "I must confess, I quite like having you to myself."

Elsa ignored the way her heart danced at his words, the fluttering in her stomach that made her feel as though she could fly. She focused on everything he needed from her.

"You don't really have much choice of company at the moment."

He leaned back a bit, looking perplexed. "What do you mean?"

"I mean that we have to be careful right now. You don't have any form of identification. We can't explain how you're here, where you came from or how you entered the country."

"If it will help, I have been working to learn modern speech patterns and adjust my accent."

"How?"

He cleared his throat and, in a passable American accent, said, "I watched a lot of TV last night before I hit the studio."

Laughter burst from Elsa's chest. She couldn't stop it. Hearing him talk like that was so incongruous.

"Was it that bad?" he asked, reverting to his normal accent.

"No, it was actually really good. I'm just not used to hearing you talk that way."

"Maybe you should get used to it." He once more adopted the accent, making her laugh even harder.

When she had regained control again, she said, "Pretending to be from this place and time is one thing.

Proving it is another. I haven't figured out how to manage that yet. And I can't ask anyone about it, because that would lead to questions that could cause problems for us."

"Do not think on it any longer," he said. "We will sort it out, eventually, and should not let it spoil the current moment."

Elsa wished she could push it from her mind, but then Dante brought them back to the subject of the ring. Working out how to get him papers would have been a more comfortable topic.

"You said my mother sacrificed everything twice for those she loved. She never spoke of any hardships with me, though I was quite young when she passed. I had only thought of her as happy."

"She took everything in stride. But she made some hard choices. She left her governess position to be with Heinrich, even though he had no real way of supporting them. Then she left Heinrich after you were born and set out on her own. It was an amazing act of courage."

Dante sat back in his chair. His chest deflated, as if her words had knocked the wind out of him.

"I had always assumed that my father abandoned us. That it was because of..." He finished his sentence by turning his face away from her, for once hiding his mask from her view.

Elsa sat up, sliding her legs over the side of the lounge chair so that she could be closer to him. Their knees touched, but she ignored the pleasant heat that spread through her body from the contact. She tightened her grip on his hand.

"She left because of Klaus. I think he was jealous of the attention you were getting."

Dante stared at her silently, waiting for her to go on. With a deep breath, she plunged forward.

"You were just a baby. Your mother left you alone with Klaus for just a few moments, and he…" Elsa's throat nearly closed up, as if trying to shield Dante from learning the horrible truth. "There was a candle. It had burned down into a pool of molten wax."

She shook her head, closing her eyes to try to shut out the memory, but it only became sharper. Dante's wailing, his mother wiping the hot wax from his face, even though it was burning her, and Klaus standing nearby, glaring at them both.

"Klaus did this." Dante's voice was barely a whisper.

Elsa felt sick. She couldn't imagine what he was feeling, what he was thinking. He stood up and stepped away from her. She couldn't let go of his hand at first, but forced herself to release him.

Straightening his shirt, he said, "If you would not mind terribly, I should like to be by myself for a little while." His voice was rough as he spoke, and he didn't wait for a response before he left.

She thought about following him, but what could she

say? His scars had caused him so much hardship.

Based on Elsa's descriptions, Garrett thought Dante might be able to have reconstructive surgery to remove some of his scarring. But it seemed an awful time to broach that topic. She wanted Dante to know that people had changed. He didn't need to alter his appearance to have a happy life. Others would accept him as he was, like she did.

The thought of Dante going through more pain because of his scars, of taking the risk of surgery, terrified her. She covered her eyes, willing herself back under control. He needed her to be strong.

Some of the fatigue from the day before was returning. She leaned back in the lounge chair, thinking she would rest a bit to give Dante time to process what he'd learned, then find him so they could talk.

Not much later, Elsa heard soft footsteps approaching. She opened her eyes and saw a man hovering over her, backlit by the sun. At first, she thought it was Garrett. The man had the same shoulder-length blond hair, but he was too short and slender.

Her stomach lurched as she realized that she didn't know this man. She started to get up, but he was so close that she didn't have room to stand. The table blocked one side and the man blocked the other. Elsa did her best to put on a stony gaze, conveying only disapproval and hiding her fear.

"It's a lovely morning," he said.

"For trespassing?"

The man laughed in response. It was a rich, throaty sound, but made the hair on her arms stand on end. He pulled over one of the chairs from the patio table and she tried to get up again, but he shifted even closer.

"Please, stay comfortable."

"If you really want me to be comfortable, you'll tell me who you are."

He sat next to her, smiling, though the smile didn't make it to his pale blue eyes. "You really don't remember me? Elsa, I'm crushed."

She didn't like that he knew her name. She tried to think of when they might have met. His features were remarkably handsome, but the smile that pursed his full lips seemed cruel, and the lines around his eyes as he squinted in the sun made him look angry.

"I thought our date went so well. I was disappointed when you didn't call." His voice was as smooth as snakeskin.

Elsa suddenly remembered a dinner Jazz had set up a few months back with one of the new artists from the gallery. Jazz called to say she couldn't make it after Elsa had already arrived, so she tried to cover for her friend. Elsa vaguely remembered listening to him talk about art and the gallery, but she had been so distracted with her plans to bring Dante to her time she'd only half paid attention.

Back then, she knew there were only a few events left in Dante's ring with strong enough imprints that she could use them to travel. She could sense the energy dwindling and she was getting desperate.

The random nature of her powers meant that she never knew when or where a piece of art was going to take her. The first time she saw Dante through his ring had been the day Heinrich died. The next trip took her to the day Heinrich offered Dante a job with the theatre—years earlier in Dante's lifetime. The third event took place between the two moments. He was helping with a performance, running around on the catwalks to operate incredible mechanisms he had developed for a play.

She had also visited times when Mary owned the ring —after the fire. Elsa knew Dante would be in the theatre while it burned. That would be the one moment when she could try to save him. And she had no idea when the ring would drop her there.

When she had met this man sitting next to her, whoever he was, she was focused on getting the play off the ground to hopefully boost her power, preparing her house for Dante's arrival, and figuring out how she could help Dante establish himself.

"I didn't know I was supposed to call," Elsa said.

A wave of anger flashed across his face, his lips tightening in a frown and his eyebrows lowering over those cold blue eyes. Elsa had seen that look too many times before. It usually preceded violence.

She couldn't move. Her heart pounded in her chest and her muscles seemed to turn to stone.

Just as quickly, his expression became placid again. He sat forward and smiled. "It's all right. I forgive you."

Elsa felt herself relax just a bit. Enough for her to ask, "How did you find out where I live?"

His smirk made her wonder if she'd find feathers in his mouth. With a shrug, he said, "Friend of a friend."

Elsa's friends would never give someone she didn't know information about where she lived. But he had found her somehow.

"What is it that you want?"

"I want us to be friends. Good friends." He leaned back in his chair. "I was thinking perhaps we could collaborate on a piece. I find you inspiring, and I think you can understand the allure of having someone to inspire you, what with the actor you've hired to live with you."

"I didn't hire Dante." There was more ire in her tone than was probably wise.

"So it isn't a professional relationship, then?" His gaze slowly slid down her body, making her wish she was wearing baggy sweats, even with the temperature starting to climb. "If I had known you liked to play dress up, maybe our date would have ended differently."

Date? As frightening as he was, Elsa was about to let

him know precisely what she thought of that. Rachel and Dante walked out from the studio doors before Elsa could let the guy have it.

"There you are, Michael," Rachel said. "Did you get lost?"

"Only a bit." Michael stood and smiled at Elsa. Her stomach churned. "I saw the garden from inside and just had to take a peek. Elsa was keeping me company."

He walked over to Rachel, then gripped her arms and kissed her passionately enough to make Elsa even more uncomfortable. Dante stepped away from the pair, glancing briefly at her before turning his attention to one of the blooming gardenias.

She suddenly needed to be closer to him. She leapt up from the lounge chair and crossed the patio to stand at his side. She tried to hide the way her legs shook.

When Michael finally released Rachel, Elsa asked, "What are you doing here?"

"We were in the neighborhood and stopped by to see how you're doing." Rachel was breathless, a dazed smile on her face. "Plus, I wanted you to meet Michael, since I already told you about him."

"My sweet little thing couldn't keep a secret to save her life." Michael tapped Rachel under the chin with his finger. "But we should go. We don't want to impose."

He didn't wait for Rachel to respond. Turning on his heel, he put his hands in his pockets, then strolled down the pathway that led to the front of the house. Rachel started after him, but Elsa took a few quick steps after her and grabbed her arm.

"Rachel, are you okay?" Elsa kept her voice low so Michael wouldn't hear.

"Of course I am. You're the one who was sick." Rachel laughed, then gave Elsa a quick hug. "I've got to go. Michael hates it when I keep him waiting."

Rachel waved cheerfully, then ran after Michael. Elsa was left standing in the middle of her patio, a knot of dread heavy in her stomach. When she felt a gentle touch on her shoulder, she yelped and jumped away, then whirled around to face the potential threat.

"I did not mean to startle you," Dante said.

Before he could say anything else, Elsa stepped forward and wrapped her arms around his waist. She buried her face against his chest.

She knew she shouldn't. She should be strong. He was undoubtedly still dealing with what she had told him. But Michael had roused her own skeletons, and their rattling bones drowned out the sound of reason.

Elsa wasn't strong enough to resist the comfort of Dante's embrace.

Chapter Thirteen

The remainder of the day passed in what Dante could only think of as bliss. Elsa had been a bit on edge, and he could not say he did not feel the same after the morning's revelation. However, after hours spent in pleasant conversation on the patio and in the studio, he was feeling more at ease than he had perhaps ever been.

Once she had retired for the night, he planned to read more of the encyclopedias. The natural light faded as the sun set, and Elsa yawned with increasing frequency. Still, she made no sign that she was preparing to return to her room.

The insects were singing loudly as she turned off the fan that kept them at bay. Elsa closed and locked the doors to the patio, her gaze scanning the garden as if some menace lurked within the azaleas. When she nearly stumbled in the short distance between her desk and the door, Dante could no longer remain silent.

"Elsa, you must sleep."

"I'm not tired." Her words were distorted by an enormous yawn that she barely managed to cover with the back of her hand.

He'd been able to finish another painting while she postponed her rest. His brushes were already cleaned and put away. Drying his hands with a cloth, he approached her, unable to tame his smile. He stopped only a few inches from her, enjoying the softness of her eyes as sleep crept in around their edges.

"You are quite stubborn." He was close enough to catch her should she fall. The way she was swaying on her feet made that a very real possibility. He tossed his cloth over the back of her chair, and she did not even protest. "You must rest. Winston has tasked me with keeping you well."

"I'm fine," she said, though she yawned once more. "Let's watch a movie. I can make popcorn."

Dante gently caught her arm as she turned toward the hall and she stumbled into him. Rather than move away, she rested against his chest, yawning again. She seemed close to falling asleep on her feet.

"What is troubling you?"

She stared at the ground, then shook her head. "It's ridiculous."

"Are you still upset from your encounter with Michael?"

"I'm probably overreacting. He's Rachel's boyfriend. I know she has bad taste in guys, but really, how dangerous can he be?"

"In matters such as these, it is always best to trust one's instincts."

"The way he showed up on the patio, the things he said… It was unnerving."

Without thought, Dante pulled her close, holding her tightly. "I will not let anyone harm you."

"I keep telling you," she mumbled into his shirt, "I'm supposed to be protecting you. Great job I've done so far."

"You saved my life," he said, but stopped himself from proceeding. She had not reacted well when he expressed gratitude about the matter before. And he respected that she did not wish him to feel indebted to her.

To lead her from the fretful path her thoughts seemed to be taking, he lifted her from her feet using a bit more energy than was strictly required. She was momentarily airborne before landing gently in his arms.

As he had hoped, she let out a brief laugh. Her smile lit the room more brightly than the electric lights. Before she could gather her wits to begin yet another argument, he carried her from the studio.

She nestled against his chest, letting out a contented sigh. She fit so perfectly against him.

When he reached her bedroom, the door was open. Dante barely hesitated before entering.

In his time, it would have been scandalous for him to be in a woman's bedroom at this late hour. He was glad to be free to assist Elsa as much as needed without worrying about her social standing, especially since she was still having some trouble with her *physical* standing.

He chuckled at his unspoken jest, and she made a soft noise in response, like a roosting dove. It was not until he set her down on her bed that she roused.

"Don't go." She gripped his shirt tightly. "Please. Not yet."

"You are perfectly safe." Dante pulled the covers from under her so that she could slide beneath them.

"I know. I just don't want to be alone. Will you stay for a little while?"

Her eyes were pleading. He was not inclined to disappoint her, given how distressed she appeared.

She slid further across the bed, making room for him. The sight of her lying there, waiting for him, brought heady images to his mind. He imagined lifting the covers to join her, sliding his arms around her waist, pulling her close and…

He scolded himself for the wayward nature of his thoughts and sat instead above the covers, then leaned against the pillows. He did grant himself the comfort of stretching his legs out next to her.

As soon as he did, Elsa tucked her body snugly against his, resting her arm across his stomach and her face against his chest. He could not resist wrapping his arms around her. Indeed, there was nowhere else for him to place them.

She made another soft sound, her breath becoming deep and even as she relaxed. For Dante, the opposite was occurring. His breath came quicker as her warmth seeped into him. He could feel the blood pooling low in his body, hardening him with desire. If she were to fully awaken, he would be mortified.

He wished he could secure more modern clothes rather than the thin slacks he wore that did nothing to conceal his current state. He thought perhaps to broach the subject, but she had gone to such lengths to make him feel at home, it seemed ungrateful to ask for more.

He kept wearing the black slacks and linen shirts to show his appreciation for how considerate she had been, but his clothes and his room only served to haunt him with memories best left forgotten.

This moment was another example of his dilemma. Trapped in his clothes from another time, the only thing he could do to conceal his predicament was turn off the lights, which would plunge him back into darkness.

At least Elsa's room had large windows and he could look up and see the stars. He kept the curtains in his room open as wide as possible, yet still, he felt as if he was back in Heinrich's theatre, buried beneath the earth. Dante wanted only the sky, the air, and the beautiful colors of the garden outside.

Each kiss of sunlight peeled away more of the life he had left behind. Perhaps he might eventually become as bronzed as Garrett. The pallor of Dante's skin was already lessening with his time in the solarium and on the patio.

All but the skin under his mask, of course. He doubted even the sun would do anything to the reddened flesh beneath.

Suddenly self-conscious for an altogether different reason, he reached over and turned off the lamp. He would lie with Elsa for a little while, until he was certain she was sound asleep, and then he would slip from her room and return to the studio.

The lounge chair on the patio was quite comfortable, and after his morose thoughts, he hated the thought of going back to his room. He would sleep in the studio, the windows giving him an excellent view of the sky and the stars. Until then, he would enjoy her warmth beside him.

In the darkness, he reached up and touched the smooth surface of his mask. If only it didn't stand between them. And yet, without his mask, the mystery that it presented, they most likely never would have met. Dante could not fool himself into believing that history would have remembered him if he had simply been a set designer for a failing theatre.

He removed his mask and held it up so that it caught what little ambient light was in the room. The smooth porcelain appeared as a pool of silver darkness, a bit lighter than the backdrop of the room.

He had tested many materials before settling upon this. Lightweight, durable and comfortable enough that he barely registered its presence.

At first, he had thought to use a flesh-colored glaze to make the mask less obvious, but that only made others' reactions worse. His experiments with decorative enamels had not been met with any less derision. He had finally ceased trying to gain the acceptance of others and left his masks unadorned.

So much of his life had been dominated by his disfigurement. Knowing that his own brother was responsible...

Dante suddenly wanted the mask away from him, even if only for a few moments. He set it on Elsa's nightstand on top of a stack of books. The silence of the room settled over them, the only sound her soft breathing.

Holding her in his arms, he almost felt normal. What if this was truly what his life was now to be? Meals shared in camaraderie with Winston and perhaps at times Garrett, days creating in the studio and gardens, evenings relaxing in Elsa's company, and nights spent like this. It was more than he dared to dream. And yet, his thoughts went further.

She cared for him a great deal. That much was obvious. And though it had only been a matter of days, he could feel his heart reaching toward her, yearning for her. How could he not grow fond of someone who inspired such loyalty in her friends, who helped others so selflessly?

He pressed a gentle kiss to the top of her head, then smoothed her silken hair against her back. She let out a contented sigh and Dante smiled, gratified that she was so at ease in his presence.

It was wrong of him to want more from her. He knew that he could not give her the kind of life that she deserved, a partner who could stand beside her in the light of day without hiding behind a mask.

She was intelligent, kind, beautiful and strong. She could have any man she wanted. Why would she ever want him?

No, the most he could hope for was her friendship. For that blessing, he would consider himself the luckiest man in the world. But for a little while, he could let himself think about what their lives could have been if circumstances were different. For a little while longer, he let himself dream.

The room was filled with a golden glow when Dante opened his eyes again. It seemed he only blinked, but he must have fallen asleep. Morning light illuminated everything within the room.

He stretched, enjoying the feel of Elsa lying at his side. She had nestled against him even closer during her sleep, the softness of her breasts pressing upon his stomach and her arms folded over his chest. He glanced at her, wanting to see her face illuminated by the morning light and relaxed in sleep, but she was awake.

One of her hands was pressed against the bare skin of

Dante's chest, the contact nearly searing him. His heart began to beat frantically beneath her palm, as if striving for her touch. Her chin was resting on the back of her hand and she was smiling at him.

Her eyes were dark in the rich light of dawn, a smoldering, deep sienna. Breathtaking.

"Good morning." She cast a smile upon him broad enough that the skin at the corners of her eyes crinkled.

He had never seen her smile so completely. It took some time for him to bring himself to speak, dazed as he was by her obvious happiness at waking next to him.

"Good morning. I trust you slept well?"

His hand reached out of its own accord, combing through the golden locks of her hair. He did not even have the pretense of tucking it behind her ear. He was just mesmerized by the light in the strands, the silken texture against his fingers. Fortunately, she did not seem to mind. In fact, she closed her eyes for a moment and leaned her head against his palm.

She let out a contented sigh. "I did. And you?"

"I am quite rested." Something was scratching at the back of his mind, a warning that intruded on his ability to enjoy the moment fully.

"I didn't realize you're already this comfortable with me. I'm so glad."

He laughed. "I have been comfortable enough to sleep next to you from the very first night."

"That isn't what I meant." A blush spread across her face that made him smile despite his forebodings.

She rose on one elbow, which brought her lips very close to his. She lifted her hand to his face and, for a moment, he thought that she might kiss him. Instead, she ran her fingertips lightly along his cheek, the gentle touch resounding through his entire body as he realized it was *the right side* of his face.

Dante was halfway across the room before he even had a chance to fully process the horror of what had just happened. Elsa, beautiful Elsa, had been looking at him, smiling at him, chatting with him. All while he was not wearing his mask.

He covered his face with his hand, hiding the scars as best he could, turning so that his right side was away from her. How could she stand to look at him? To touch the marred flesh that had destroyed his chances at a normal life?

He started back to the nightstand to find his mask, but it was not where he thought he placed it the night before. Perhaps it had fallen among the books she kept at her bedside. Or Leonardo could have knocked it off the nightstand during his nightly prowls.

Dante dropped to his knees, reaching under the bed to see if it had fallen below. It was neither under the bed nor the bedside table. He rifled through the stacks of books, knocking them over in his frantic search for his mask.

Where was it?

"Dante…" Elsa's voice was quiet and thin. He had never heard that tone from her before. She sounded afraid. The thought tore through his heart, freezing him in place.

He closed his eyes, taking a deep breath and letting it out slowly. His whole body was shaking with the effort to calm himself. But he was frightening her, and why shouldn't she be frightened? He was used to those who saw his face reacting quite worse than Elsa had. At least she had not screamed.

In fact, she had spoken to him, smiled at him, even touched the scarred skin without seeming troubled at all.

The depths of her kindness went beyond what he had realized. Kindness or pity, the one reaction he found even worse than fear.

Dante opened his eyes, keeping his hand over his face. Elsa was on her knees on the bed, clutching the sheets to her chest and staring at him. Her face was bloodless, a deep crease wedged between her brows. Whatever her initial reaction had been, fear had unmistakably taken over.

He stood and turned his back to her, unable to bear her gaze. "I apologize. It was careless of me to sleep without my mask. I will not let it happen again."

He was halfway to the door when he heard her slip from the bed and quickly cross the room to him. She grabbed his shoulders with her slight hands, as if she could hold him in place. He decided to humor her and stopped.

Her fingers trembled.

"Dante, look at me."

He did not think he had the strength to turn around. He could not stand to see those eyes, those frightened eyes, staring at him. He wanted to find some dark corner in the house where he could hide.

When he did not turn, she circled to stand in front of him.

"You startled me," she said. "I don't like it when people get angry."

"I was not angry. I was terrified."

She seemed genuinely confused. "Why?"

"You should never have seen me like that. I should not have let you."

"I'm grateful that you let me see you. I want you to be comfortable with me. As comfortable as I am with you." She stepped in closer. "I don't care about what you look like. I care about who you are. You don't have to wear your mask with me. Not ever."

"A noble sentiment, however, I could not subject you to —"

"I've seen you without your mask before today."

He sought through his memory, but could not think of another time he had been without his mask while they were in the same room. "When?"

Her chest stilled, as if she was trying to keep the answers he sought from escaping with her breath. She bit her lower lip to further trap the truth within her.

"Elsa, what are you not telling me?"

"I did tell you. That I had observed you before."

"When Heinrich died. And the night of the fire, of course."

A sick feeling coiled and rattled in Dante's stomach. Elsa had also mentioned seeing Mary when Edgar gave her Dante's ring. And there were the travels where Elsa had observed Dante's parents. Dante hadn't given it much thought beyond that, his mind too filled with all that he had experienced since coming to stay with her.

"How much of my life have you witnessed?"

"My travels were usually brief, since they centered on moments of extreme emotion. Do you remember when you finally figured out the trick with mirrors and pulleys that you used to make Edgar disappear in your first production with Heinrich's theatre?"

"That hardly seems like something important enough to allow you to…"

The dread in his stomach lashed out, striking Dante's heart and pumping stinging venom through his veins. If such a relatively small accomplishment was strong enough for her traveling, what else had she seen?

"How many events in my life did you witness?"

"A few…dozen." She clasped her hands in front of her chest as if she was begging for forgiveness. At the moment, Dante was too shocked to offer any.

"Dozens? Dozens!"

She took a step toward him, but he lurched back. For the first time, he didn't want to feel her touch. What had once been intimate now seemed invasive. He had the most unsettling feeling, as if she was seeing through his clothing and there was nothing he could do to cover himself.

"What all have you seen?" he demanded.

She looked stricken, and a part of his heart went out to her, wanting to give her comfort. He would not let it win.

"Highlights, mostly." Her voice was small, her gaze fixed on the floor as if she could no longer face him. At least she had the decency to seem abashed. "I saw the night when you met Heinrich at the circus. When he offered you a job at his theatre. I saw how filled with hope you were when you arrived."

Dante's jaw began to ache from how tightly he was clenching his teeth. That was a very private moment. Knowing that someone else had been watching, even Elsa, felt like a violation.

"Go on." He kept his voice as cold as he could.

"I saw how they treated you when you arrived. How it drove you to seclusion beneath the theatre."

Elsa looked at him again, a fire blazing in her eyes. There were ample memories for her to have seen to explain her anger. His treatment at the theatre had been quite horrid, especially in the beginning.

The others made it clear that he had no place among

them. Even Heinrich had been distant, though Dante now better understood the origins of his behavior.

"Would that I had known the door was not keeping out all prying eyes."

She gasped, her mouth dropping open. Even now, as angry as he was, Dante longed to reach out and stroke the soft flesh of her lips. That fact only angered him further.

Apparently, his comment awoke a similar spark within her. Her eyes narrowed, and she dropped her hands to her sides.

"I know you watched people from the catwalks when they didn't know you were there."

"I had no recourse. I was reviled! The only people who would speak to me were Heinrich and Mary."

"What makes you think it's that different for me?"

"Don't be absurd. You are surrounded by people who care for you. You can go out in a crowd without people staring, without children pointing, without women fainting or screaming."

"Only because they don't know!" The vehemence in her voice was shocking. As was the bleakness of her expression as she spoke. "If people knew what I could do, they would hunt me down and dissect me."

"You cannot believe—"

"I know it," she said, cutting him off.

Dante was silent for a few moments, wondering at how deep her fear ran within her, how very blind she was to the people around her.

"Even Garrett? Even Winston?"

Elsa looked away, grabbing her left arm with her right as she half hugged herself and stood as stiff as a mannequin. She truly believed that even those closest to her were capable of turning on her viciously. Dante wondered what could have happened to make her have so little faith in those who cared for her so very much.

"And what of me, Elsa?"

When she looked up at him, her eyes were shining with tears, but not a one strayed over her lashes. Her voice was small when she spoke.

"I suppose I'm at your mercy."

Even more than her words, the complete and utter lack of hope she expressed shook him to his core. He thought that risking her life was the greatest threat she faced in saving him. Now he knew her act had a much higher price. She had sacrificed her sense of safety. As he had done with her on that first night, she had placed her life in his hands.

His anger evaporated in an instant. Dante took a slow step toward her. Elsa was on the edge of an emotional precipice. If he was ever to truly reach her, he must take a leap of faith himself. And despite what he had learned, he still wanted to reach her, to be with her.

When he was quite close, he took a deep breath and lowered his hand from his face.

Hope slowly seeped back into her expression, and it

seemed to him like the morning sun rising over the horizon. Her lips parted on a quick intake of breath.

He reached out to cup her cheek. His voice rasped low from his throat. "I would never do anything to harm you."

Elsa pulled her lower lip between her teeth, biting it firmly enough that he feared she might draw blood. He finally gave in to his desire, gently brushing his thumb along her lower lip, coaxing her to release it. She took a deep, shuddering breath as she did.

Dante continued to trace its satin surface. The entire time, her gaze never strayed to his scars, almost as if she did not notice them.

Grasping his hand, she pressed her cheek into his palm and closed her eyes. "I believe you."

Her skin was soft and warm. He had no doubt her lips would be much warmer, much softer. He dipped his head toward her, unable to resist the temptation to find out.

Before their lips met, a crashing sound downstairs startled him. Both of them jumped, the moment vanishing.

"What was that?" Elsa asked.

Before he could speculate, he heard Winston shouting profanities that made Dante want to cover Elsa's ears. It was too late for that, as she had already fled to the door and disappeared down the hallway. Dante followed.

They found Winston in the kitchen, lying on the floor. Elsa ran to his side, placing her arms on Winston's shoulders. She looked panicked.

"Winston, what happened?"

Winston let out a low grunt. "What's it look like happened? The old geezer fell down."

"Don't talk about yourself that way. Are you hurt?"

"My ego more than anything else."

"This isn't a joke," Elsa said.

Dante could see her pulling herself together, taking control of the situation.

Her voice was low and level when she next spoke. "Take a moment and assess yourself. Do you have pain anywhere?"

"Only on my arse, where I fell."

"Dante, call Garrett," Elsa said. "The phone is on the shelf by the door."

Dante crossed the room and picked up the device, making a quick study of the buttons on the number pad. He had read about phones, but had not used one as of yet. She rattled off a series of numbers, and he pressed each one in turn, then the talk button at her direction. When finished, he held the phone to his ear as he had seen done on the television.

"This is Garrett." Garrett's disembodied voice came through the phone.

Dante wished he had more time to marvel at the technology, but he needed to keep his focus on Winston.

"Garrett, it is Dante."

"Oh hey, Dante. What's up?"

"I fear it is a matter of what's down." Dante heard Winston chuckle, but when Dante looked over his shoulder, Elsa was scowling at him. Clearing his throat, he continued. "Winston has fallen."

"I'll be there in ten minutes. Make sure he stays still and doesn't move around too much."

"I fear that is easier said than done."

"I don't doubt it. Just have Elsa sit on him. That should do the trick."

"Indeed."

Elsa spoke up, saying, "Tell him we're in the kitchen. That way, he'll come to the right door."

Before Dante could relate this to Garrett, Garrett said, "Got it."

Dante pressed the end button and set the phone back in its cradle. He then returned to Elsa's side. "Winston is to remain as still as possible until Garrett arrives."

"Like hell I will," Winston said.

"Like hell you won't." Elsa moved so that she could sit near Winston's head, crossing her legs and pulling him down so he was using her knees as a pillow. "I don't play the boss card very often, but I'm laying it down right now. You are not moving."

"I'm going to get more stiff lying on this damn floor than I would if you'd help me up to one of the chairs."

"Then I guess Garrett will have to prescribe some painkillers for you. And I'll schedule you a massage or something."

"Hmph."

Dante watched the exchange with a growing sense of tenderness. Elsa had one hand on Winston's shoulder, and the other she used to stroke his hair. Winston would never admit it, but Dante could see the fear on his face. It was mirrored on Elsa's.

"I'll get a blanket," Dante said.

"Thank you." Elsa looked so stricken when she glanced at him. As Dante left the room, he gently touched her shoulder, and Elsa rewarded him with a faint smile.

The closest blanket that Dante knew of was in the entertainment room. He ran to it as quickly as possible and pulled the soft plum-colored throw from the back of the couch. As he turned toward the hall, he noticed one of the doors to the cabinet at the bottom of the movie shelf was open.

Elsa loved for things to be just so. Dante was certain the cabinet door had been closed when last he was in the room. Between that and his mask disappearing, an uneasy feeling stirred in his stomach.

He had no time to contemplate it further. He ran back to the kitchen and spread the blanket over Winston, then knelt at Elsa's side.

"Thanks," Winston said. Lines were etched around his eyes that had little to do with his age. He might profess that he felt fine, but Dante recognized the signs of pain.

"Was it Leonardo?" Elsa asked. "He's always trying to trip people."

"That cat will never get the best of me," Winston said. "I know how to deal with him. No, I stepped on something. Foot flew right out from under me."

Dante scanned the floor as he searched for what could have caused Winston's fall. His gaze lit upon a small object reflecting the morning light from the windows. He reached under the table to pick it up, then stood, holding it so Elsa could see.

"That's the key to the kitchen door," Elsa said. "We always keep it in the lock. How did it get on the floor?"

Dante glanced at the door, thinking back on the cabinet and his missing mask. "How, indeed."

Chapter Fourteen

The minutes that passed between Dante calling Garrett and Garrett's arrival were some of the longest of Elsa's life. Dante stayed at her side, his hand resting on her back.

She was meticulous about keeping everything in place to protect Winston. The key to the kitchen door stayed in the lock, like the one in the studio. Neither had fallen out before. The doors were old-fashioned, with antique keys that were part of the charm of the house. Elsa would install modern deadbolts as soon as possible to make sure this never happened again.

Garrett didn't bother to knock. When he arrived, he opened the door and came right in. Winston must have unlocked it earlier.

But that didn't make sense. If he had, he would've heard the key fall from the door. Elsa would have to figure it out later. Winston needed her full attention.

"Hey, Winston." Garrett smiled as casually as always, joining them on the floor.

"Hey yourself," Winston snapped.

"Garrett is here to help you," Elsa said. "The least you can do is be civil."

"Why start now?" Garrett winked at Elsa, ignoring her scowl. He placed his hands at different points along Winston's body. "How bad is the pain?"

"I'm fine," Winston said. "I tried to tell Elsa."

Winston let out a yelp as Garrett touched a spot on his back. "Fine, huh?"

Elsa hated seeing Winston in pain. She couldn't believe she had let this happen. "Is it bad?"

"Seems like you bruised yourself up pretty good," Garrett said. "But nothing that won't fix itself with a few days' rest."

"A few days?" Winston chuffed. "We'll all starve."

"We will not." Elsa tried to feign a confidence she didn't feel. "I can cook."

Winston groaned and Garrett said, "Dante, you better make sure you have my number on speed dial."

Laughing, Winston piled on. "The only thing you can cook is a peanut butter and jelly sandwich. And only then if it's not on toast."

"I would be more than happy to take over the cooking duties," Dante said. "It is the least I could do after all your hospitality."

"There. No one is starving." She wasn't sure Dante could make good on his promise, since he'd never even seen an electric range until a few days ago. Elsa was just glad Winston felt well enough to make jokes.

"Let's get him to his room," Garrett said.

"Finally." Winston waved in the general direction of Garrett's voice, pushing away from Elsa's lap. She supported him as best she could while Dante and Garrett lifted Winston to his feet.

They half carried him to his room, then worked as a team to settle him in bed. Garrett gave Winston some painkillers and strict instructions for bed rest and to sleep. Elsa knew she and Dante would have their work cut out for them to keep Winston resting. Winston was stubborn, but outnumbered now that Elsa had Dante to help.

Once Winston was asleep, Elsa returned to the kitchen with Dante and Garrett. Garrett leaned against the counter and Elsa sat at the table. Dante's presence at her side was a welcome comfort.

"Is Winston really going to be okay?" she asked.

"I think so." Garrett's tone was less than convincing. "I'm more concerned with why he fell. It isn't like Winston to be clumsy."

"The fault was not with him." Dante had placed the kitchen key on the table after finding it. He picked it up to show Garrett. "He slipped on this."

"Did it fall out of the lock?" Garrett asked.

Dante hesitated before responding. "I do not think that is the case."

"What do you think happened?" Garrett crossed his arms.

"My mask is missing. And the cabinet door on the shelf

in the entertainment room is ajar."

They hadn't watched TV last night, and Elsa was certain Dante shut the door to the cabinet after getting out the movie they watched the night before. Winston never went into that cabinet. But if none of them had done it...

"Maybe Leonardo somehow opened it," she said. "And he probably knocked your mask behind my nightstand."

Dante sucked in a quick breath of air and cast a wary look at Garrett. It took Elsa a moment to realize she'd just basically told Garrett that she and Dante had spent the night together. Honestly, she had other things to worry about at the moment.

If Garrett was surprised, he wasn't letting on. "It seems a bit much mischief for one night, even for Leo."

Elsa didn't want to contemplate the only other possibility, but she forced herself to face it. "You don't think someone was in the house last night, do you?"

"We must not dismiss the possibility," Dante said.

"Why would they only take your mask?" Garrett asked.

Elsa's cheeks tingled and her heart clenched in her chest as she ran through different scenarios. She had valuables out in plain sight. Taking Dante's mask and leaving everything else made this personal, like someone was taunting them. Her stomach churned at the thought.

"And how did they get in?" Garrett nodded toward the door. "Did Winston forget to lock up?"

"He wouldn't do that." Elsa reached for the key. "May

I?"

Dante handed her the key, his fingertips lingering a bit as they traced over her palm. Even with the fear, or perhaps because of it, his gentle touch sparked a shiver down her spine. She hoped it wasn't too obvious.

Elsa stood and walked to a drawer that held several sets of chopsticks. She grabbed one, then went to the door and pulled a piece of paper from the shelf under the phone. She put the key in the lock, then opened the door and stepped outside.

She slid the paper under the closed door, then fiddled with the chopstick until she felt the key jiggle loose. It almost bounced off the paper she had ready below, but she was still able to gently pull the paper toward her until the key was in her hand. She opened the door again, stepping back inside and holding up the key.

"Of course," Dante said.

Garrett shook his head. "How do you know this stuff?"

"I'm a writer. It's my job to know this stuff."

"That's it." Garrett pulled out his phone. "I'm calling the cops."

"No!" Elsa was standing close to Garrett now, and she reached out and grabbed his arm.

"Why not?"

That was a good question. Elsa didn't have an answer ready. She blurted out the first thing that came to mind. "We don't know for sure that someone was here."

"You're kidding, right?"

"It's my decision." She wouldn't let him argue with her about this. The police would have too many questions. They'd want to know about Dante and might ask him to prove his identity. She couldn't risk that.

Garrett let out a sigh, and she knew she'd won. She let go of his arm as he put away his phone. She'd never seen him so serious.

"Fine." Garrett picked up his bag, then fished around inside. He pulled out a small piece of black fabric. Brushing past her, he walked over to Dante. "I picked this up for you."

"Thank you." Dante took the item and turned it over in his hands. It was a mask.

Garrett stepped in close. As tall as Dante was, Garrett loomed over him.

"You listen to me." Garrett's voice was a low growl. "Elsa and Winston are very important to me. They get hurt, and I'm coming for you."

"Garrett!"

Neither man reacted to her exclamation. In a quiet and calm voice, Dante said, "I will protect them both with my life. I promise you."

"See that you do. I'll be back to check on everyone tonight."

Garrett didn't say another word to Elsa. He stalked out the door and slammed it behind him.

"I'm so sorry," she said. "I've never seen Garrett act that way."

"He cares for you a great deal. I am glad for that."

"That doesn't mean he should talk to you that way."

"I believe I would react much the same if our roles were reversed." Dante went to the door and turned the key, then tried the handle to make sure it was locked. He stared out the windows for a few moments before turning to face her again. "Would you have hesitated to contact the authorities if I were not here?"

She couldn't say that she would have. "It doesn't matter what I might have done. You're here and I'm doing what I need to do to protect you."

"This is because I have no way to prove who I am."

"Dante Lucerne died over a hundred years ago. How am I supposed to explain you being here?" She shook her head, all the different ideas she had come up with so far churning through her mind, each with its own challenges. The best idea involved Dante feigning amnesia, and that was pretty weak.

"It is not worth risking your safety."

"It absolutely is." Elsa spoke with more force than she intended. She wanted to cover her outburst, but couldn't think of anything to say.

"I must have been on my best behavior when you observed me to have made such an impression upon you."

Elsa didn't trust herself to respond to that. It wasn't just witnessing his genius or his kindness. His isolation had struck a chord with her. She knew that. But he actually had a chance to form real, honest relationships with people in her time. To be accepted for who he was. She hoped that he was starting to realize that.

Turning his new mask over in his hands, Dante smiled softly. He looked down at it for a moment, then set it on the table.

"Shall we finish breakfast? Winston may be hungry when he awakens."

Her heart seemed to bloom in her chest. Dante was choosing to let her see him, leaving his mask behind. Even with everything else going on, Elsa couldn't help but smile.

Chapter Fifteen

This was perhaps the happiest that Dante had ever been in his life. It was not just that he had a home, but that he had people who counted on him. He felt a sense of belonging he had not experienced since his mother passed away.

Winston was sleeping comfortably after sharing a dinner with Dante and Elsa. Dante had convinced her to relax and indulge in a bath while he watched over Winston. After rinsing the last dish, Dante set it in the rack to dry. He pulled the plug free and watched the soapy water swirl down the drain, thinking of Elsa in her bath.

The image of her in the large tub in her bathroom sparked a heady warmth in Dante's chest, dropping quickly to lower parts of his body. They had spent the entire day together and she never once stared at him or seemed uncomfortable.

Drying his hands, he walked to the table and picked up his new mask. He had not touched it since Garrett had left.

Even though he'd directed considerable anger and suspicion toward Dante, Garrett had still made this thoughtful gesture. Dante would work to earn Garrett's trust. He truly hoped they would become friends.

Garrett was as nonplussed by Dante's appearance as Elsa. Perhaps no one would have the visceral reactions as those in his time. It seemed impossible.

As impossible as time travel. Dante chuckled.

The bell sounded, and he set down his mask, heading for the front door. Garrett must have arrived to check on Winston. This would be Dante's first chance to regain some of the lost camaraderie he had shared with Garrett on that first night. Showing him that Winston and Elsa were both well would be a good start.

Opening the door, Dante smiled and began a greeting. The words died in his throat as he saw that it was not Garrett who had come calling.

A slender Asian woman stood before him. Her smile vanished when she saw Dante's face. Her eyes grew wide and her mouth dropped open, emitting a brief shriek.

Dante backed away from the door, covering his scars with one hand. He began apologizing, not even certain what words he was using, and raced toward the kitchen.

What had he been thinking? Opening the door without knowing who it was or how they would react. Of course people would still be shocked by his appearance. He pulled his new mask into place. It fit snugly with straps that stretched to conform to the dimensions of his head.

Though it was more comfortable than his previous mask, he was already becoming accustomed to going without. He had never realized how wearing a mask chafed the raised flesh of his scars, or how stifling it was to have half his face covered.

"It's rude to leave visitors alone in your foyer, you know."

Dante jumped at the woman's voice. He turned to find her standing in the center of the kitchen, hands on her hips, one of which was cocked to the side in a cavalier manner.

She wore black leather pants that hugged her legs like a second skin, with boots that rose to her knees. Her thin white shirt dipped down at the neck in a V and fit her thin frame perfectly. Thick black hair trailed down her back and hung about her face in windswept layers. One dark brow was arched at him, and she was frowning.

"I beg your pardon, madam." He tried to maintain as much of a dignified manner as he could. "I did not mean to startle you."

"You're lucky I didn't use my pepper spray on you."

"I beg your pardon?"

"I heard about the break in. Don't worry. I locked the door behind me."

She walked to the sink and took one of the glasses Dante had just washed, filled it with water and took a long drink before turning around again. Her gaze was scrutinizing until a broad smile brightened her face.

"You're the Phantom that Rachel talked about! The actor Elsa hired to help with her book."

"I am Dante Lucerne."

He was eager to separate himself from the character, especially if he was to become part of Elsa's life. She seemed focused on enabling him to move on, but even with a new world to explore, he found he could not bear the thought of leaving her.

"Good name." The woman looked Dante up and down as if she was assessing every part of him.

Her gaze lingered on the exposed skin of his chest for long enough that a blush swept over his face. The woman, oblivious to his discomfort, began a slow circuit around him. She stopped when they were facing once more.

"You are amazing. The mask is all wrong, though. Way too modern."

"It serves its purpose. Had I been wearing it when I answered the door, perhaps you would not have been so surprised." He didn't bother to hide the ire in his tone. He was only grateful that Winston and Elsa had not seemed to hear the disturbance.

"Maybe. Maybe not. I didn't know who you were and someone just broke in."

"Indeed. But was that truly the only origin of your outburst?"

The woman did not seem offended by Dante's bluntness. Her smile turned to a wry smirk.

"Is it makeup?"

"No."

"You're the real thing, then."

Dante did not bother to respond. He held her gaze as she boldly stared at him, her eyes calculating. He wondered if her mind ever stopped turning behind the deep sepia of her irises.

"Okay," she said. "Yeah, I was startled when I saw you. Your face is unusual and I wasn't expecting it. Deal with it. Let's move on."

"I beg your pardon?" He was quite taken aback. He had never heard anyone speak of his disfigurement with such nonchalance.

"Back to begging?" She crossed her arms and smirked.

"Who are you?" Each word came out as a gasp, exasperation winning out over his manners.

"I'm Jazz." She smiled brightly as she held out her hand. Dante took it, bowing curtly and pressing a quick kiss on the backs of her fingers. She arched an eyebrow. "Wow, you really are the real thing."

Perhaps that social custom had changed over the decades. He dropped her hand as he stood, then stepped away from her.

This was Elsa's oldest and dearest friend. He should try to make a good impression, but he was finding her quite overwhelming. Continuing in that vein, she grabbed his wrist with an alarming speed. Closing the space he had created between them, she pulled his arm closer to her face for further scrutiny.

An insect under a microscope might feel similarly exposed while being examined. She ran her finger over paint stains on his sleeve, pale greens and blues from his latest landscape. He had meant to change shirts, but had been too busy enjoying Elsa's company.

"You're a painter," Jazz said.

"Yes. Though I do not know what business that is of yours." He wrested his arm from her grasp as politely as he could.

"It is exactly my business." Her gaze turned almost hungry. She pulled a small card from her back pocket and handed it to him. It read *Jazz Gallery—Cutting Edge Art for the New Millennium.*

"Yes, you own a gallery." He had been so flustered, that fact had slipped his mind.

"This is just too good. You have to let me sell you."

"I assure you, I am not for sale."

"All you artists." Jazz waved her arms at him and made tching noises as she shook her head. "You're so concerned with not selling out. I'm concerned with putting food on your table. Let me represent you and I promise you will become one of the most famous artists of the decade. Not to mention all the money you'll rake in. After my cut, of course."

"You have not even seen any of my work."

"I don't need to see your work. I don't sell art, I sell artists. And the biggest draw for an artist is mystique." She made a point of looking him up and down. "Believe me, you have that covered. This whole Phantom persona is epic. Brilliant marketing. Your paintings could be stick figures and I'd still be able to sell them."

With a revenue stream of his own, Dante would not be reliant on Elsa for things such as a modern wardrobe. She was always so pained when she spoke of helping him to establish himself. With Jazz's help, perhaps he could do so without Elsa's involvement.

The idea was very appealing. He stared at the business card in his hand.

"Don't tell Elsa." He spoke before the thought had even fully formed.

"Why?"

Dante smiled, excitement brewing within him. "I would rather surprise her."

"I like the way you think." Jazz returned his smile.

If only she knew the maelstrom of thoughts circulating through his mind. Beyond his plans for what to do should he be able to support himself, he was beginning to wonder just how much of a hindrance his appearance would, or rather, would not be in this time.

Rachel had complimented how he looked. She had not seen all of his face, of course, but it was still encouraging. Jazz had seen his face, and yet the way she stared at Dante was enough to make him blush.

And then there was Elsa, with her shy looks and soft

touches. A thrill passed over his skin, the mere thought of her hands on him causing gooseflesh to spread over his arms.

If he could come to her as an independent man, if he had more to offer her, perhaps the misgivings that always seemed to creep into her gaze would vanish.

Jazz walked to the counter and started to wash the glass she had used. "Now that we have that out of the way, how is Winston? I heard he fell."

"Garrett predicts a full recovery. Winston is sleeping at the moment."

"It is kind of late. I had to wait until I finished up at the gallery before I could stop by."

"Your circle of friends seems to be quite closely knit. I am amazed how quickly news has spread."

Jazz shrugged. "I had lunch with Garrett today. He's one of my best customers and a good friend. I introduced him to Elsa, in fact."

"Another of your dates?" Dante did not mean to say it so harshly, but Elsa had explained that Michael was the man Jazz had attempted to set Elsa up with. Garrett, Dante could understand. Michael had been a woeful error in judgment.

"What can I say? I'm a sucker for the romantic." Jazz set aside the glass and dried her hands. "But don't worry, no more blind dates from me. I can see Elsa's off the market."

"I beg—" He cleared his throat as he decided on a different turn of phrase. "Excuse me?"

If Jazz really thought that Elsa would consider having a romantic relationship with Dante, even after seeing him without his mask... He thought back to his earlier interlude with Elsa in her bedroom, when he'd been overcome with the urge to kiss her. If Winston's fall had not interrupted them, Dante now wondered what would have happened. She had not looked like she was going to pull away.

"Come on. Aside from Winston, Elsa has lived with exactly two other people in her life. Me and you. And the only reason she lived with me was out of financial necessity. The way she doesn't talk about it, I don't even think she ever lived with her family. I swear that woman stepped into this world fully formed."

"You put too much upon her, viewing her in such a manner." He did have to admit that Elsa was the most independent woman he had ever met. And though she spoke freely of his family, she had yet to mention her own.

Jazz shrugged. "All I'm saying is, I've known Elsa longer than anyone and you are the first person other than Winston that she has chosen to live with of her own free will." She leaned in very close. "I will expect an invitation to the wedding."

"Elsa and I are simply friends." Or were they? The excitement growing within him surged through his body, his soul practically thrumming with delight.

"I have a feeling there's nothing simple about this relationship. Anyway, I won't intrude. Please give Winston my regards."

"You do not wish to wait for Elsa?"

Jazz grinned. "I'll leave you lovebirds alone."

"As I said, our relationship is—"

"Yeah, I heard you."

Dante followed Jazz to the front door. She turned to face him once more before leaving.

"It was nice meeting you, Dante. I look forward to doing business with you and getting to know you better."

"And I, you, madam."

"Don't call me madam. It's Jazz."

"Of course. Jazz."

"That's better."

And then she was gone, leaving him alone in the foyer, not quite sure what to do with himself. He locked the door and headed to his room, taking the stairs slowly as he thought over what had just occurred.

He had a potential source of income, and Jazz believed that he had a chance at a romantic relationship with Elsa. It was all quite exhilarating.

Of course, working with Jazz meant the issue of his lack of identity might come up sooner rather than later. Dante felt it was best to deal with the matter right away. Perhaps she would have some contacts who could help him. He would need to acquire funds to assist with his new beginning, but the only thing he had of worth was his mother's ring.

He smiled, knowing exactly what his mother would say on that point. He would call Jazz first thing in the morning while Elsa was tending to Winston, and set up a meeting. That in itself would be a bit difficult, however. He and Elsa were seldom apart.

The realization stopped him in his tracks. Since Dante had arrived, they had spent almost every waking moment together, as well as several nights. He thought back to Jazz's comments about the nature of his relationship with Elsa, and he found he wasn't sure what it truly was.

He happened to have paused just outside the door to Elsa's bedroom. She had left it open a crack. He ran his fingertips lightly down the wood, enjoying the coolness of its surface. Taking it as a good sign, Dante retired to his room to prepare for an evening relaxing in her company.

Chapter Sixteen

Even after her bath, Elsa couldn't relax. She sat at the kitchen table drinking yet another cup of chamomile tea, trying to soothe her frayed nerves. The thought that someone had been in her house was beyond unsettling. She was still hoping that they were wrong, that there was some other explanation.

Maybe they had left the door to the cabinet open themselves. Maybe Leonardo had knocked Dante's mask onto the floor and it bounced under the bed somewhere. Maybe the key had caught on Winston's shirtsleeve as he locked up the night before and it'd fallen to the floor.

None of those scenarios seemed likely. Elsa insisted that everything was just so. She had to admit it wasn't only because she was watching out for Winston. Her friends thought of her as a control freak, and they were right. They just didn't know how much of her life she had felt completely out of control.

She'd crawled under her bed with a flashlight and searched everywhere for Dante's mask with no luck. Winston might be blind, but he had a keen sense of hearing. If he had been in the room when the key hit the floor, he would have heard it.

Elsa couldn't rationalize any of the occurrences away. The most likely explanation was that someone had been in the house the night before, someone who had picked through her things and watched Dante and Elsa as they slept.

Another shudder swept over her body. Elsa held the hot mug closer to her chest. The warmth did little to comfort her, but at least she could distract herself a bit. She focused on the sensation of the steam as it floated around her face, calming herself as she breathed in its earthy scent.

Someone knocked at the kitchen door. She jumped, spilling the tea on her chest. Luckily, she was wearing a baggy T-shirt, and leaned forward quickly enough to avoid being burned.

Garrett was standing outside, rattling the handle. She could see the concern etched in his features through the door's window. Elsa trotted over to let him in.

"Are you okay? I didn't mean to startle you."

"I'm fine." Elsa stepped aside as Garrett entered the kitchen, closing and locking the door behind him. "It was my fault I jumped. I was distracted."

Garrett stared at Elsa's chest, where her T-shirt had plastered itself against her breasts. She pulled the fabric away. The tea on her front was quickly becoming cold, which was just making the situation more embarrassing.

"Sorry." Garrett looked away.

"It's okay. I'll change later."

"How's Winston doing?"

"Grumpy. He says he wants to get up, but I saw him going back to bed from the bathroom and he was walking stiffly."

"That's to be expected. I'm sure he'll shake this off after a couple days of rest. And moving around a bit will be good for him."

"Well, don't worry about us starving. It turns out Dante is a great cook." Which was a good thing, because when he let Elsa make the toast that morning she managed to burn half of it. As in, all of the toast was burned on one side.

"About Dante…" Garrett's mouth was still open, but no words came out.

"What about Dante?"

"I know he's the reason you didn't want to call the police."

"Why would you say that?"

"Listen, this guy isn't who he says he is."

Garrett made his statement with entirely too much conviction. Elsa's cheeks began to tingle, the blood draining from her head and making her dizzy.

"What did you do?"

"My friend Finn is a private investigator. I gave him a call and asked him to do some digging."

"You did what?" Elsa's sense of foreboding blossomed

into a full panic attack. Her heart threw itself against her ribs, seeking to flee, while her body felt leaden and rooted to the ground.

What kind of digging? What had he found?

Memories churned through her mind. *"Abomination! Which of my sins was so bad that I was burdened with you?"*

She shoved the pain away. She had to stay focused. Damage control. Assess the threat to herself and Dante.

"How could I not?" Garrett said. "You refused to go to the police after someone broke into your house, and you're shacking up with a guy who is lying to you."

"Dante has never lied to me. Ever."

"Are you sure about that? Because my friend says there is no record of a Dante Lucerne entering the country. In fact, the only Londoner he could find by that name died back in 1881."

"I can't believe you went behind my back and did this."

"What did you expect me to do?"

Rage overwhelmed her fear. "Respect my wishes? Not invade my privacy?"

"I thought you were in danger. I still think so. This guy is conning you. He's playing on your sympathies—"

"Stop. Just, stop." Elsa took a few deep breaths, trying to calm herself down. "If you ever, ever, disparage him like that to me again, you will no longer be welcome in my home. Do you understand me?"

Garrett's mouth went slack, his shoulders slumping. She regretted hurting him, but she couldn't stand by and let Garrett say such things. Especially when Dante was keeping silent to protect her.

Snapping his mouth shut in a frown, Garrett glared at her. Deep furrows formed on his forehead, and she could practically hear his teeth grinding together.

"Yeah, I get it."

Elsa heard a soft voice behind them say, "Am I intruding?"

She turned around to see Dante standing in the hall just outside the kitchen. His eyes were wide and he looked about as stunned as Garrett had a moment before.

"No," Garrett said. "As Winston's doctor, I'm here to check on him."

As angry as she was, Elsa still felt her heart constrict watching Garrett leave the room. He was one of her best friends. She didn't want to lose him over this, but she couldn't think of a way to make him understand without telling him everything.

For a moment, she considered doing just that, but immediately dismissed the idea. Garrett had gone behind her back. He might have been doing what he thought was best, but she had made herself clear and he hadn't respected that. At least he had gone to a private investigator and not the police.

Dante was counting on her. She had to protect him.

Elsa grabbed her mug and stalked to the sink to wash it. Her shirt was still cold and wet, thanks to Garrett as well. Why couldn't he have left it alone?

Dante crossed the room to stand next to her. He spoke in a low voice. "I do not mean to cause rifts between you and your friends."

"You didn't cause this problem. Garrett not respecting my wishes caused this."

She managed to slam her hand against the side of the sink, hitting her thumb just right to make her yelp. She set the mug down a bit more forcefully than was probably wise, shaking her hand to make her thumb stop stinging.

"Did you injure yourself?" Dante reached for Elsa's hand, but she clutched it against her chest.

"It's nothing."

"You must learn to let others help you."

Right, because that had worked out so well for her in the past. Elsa bit her lower lip to keep the sarcastic comment from spilling out. She did let him take her hand and put it under the tap.

Her anger dissipated as he rinsed the soap from her hands, his fingers gliding over her skin. Tingles of pleasure raced up her arms at his gentle touch. Dante turned off the water and held her injured hand close to his chest. He ran his fingertips lightly over her thumb. "Does it still hurt?"

"Not really." Elsa's voice came out a squeak. He stared

into her eyes, still lightly caressing her hand with his. She cleared her throat and said, "Thank you."

Dante brought her hand to his lips, pressing a gentle kiss on her thumb. "You are most welcome."

His gaze slid to her lips and he leaned closer, his head bending toward hers. Elsa could feel the heat of his body, as if their skin was already touching. He was going to kiss her—she was sure of it. And suddenly, she couldn't remember any of the reasons she had to stop him.

"Winston is fine, in case you're wondering." Garrett stood in the doorway. His harsh voice scattered the clouds in Elsa's mind.

She couldn't believe she had let that moment go so far. That she and Dante had almost kissed. And here was Garrett, angry because he thought that Dante was trying to take advantage of her. If only Garrett knew the truth.

Dante looked momentarily abashed. "That is welcome news."

"I bet." Garrett scowled at Dante, but didn't even look at Elsa.

She grabbed Garrett's arm as he passed her. "I appreciate you coming to check on Winston."

"It's the least I can do for a friend."

"I know you're only trying to help, and I appreciate that too," she said. "But on the other matter, can you please trust me that I know what I'm doing?"

Garrett shook his head and let out a sharp, low laugh.

"Funny. You're so good at asking for trust, but do you ever look at how much you give out? It's a two-way street."

"Garrett, I—"

He didn't let her finish. "I'll call my guy off. Don't worry about it."

How could she not worry? He was asking her to trust him, and she wasn't sure she knew how. His harsh accusation rattled like chains in her mind. But another voice broke into her thoughts. Dante's voice, their conversation from earlier in the day playing through her mind.

"You are surrounded by people who care for you."

"If people knew what I could do, they would hunt me down and dissect me."

"Even Garrett? Even Winston?"

Would they really hurt her? Elsa's mother had been a drunk and a religious fanatic. Winston and Garrett cared for Elsa. They had proven how they felt time and again. But was she brave enough to trust them, too? Like she was learning to trust Dante?

Garrett had only spoken with a private investigator. A friend. He could handle telling the guy to back off. Maybe if she could try to trust Garrett on this one thing, she could mend a little of what had been damaged between them.

"Okay." She loosened her grip on Garrett's arm.

Garrett lingered as if he was waiting for her to say more. He probably expected a long litany of instructions.

But she was going to trust him to take care of this, even though it felt sort of like stepping off a cliff.

"Well, all right then."

Garrett's eyebrows scrunched together and he cocked his head to one side as if he was trying to puzzle out what was going on. He hesitantly leaned in to hug her. Elsa stood on her toes to hug him back, which pushed her cold clothing against her skin.

When he let her go, his signature smile was back in place. "Dante, make sure she changes into something dry before she catches a cold. Winston is enough of a handful. I don't think we can stand tending to them both."

The tightness around her heart vanished at Garrett's words. She hadn't lost him. More than that, he had included Dante, as if the two of them were a team. Elsa didn't miss the way Dante's expression relaxed.

"I shall make that the next order of business," Dante said.

"I'm sure." Garrett's smile turned a bit wry, but that seemed to be the end of it.

After Garrett left, Dante locked the door. He put the key on the shelf nearest the door instead of leaving it in the lock. "You should change your shirt."

"I'll just check on Winston first. I think I'll sleep on the couch tonight. I want to be close enough to hear him if he needs anything."

"Garrett was right." Dante grabbed the edge of his shirt,

then pulled it over his head and held it out to her. "If you will not take the time to go upstairs and change, at least put this on instead."

Elsa might have if she was able to move, but she was paralyzed at the site of Dante half-naked in her kitchen. The dark hair that lightly covered his chest contrasted against his pale skin, accentuating the broad planes of his muscles and flowing like a waterfall down his flawless stomach. It disappeared beneath the waistband of his pajama pants.

Fireworks exploded through her. Her arms tingled, as if begging her to reach for him. She could barely breathe. The air passing over her parted lips felt like a caress. She longed to touch his chest, to trail kisses along his stomach, to explore every inch of his body…

"Are you all right?"

He took a step toward her, jolting her back to reality. She kept her eyes locked on his, only his eyes, and tried to block out everything she was seeing in her periphery.

"I'm fine, thanks."

She reached for his shirt, but since she wasn't looking, she wound up brushing her hand against his. The physical contact was like touching a live wire. She still managed to grab his shirt and started to pull it over her head.

"Elsa…" Dante stepped closer and grasped her arms to stop her. He was so warm. "You should take off your own shirt first."

She peered at him through the open neck of his shirt, her arms still held above her head. "You want me to…"

A flush spread across his neck and chest, creeping over his face as well.

Elsa would not let this happen. Not until he had met other women, spent time with them, and realized that he had options besides her. If she gave in now, she'd never be sure that he would have chosen her.

She lowered his shirt and backed away from him, forcing a smile. "Of course. I'll change in the laundry room."

She fled from his presence as quickly as she could, heart beating like a frightened rabbit thumping out a warning. The laundry room was just off the kitchen. Elsa closed the door behind her, leaning against it as she brought herself back under control.

This was going to be harder than she thought. Dante was kind, intelligent and beautiful. She loved spending time with him. She was already attracted to him, and that was before what she had just seen. Elsa had never wanted anyone so intensely.

His body was gorgeous, and she had slept right next to *that* not once but twice. She shivered just thinking about it. Her mind filled with images of exploring his chest, her fingers tingling as she imagined trailing them all the way down that dark path.

For once, she was glad for her insane cycles—they had

driven her to get an IUD that secreted hormones to lighten her periods. At least if she did give in to her desires, she wouldn't have to worry about birth control.

That was not what she should be thinking about.

She would have to be stronger. With renewed determination, she tore off her shirt and threw it aside, then pulled Dante's over her head. She only realized her mistake after it settled over her shoulders.

The scent of sandalwood enveloped her. His shirt was still warm from his body. His heat seeped into her chilled flesh. She could feel him surrounding her. She moaned and leaned against the wall, unable to make herself take it off.

If it felt this good just to think about touching him, what would it be like if she gave in? But if she did give in, she'd never know if what they had was real.

Changing their relationship would also absolutely change how they behaved toward one another. What if it didn't work out? What if giving in to their attraction brought out dark sides of their personalities? What if they lost what they already had?

Everything would intensify—attraction, passion, rage...

Elsa needed distance. If she kept her hands to herself and tried to avoid physical contact, she could resist the temptation he presented. Clinging to that thought helped as she summoned the courage to open the door to the kitchen again.

He was nowhere in sight. She was both relieved and

disappointed. She headed to check on Winston, glancing into the entertainment room as she passed by. Dante wasn't there either.

Winston's door was slightly open. His room was dark, but the light spilling in from the hallway was enough for Elsa to find her way to his bedside. He was sound asleep. The weathered lines around his eyes and mouth had softened.

She watched him sleep for a few moments, reassuring herself that he was okay, then tiptoed back to the door. She left it open a bit to hear him better if he needed anything during the night.

Passing the entertainment room again, Elsa noticed blankets and pillows stacked next to the couch. Dante must have been there, but he had already left. She backtracked to the kitchen, where she found him pouring two glasses of tea. Thankfully, he'd put on another of his shirts.

"I didn't know you were expecting company." She tried to feign a sense of ease she didn't feel.

He set the tea pitcher back in the refrigerator and closed the door. "I thought perhaps we could watch a movie together."

"Okay." The word slipped out before she could stop herself. What was she doing? This wasn't avoiding temptation. This was barreling right into it.

Disgusted with herself, Elsa stormed to the cabinet and pulled out a bag of popcorn. It took her three tries to get it out of the plastic wrap, each more frustrating than the last. She threw the bag in the microwave when she finally managed it, pounding the buttons into obedience.

"Do you need assistance?"

Dante's voice was right at her ear. At least, it felt that way. She spun around to find him standing next to her. She hadn't heard him approach.

"I apologize. I did not mean to startle you."

"It's okay. I guess I'm still jumpy."

He placed his hands on her arms. He was too close for her to step aside. "You do not need to worry. I will not let anything happen to you. Not while it is in my power to protect you."

"I didn't bring you here to protect me. I can take care of myself."

She turned around as the microwave beeped, grateful for the excuse to move away from him. Elsa took out the popcorn and set it on the counter, then opened the bag so it could let off some steam.

"I am well aware of this." There was a bit of an edge to his tone. "As you have repeatedly told me it is so."

She turned to face him again, leaning against the counter. "I'm sorry. I didn't mean to say that so harshly. This is frustrating, though. You aren't supposed to be helping me. That isn't why I brought you here."

"It is no trouble at all."

"But it is. You shouldn't have to worry about any of

this. I should've had a plan in place. I should've had paperwork ready. You shouldn't be stuck here with Winston and me, taking care of him and making sure that we're safe. I'm supposed to be doing that for you."

Dante stepped closer, his eyes the rich blue of deep water as he gazed down at her. "It is an honor to be able to care for Winston and to protect you both. I have never had someone to take care of. Not like this. It warms my heart more than you could ever imagine. Please do not begrudge anyone for that, least of all yourself."

How was she supposed to keep herself at a distance when he said things like that?

"I appreciate the sentiment, but there are other people you could be taking care of. You should be free to go wherever you please."

"There is no place in this world that I would rather be than here."

"You've never been anywhere else. How can you possibly know that?"

"Because this is where you are."

Elsa's heart felt like it had suddenly swollen and was about to burst. It would be so easy to give in. All she had to do was lean forward and kiss him. The way he was staring at her lips, she knew he was thinking it too, just like earlier.

She should've stopped him then, and she knew she should put a stop to it now.

"And this is where I'll always be." She smiled, trying to keep the longing she felt from clouding her tone.

A flash of uncertainty crossed Dante's face. She needed to stop sending him mixed signals. But to do that, she needed to get her heart under control. If only her heart didn't want him so much.

Chapter Seventeen

The studio doors were open as Dante worked on yet another painting. Natural light poured in from above and filtered through the windows facing the gardens and patio. He and Elsa must certainly have tea outside, if he could convince her to leave Winston's side for a little while.

Winston was feeling better, and as such, it grew harder to convince him to rest. She had been with him throughout the morning. Dante felt selfish to admit it, but he missed her.

He knew he would not be without company for long. Precisely on time, Jazz appeared in the patio doorway, peeking her head into the studio. She smiled when she saw him, then glanced around.

"Elsa is not here." Dante touched his mask to be sure it was in place. After Jazz's initial reaction, he thought it best to wear in her presence.

"She's with Winston?"

"Yes. But I do not know how long she will be, and they are just down the hall."

"I know where Winston's room is." Jazz stepped into the studio. "I've been around here a while longer than you."

"Of course. I am a bit distracted at present."

"Let me see." She walked around Dante, nodding as she viewed his latest work. She pursed her lips and tilted her head to the side. Finally, she smiled. "Oh, yes. I definitely see a future for you."

He laughed inwardly at her ironic choice of words. If not for Elsa, he would have no future in so many ways.

Jazz turned to face him. "There are others?"

"Yes. These new acrylics dry so quickly." He pulled out the stack of canvases he'd filled since he arrived.

"What kind of acrylics do you use?" She picked up a tube of paint near his easel.

Dante's heart fluttered nervously as he realized his error. For all he knew, acrylic paints had been available for decades.

"I suppose they are the common kind. However, I have never worked with them before. Hence, they are new to me."

One of her eyebrows rose, but she said nothing more. Eager to distract her further, he began showing her his other paintings.

"These are good, Dante," Jazz said. "Very good. The use of color and the brush strokes…" She leafed through the paintings, pausing occasionally to examine one in more minute detail. "How long have you been here?"

"It will be one week tomorrow."

"And have you slept since you arrived?"

"A bit." The nights he had spent with Elsa curled up beside him rose to the surface of his mind. He would certainly sleep more often if he could spend each night in such a manner.

"Well, I'm impressed. You almost have enough for a show already." She pursed her lips again, no doubt puzzling something out. "I had a last-minute cancellation for an opening show next week. Do you think you could have three more of these by then?"

"At least."

Jazz smiled broadly. "Then, my friend, we are in business."

Dante took her hand when she offered it, having studied interactions more closely on various television programs. She shook his hand vigorously and then released him.

"Since we are now business partners, there are a few other matters I would like to discuss."

"I'm intrigued." Jazz walked over to Elsa's writing desk, then leaned against it and crossed her arms.

"The first is a matter of funding. I do not wish to continue to impose on Elsa's hospitality."

"You want an advance from the show?"

"Not at all. But I assume you have contacts who appreciate fine pieces." He took off his mother's ring and held it out to Jazz. "I should like to find a buyer for this."

"This is Elsa's ring. She gave it to you?"

"It is a bit more complicated than that." He struggled to find a way to explain that would not betray Elsa's confidences. "Elsa returned the ring to me the night I arrived. It was made by—"

"Heinrich Gerhardt." Jazz took the ring. She ran her fingers over the intricate design covering its surface.

"You have heard of him?" Dante was unable to hide his astonishment.

"Who do you think found this ring for Elsa? Heinrich was a German goldsmith who only produced for about a decade around the mid-1800s. Which is a shame, really. The man was a genius."

Dante could hardly believe what he was hearing. It seemed everyone knew more about his family than he did.

"Elsa's been obsessed with Heinrich's mistress, Deirdre Lucerne, for years." She stared at Dante, her eyes slowly widening. "Wait a minute. How could I not have realized? Dante Lucerne. You're descended from them!"

He let out a breath of relief. He could hardly deny what she said, and it enabled him to protect Elsa's secret without lying to Jazz.

"I am."

"Wow, Elsa really is collecting everything she can get her hands on."

"I am not an item to be collected by anyone."

"I'm just teasing. But I get it now. How you guys met and why she's letting you live here. I don't get why you want to sell that ring, though."

"I need to make a fresh start free of debt to anyone. My
—" He caught himself before he made another slip. "I
believe Deirdre would want me to be able to do so."

"Do you owe someone money?"

"Not as such. However, I am imposing on Elsa's
generosity. It is not a position in which I am content to
remain."

Jazz grinned. "You know her pretty well."

"I hope to know her better." Of all the confessions he
could have made, those words did little more than
embarrass him. Jazz only grinned the more.

"I bet you do. And I will help with that."

"You will?"

"Elsa has been alone for a long time. Too long. I think
you have a shot with her, so I'm going to back your play."

"I...thank you."

Dante could scarcely believe that Jazz thought he had a
chance of a lasting happiness with Elsa. He had suspected
that Elsa wanted a relationship with him, perhaps even as
much as he wanted one with her. Jazz's words
corroborated his theory.

Now that he had an ally in Jazz, he was confident
enough to ask his next question. "There is one more thing
that would help in that regard."

"Spill it."

"I am truly starting over here. My previous situation

was untenable. I broke no laws and owed no money, I assure you. However, I find myself in the position of having utterly nothing aside from this ring."

"You don't need to worry. Once I sell that ring, you'll have plenty of money for canvases."

"My needs go beyond that. Elsa arranged for me to come here and is providing for my needs. As you can imagine, it is not the most favorable position for me to begin courting her."

"You want to come to her on your own two feet."

"Precisely. But that is difficult given my circumstance."

Jazz tucked the ring into the front pocket of her pants. "Just tell me what you need."

"I am not even certain how to ask. Sufficed to say, when Elsa brought me here, I was required to leave everything behind. Including the man I was."

Jazz's brow furrowed, her lips pursing as she pondered his words. Finally, her eyebrows rose and her eyes widened.

"Oh! I get it." A devilish look that made him a bit uncomfortable swept across her face. "I'm going to have some fun with this. You have come to the right person. You don't know how lucky you are."

"I am unsure if—"

She did not let him finish. "No take-backs. It's done. My business is making people. And I have never had a blank canvas before." She looked him up and down again and shrugged. "Well, mostly blank. Dante is good. We'll keep Dante at least. And using your personal circumstances to create this Phantom persona—"

"Was never my intention. Not for my career as a painter."

She let out a sigh. "Well, you let Elsa play with it, so you have to let me have some fun too. No wardrobe changes or anything until I've introduced you around. After your unveiling, you can change your look or let Garrett's doctor friends do whatever they want to you."

Dante wasn't sure what Jazz meant by that. He didn't have a chance to ask, as he heard Elsa's voice behind him.

"Jazz? What are you doing here?"

"Elsa! I'm just here to check on Winston." Jazz walked around Dante, crossing the room to give Elsa a hug.

"In the studio?" One delicate brow was arched on Elsa's forehead.

"Well, it'd be rude not to say hello to Dante."

"I didn't know you'd met." Elsa's tone was terse.

Dante was eager to divert the conversation. "I fear I forgot to mention that Jazz stopped by a few evenings ago."

"That seems an odd thing to forget mentioning." Elsa turned her skeptical gaze upon him.

"I was preoccupied with other matters."

"Such as?" She crossed her arms, curiously like the posture he had seen Jazz adopt.

"He was telling me about Winston." Jazz wrapped her arm around Elsa's shoulders. "Isn't that right, Dante?"

Elsa looked back and forth between them, her eyes narrowing. Finally, she turned to glare at Jazz. "What are you trying to drag him into?"

Jazz lifted her hands, her shoulders creeping toward her ears. "Why is it always me?"

"Because you're always up to something."

Dante did not wish to be the cause of yet another rift between Elsa and her friends. As much as he wanted to surprise her with his plan, he could not in good conscience let Jazz take the blame for something she was not responsible for.

"The truth is—"

Jazz jumped in before he could finish. "You caught me. I am up to something."

"What is it this time?" Elsa asked.

"A dance!" Jazz waved her hands through the air as if calling their attention to an imaginary marquee. "Everyone who's anyone will be there, so of course, you and Dante have to come."

"We can't make it." Elsa's frown would brook no disagreement.

"Aren't you going to ask Dante? I'm sure he wants to go."

He wondered if this was part of what Jazz alluded to when speaking of his unveiling. "By all means."

Elsa said, "Dante, you don't know what you're agreeing to."

"And neither do you," Jazz said. "I haven't told you the best part."

Elsa groaned. "I know I'm going to regret this, but what would that be?"

"It's a masked ball."

"Jazz." Elsa's tone turned foreboding.

"You won't have to worry about anything. I'll take care of your costumes. I'll even send a car. But you both have to come."

Elsa shifted closer to him, her warmth seeping through his shirt. "Absolutely not. Dante just got here, and I'm not going to have you parading him around as part of some marketing ploy."

"If I might interject," Dante said. "Jazz has come up with an idea to introduce me to those in your social circle in a manner that I would be most comfortable with. If others are wearing masks, I will not stand out. It is quite a clever idea."

Very clever. Jazz was both covering for their meeting and attempting to launch his career as an artist.

"Finally someone appreciates me," Jazz said.

Elsa began to chew on her lower lip, her shoulders hunching as if a weight was settling upon them. He could bear her discomfort no easier than causing strain between the two friends.

"Jazz, if you would be so kind as to give Elsa and I a moment."

"Sure, I'll go see Winston."

"I am certain he shall enjoy your company."

Dante waited for Jazz to leave the room before closing the distance between himself and Elsa. "Tell me."

"People will have questions." Elsa's voice was tight.

"And we shall have answers. We met through a mutual love of art. Is that not so?"

Her lips twitched up in a wry grin for a moment. He seized on that. He brushed her hair back past her shoulder, then tucked a few stray strands behind her ear.

"This is a chance for me to meet others in a safe manner. It is an opportunity we dare not let slip by."

Her smile faded. "What if something goes wrong?"

Dante slid his fingers beneath her chin and tilted her head up to him. "What if something doesn't?"

Chapter Eighteen

Two of the best days of Elsa's life passed after Jazz's visit. In the sunlit hours, Dante painted while Elsa wrote in the studio. They spent their evenings relaxing with books or watching movies.

During meals shared with Winston, Dante would teach them about what he was studying. Elsa knew how to drive a car, but had never bothered to learn about engines. The way Dante explained everything was fascinating. If he decided not to be a painter, he'd make a wonderful teacher.

Winston was doing so much better. Watching him ask questions, thoughtfully nodding as he listened to Dante's answers, was quickly becoming one of Elsa's favorite things in the universe. Winston had even started downloading audio books on some of the subjects they discussed, his curiosity piqued by Dante's enthusiasm.

Garrett's visits were encouraging too. He had kept his promise and Elsa was beginning to feel more at ease about letting him call off his friend. Nothing bad had come of the private investigator poking around and she felt like she and Garrett were closer than before. Their friendship was stronger from the trust she finally felt able to give him.

The only cloud hanging over her was the thought of Jazz's dance. It crept ever closer until the dreaded day arrived, along with two large packages. Elsa carried them to her bedroom, hoping to inspect what Jazz had sent before Dante had a chance to see the outfits. He happened past her bedroom door just as she was setting the boxes on her bed.

"Have the costumes arrived?" He joined Elsa by the side of her bed.

"I think so."

"Allow me to assist you." Dante opened the first box, stiffening when he caught a glimpse of what was inside. He lifted a white half-mask from within, then sighed. "I begin to understand what you meant by my not knowing what I was getting myself into."

"She didn't!" Elsa turned back to the box, picking up the top item of clothing. It was a long black jacket with dark burgundy accents in a satiny fabric. She dropped it back in the box, then turned toward the door. "That's it. I'm calling Jazz to tell her we aren't coming."

Dante caught Elsa's arm and spun her in a circle till she was facing him again. Elsa stifled the urge to giggle. When she looked up into his eyes, there were playful crinkles at the edges as he smiled. He hadn't worn a mask since Jazz's visit.

"If Jazz would like me to attend as the Phantom of the Opera, I shall not disappoint her. Besides…" He held the mask up to his face. "It is a role I am well prepared to play."

Elsa laughed and shook her head. "You're taking this all pretty well."

"I have had quite a few opportunities to practice adapting of late. It has become second nature." He put the mask back on top of his costume, then drew his fingertips slowly over the unopened box. "Also, I am quite eager to see what she has prepared for you."

"That makes one of us."

"Do you mind?"

"Go ahead."

Elsa watched as Dante opened the other box. She couldn't suppress a gasp as he pulled out an eye mask covered with pale gold feathers in an intricate design. It was absolutely gorgeous. A bed of rich gold silk with chestnut accents lay beneath the mask.

"Rachel had to be involved," Elsa said. "She's amazing with colors and fabrics."

"Then I am beholden to her."

He set aside the mask and gingerly lifted Elsa's dress from the box. He held it in his arms like he had carried her when he first arrived. His eyes darkened to a blue as rich and deep as an autumn sky at dusk.

In a quiet voice, he said, "I should very much like to see you in this."

"I…" Elsa stammered. "Okay."

Dante placed the dress on her bed, a soft smile on his lips. "In that case, I shall retire to my room to prepare for our evening."

He replaced the lid on the box that held his costume, then tucked it under his arm. He lifted her hand once more and pressed a kiss onto her palm, his gaze locked with hers. There was a spark in his eyes, an intensity that flooded her body with warmth.

And then he was gone, closing the door to her room behind him as he left. Elsa sat on her bed, running her fingers over the smooth fabric of her dress, its coolness seeping into her skin. She lifted the mask and stared into its empty eyes.

Scenarios ran through her mind, each more terrible than the last. Dante was set on going. She knew she couldn't talk him out of it, so she would be at his side to help him.

It was going to be a long night.

Elsa spent more time getting ready for Jazz's dance than she'd spent preparing for every other date of her life combined. Not that this was a date. She was accompanying Dante to help him meet other people in a relatively safe setting. That was all.

Standing in front of her armoire's floor-length mirror, she had to admit her efforts were worthwhile. She'd opted to pull her hair back, leaving a few soft tendrils around her face. The bodice of her dress hugged her chest and waist perfectly, lifting and slimming in all the right places. The skirt flowed around her legs like a pool of sunlight.

Rachel was a genius.

Elsa heard a soft rap on the door. "Come in."

Dante appeared in the mirror behind her. She was so stunned she couldn't turn around. She watched his reflection approach. He hadn't worn such an ornate and flattering outfit in any of the times she observed him.

The tails of the black jacket made him look even taller, the tailored pants showing off his long legs. Only the very edges of a white shirt showed beneath the vest under his jacket, everything offset with that rich burgundy satin. His hair was slicked back with something—all but a stray lock that had fallen over the mask he wore.

He strode up to her, resting his hands on her arms and stopping close enough that she could feel his warmth against her back. Even without the tightness of her dress, Elsa would've had trouble catching her breath just from the sight of him. He looked so serious, a strange energy about him that was new.

He leaned in even closer, his lips hovering just above her neck, and whispered, "Do I look the part?"

Elsa stammered until she saw his lips pull into a broad smile.

"Very funny." She stepped away from him. Her stomach was doing flip-flops, and the skin along her neck was still tingling from the warmth of his breath. "Are you enjoying getting into character?"

"I am making the most of the evening. I must confess, it is an interesting exercise to pretend to be the legend that stemmed in part from my life."

"'Interesting' is one word for it. We can still back out if you want to."

"I wouldn't dream of it. Besides, in all honesty, I fear what Jazz would do if we did not make an appearance at the very least."

"That point I cannot argue."

"And it will also be quite some time before I have had my fill of seeing you like this. You look…" His gaze trailed down her body, leaving a wake of sparks that burned through her. "'Beautiful' is not a strong enough word."

She tried to shake off the effect of that look—the urges that rose in her. She needed to stay focused. Who knew what the evening held?

Not sex. Definitely not sex.

Dante lifted Elsa's hand and threaded it through his elbow. "Shall we?"

She took a deep breath, feeling as if she was about to dive into murky water, then nodded.

"Let's go."

Chapter Nineteen

Dante had thought his logic sound when they left the house, but once they were on their way to the gallery, he found himself plagued with doubts. Even the clear view of other cars in the fading sunlight could not distract him.

It had not escaped his notice that Elsa was in a similar state of mind. She was practically wringing her hands as she stared out the window and chewed on her lower lip. He longed to tell her that everything would be fine, but in honesty, he was uncertain.

Uncertain and uncomfortable.

The mask Jazz had provided was made from some sort of clay. It was quite heavier than he was accustomed and was not fitted to the contours of his face like the porcelain versions he had crafted. Already, he looked forward to returning to Elsa's home, where a mask would not be required.

The car stopped in front of a row of shops and buildings nestled so close, there was barely telling where one began and the next ended. Only the color of the bricks and the architectural accents on the upper stories differentiated them.

On the ground level, the walls were made of glass and metal, allowing passersby to see right into the storefronts. *Jazz Gallery* was emblazoned in red lettering above an open door. Dante could hear faint music from within the gallery.

When the driver opened the car door, Dante exited first, then reached down to help Elsa step onto the sidewalk. She was truly a vision.

The burnished gold of her dress made her hair shine like pale honey. Her eyes fairly glowed. For a moment, he simply stood on the sidewalk, mesmerized by her.

She lifted a hand to her face and touched her cheek, the gesture oddly reminiscent of how he checked the positioning of his mask. "Is everything okay? You're staring."

"I am riveted. There is a difference."

The blush that came to her face buoyed his confidence. Pulling her hand through his elbow again, he led her inside.

The press of bodies was oppressive, especially compared with their quiet existence at Elsa's manor. Dozens of people filled the rooms beyond the foyer, milling about and looking at the art upon the walls or gathering in clusters to converse.

Elsa clung to Dante, staring at everyone as if they were an angry mob merely awaiting a target. He knew she was not just worried for him. If people questioned him about his origins and his answers were anachronistic, her secret would be at risk.

The artwork was another danger. They were contemporary, but Dante's first painting had been enough to trigger her ability outside of her control.

He had not truly considered that before and chided himself for his oversight. His resolve to protect her grew. He slid his arm around her waist as he pulled her closer and walked deeper into the throng.

The central room held no art, but was dominated by an open area being used by several couples for a waltz. Everyone was dressed in costumes that spanned the history Dante knew and some he did not. He and Elsa were hardly the most outlandish couple. There was a pair dressed as Marcus Antonius and Cleopatra.

Dante paused as he realized he thought of himself and Elsa as a couple. He wondered if perhaps she felt the same, with the way she pressed herself ever closer into his embrace. It was becoming easier to believe that there was more to their relationship than friendship.

"You made it!" Jazz navigated the crowd to reach them, wrapped her arms around Elsa's shoulders and gave her a kiss on the cheek. Dante was rather surprised when Jazz greeted him in the same manner.

She was dressed as some sort of sailor, he thought, with a ruffled white shirt under a deep red jacket. A matching bandana was tied over her dark hair. Her leggings were tan, though most of her legs were covered in high black boots adorned with many buckles.

"I have so many people I want to introduce you to."

Elsa sighed. "Isn't it enough that we're here?"

"It's great that you're here, but you hardly ever come out, so I have to show you off when I have the chance. Plus, I want Dante to meet everyone."

A server passed with a tray of tall flute glasses filled with gold liquid and chopped berries. Jazz grabbed a pair and handed one to Dante. Rather than give the other to Elsa, Jazz took a sip herself. Dante offered his glass to Elsa, but she shook her head.

Jazz clicked her tongue at Dante. "See, if you two went out more, you'd know that Elsa doesn't drink."

"It's okay," Elsa said. "Go ahead."

Dante would need to ask later if there was some reason for her abstinence. There was no time at the moment, as Jazz led them through the room. Elsa clutched Dante's hand and cast a nervous glance at him. He forced himself to smile, hoping to ease her nerves.

Jazz had not been exaggerating about the number of people she wanted them to meet. Faces, masked and otherwise, blurred together until at last a pair that were familiar neared them.

Rachel waved, though it was hardly necessary. Both she and Garrett were quite tall. Dante easily saw them through the crowd, even without the people stepping aside as they approached.

Rachel's gown was such a pale blue it was nearly white, with full skirts offset by a corset that seemed tied a bit too tight. Her hair was piled in curls atop her head in an overly intricate manner.

With the gloves she wore and the fan she carried, Dante was reminded a bit too much of his own time. He was glad at least that Elsa's dress was more understated. Dancing with Elsa would be much easier with the slenderness of her skirts. He would be able to hold her close.

Garrett trailed after Rachel, wearing a dark suit and crisp white shirt with a small black tie at his neck. He nodded curtly, but said nothing.

Rachel let out a delighted squeal when she reached them. "Oh my God! You guys look great!"

"Where's your new boyfriend?" There was an edge to Elsa's voice, the strain of the evening no doubt showing through.

"He couldn't make it, but Garrett was nice enough to be my date."

"That's me," Garrett said, his hands in his pockets. "Mr. Nice Guy."

"Doctor Nice Guy." Rachel patted Garrett's arm. "My mother would be so proud."

"Elsa tells me that I have you to thank for the exquisite dress she is wearing tonight," Dante said.

"You caught me." Rachel was smiling, but it did not

quite reach her eyes. In fact, there was a haunted look to them, as if something was upsetting her. She grabbed Dante's elbow and pulled him toward the dance floor. "We have to have a dance."

Elsa stiffened, but then she released Dante's arm. "You should go."

"Don't worry." Garrett stepped forward, a polite smile etched on his face. "I'll keep Elsa company."

Dante did not want to dance with Rachel. He wanted to dance with Elsa. But she had already backed away, Garrett following. There was nothing for Dante to do but allow Rachel to usher him onto the dance floor.

The waltz was simple enough that he could proceed through the motions without concentrating overmuch. This was good, because he was preoccupied with thoughts of Elsa. Being taller than most of the crowd himself, he could keep her in his sight as he and Rachel danced. Garrett and Elsa appeared to be having a heated discussion. Dante could only see Garrett's face, but he looked upset. Garrett shook his head and walked away, leaving Elsa alone.

The crowd parted as he left, and Dante caught a glimpse of her. Her gaze met Dante's briefly, and he was uncertain if the longing he detected was her own, or a projection of his feelings upon her. The crowd shifted and he lost sight of her again.

"It's really great that you're helping Elsa with her book," Rachel said. "And you're so into the part. Have you been acting for long?"

With chagrin, Dante realized that Rachel had been speaking for quite some time, but he had not been paying attention. Only at the very end, when she asked her question, had he recognized that she was addressing him.

"I am not an actor."

"Oh come on. You have this character down so perfectly. Are you a specialist that only plays the Phantom? I've heard of that before."

She laughed, a high pitch to the sound that hinted strangely at hysteria. It was enough to call Dante's full attention to her. The lines of strain around her eyes had deepened.

"Is everything all right?"

"Of course it is." Rachel gave another shrill laugh. "It's just that I have a wager going on about whether you're a method actor or not."

"I do not know what you mean."

"You know." She looked pointedly at Dante's mask. "I bet you have makeup on under there. To fully embody the essence of the Phantom."

"I assure you, that is not the case." Dante bristled despite his concerns for her.

"Come on. I can see it around the edges of your mask."

As much as Dante wanted to help Rachel with whatever challenge she faced, he was finding their conversation intolerable. He ceased the waltz and said, "If you would excuse me. I believe I will take my leave of you now."

Rachel looked stricken for a moment, and then she lashed out, grabbing Dante's mask and tearing it from his face. Her grip was precarious, and it slipped from her fingers.

The brittle clay shattered as it hit the floor. Rachel was so intent upon him, she barely seemed to notice.

Gasps and whispers spread out from the two of them like ripples from a pebble dropped in still water. One by one, all of the people around them stopped and turned to stare at him. And first among them was Rachel.

"See! I told you," she said.

Dante was too stunned to step back as she reached out and touched his face. A troubled look crossed her gaze, her fingers exploring the raised, rough flesh. The confusion was soon replaced with shock and then horror. Rachel snatched her hand back—yet another misguided soul who thought scars could be transferred by touch.

He waited for the rest. The repulsion. The screams. But they never came. All he could hear were whispers from the crowd around them.

"Oh my God, Dante," Rachel said. "I'm so sorry. I didn't know."

Tears welled in her eyes, quickly spilling down her cheeks. She dropped to the floor and gathered the pieces of his mask in her trembling hands. Dante cleared his throat, trying to find his voice. When he did, it was rough and tight.

"Leave it."

"But your mask… I broke it." A sob escaped her, her breath uneven and her tears continuing to flow.

He knelt beside her, ignoring the stares of the surrounding crowd, and placed his arm over her shoulder. "I can always get another. But you must not try to gather these pieces when you are so distressed. You might hurt yourself."

Dante pulled out his handkerchief and gave it to her. Rather than using it for herself, she opened it on the floor and started placing the pieces of his mask within. He assisted, eager to end the scene the incident had created.

When the pieces had been collected, he tied the corners of the cloth together and placed the bundle in his pocket. He helped Rachel to her feet as he stood and was shocked when she leaned against his side and wrapped her arm around his waist.

She looked up at him, and Dante saw no hint of discomfort or repulsion in her gaze. Only regret.

Elsa and Jazz appeared among the crowd surrounding them. Garrett was standing nearby. Dante did not know how long Garrett had been there.

"Dante, are you all right?" Elsa looked at the scars on his face for what seemed the first time. Her jaw went slack, but then she snapped her mouth shut and turned to Rachel.

"I didn't mean to." Rachel shrank away from the intensity of Elsa's stare.

"What did you do, Rachel?" Elsa's tone was cold and level, the calm before a gathering storm.

"It was an accident." Dante wrapped his arm around Rachel's shoulders. "She did nothing wrong."

Elsa blinked and jerked her head back as if she had been slapped. Her gaze lingered on Dante's hand resting upon Rachel's arm.

"It was my fault." Rachel's breath came in gulps, her eyes filling with tears once more. "I thought he was just playing a part, you know? Helping you with your—"

Elsa did not allow Rachel to finish her sentence. "You pulled off his mask, didn't you?"

Rachel nodded. She squeezed Dante's waist tightly, and he pulled her closer.

The storm broke, but it was not a blizzard. Flames of rage sprang to life in Elsa's eyes. "Of all the inconsiderate, impulsive acts you've done, this has to be—"

"An accident." Dante summoned his most commanding tone as he cut in. "Rachel had no idea of my disfigurement. You could hardly expect her not to be curious as to what lay beneath my mask."

"But I can expect her to respect your personal boundaries," Elsa said, that fire now directed at him. He did not shrink away from it.

"It is I who decide my own boundaries. And it is I who

have the right to offer forgiveness, which I most certainly do."

Elsa's eyes flashed with anger, but she held her tongue. Beside her, Jazz was smiling, as if this spectacle amused her. The thought irked Dante as much as anything else from the evening.

Was this the introduction that Jazz had planned for him? If so, he would most certainly have words for her. To start, he wanted to know if she was the one who had put Rachel up to this. He had seen enough manipulation in the theatre to know when someone had been goaded into action.

In the meantime, Dante found himself at the center of too much attention. A few people turned away when he met their gazes, lips curling in distaste, but most simply seemed curious. Many had already moved on from the matter, going about their own business.

There were whispers and stares, but no screams, no pointing. There was no fear.

Jazz raised her arms over her head and clapped loudly. "Okay, everybody. This isn't performance art. This is a dance. Get back to it and cut the gawking."

She cast one final grin toward him, then whispered something in Elsa's ear. Elsa's eyes widened for a moment before she turned to glare daggers at Jazz as she walked away.

Dante wanted to retreat, to cover his face and find the

nearest shadow where he could hide and get his bearings. But that would be letting himself be cowed by the few lingering stares still cast his way.

This was a new world, and he would be a new man in it —a man who was not ashamed or afraid to show his face.

"Are you okay?" Garrett was standing just behind Dante, and he started at hearing Garrett's voice so close.

"Yes, I am fine."

Garrett rewarded Dante with a smile and even briefly placed his hand on Dante's shoulder. Looking to Rachel, Garrett said, "I'll be in the back showroom when you're ready to leave."

"Thanks." Rachel sniffled loudly as Garrett left the dwindling group. She smiled up at Dante. "Jazz is the boss. Can we finish our dance?"

"Of course."

Elsa's head whipped back toward Dante and, for a moment, she looked stricken. He could see her pushing away whatever was paining her, just as she shoved away her fear when Winston had fallen.

This time, her expression became completely blank. No fire, no ice, no warmth. No Elsa.

In that moment, Dante felt that she was more distant than when decades stood between them. She turned away, quickly disappearing through the crowd.

Rachel stepped in front of him, lifting his hand in hers as she pulled them into the dance again. The waltz could not end quickly enough. He kept staring out over the crowd, no longer caring at all that he was without a mask. He only wanted to catch a glimpse of Elsa.

"I really am sorry," Rachel said, drawing him back to his present company. "I had no idea."

"And I truly forgive you." Dante managed to glance at Rachel for long enough to smile at her. Her eyes were red-rimmed, the forget-me-not blue of her irises shining brightly from the contrast.

"How did it happen?" Her voice was soft and timid.

He considered how to respond to her inquiry and found he could not malign his brother. Finally, he settled on saying, "A much more unfortunate accident."

"I'm sorry."

"It was a long time ago." How very long indeed.

"Is Garrett your doctor?"

"I suppose you could say so."

"He's a great doctor. I didn't know he did plastic surgery, though."

"How would one perform surgery on plastic?" Dante had researched the material after it came up so often in his other reading.

Rachel gave a tittering laugh. "Very funny. Is Garrett going to perform the surgery, or is he working with someone else on your case?"

"I have no plans for surgery of any kind in my future, if I can avoid it."

"Oh, I'm sorry. I just assumed he was helping you with…"

"With what?"

"You know. Your scars."

Dante stopped dancing quite suddenly. Their momentum caused Rachel to stumble, but he caught her up against his chest so she did not fall.

"I apologize," he said. "That was careless of me."

"It's okay."

"If you could clarify…" Dante's mind was reeling from the thoughts speeding past.

In his time, he had heard of techniques that were being developed to change peoples' appearance. Nothing showed enough promise to give him hope, but that had been over a hundred years ago. With the advancements in other areas he had seen, he wondered what had been accomplished in this field.

"Are you saying that Garrett could perhaps remove the scarring on my face?"

"I don't know for sure, but you should definitely talk to him if you haven't already. Maybe he can refer you to a specialist. There are plenty of people out there who can do reconstructive surgery. If it's something you want, you should keep looking until you find someone who can help you."

"Reconstructive surgery…"

Dante felt a rush of adrenaline spread through his body

at the thought. As he soared on the surge of hope, his stomach suddenly clenched, the leaden weight of it dragging him back to cold reality.

Elsa would know of this. This was her world, after all. She would know that there were surgeons who might be able to help him. But then, why had she not mentioned this yet? Why would she keep this possibility from him?

"Are you okay?" Rachel asked. "You look angry."

"I am quite fine, I assure you." Dante reined in his temper and put forth a placid expression. He might not have ever taken to the stage, but he had spent over a decade in the theatre. He knew how to act. "I do find myself growing tired. It has been quite an eventful evening."

"I suppose I didn't help any."

"On the contrary." He lifted Rachel's hand to his lips and pressed a gentle kiss on her knuckles. "I found your company most illuminating."

Rachel laughed, but some of her nervousness had returned. Perhaps she was not as comfortable with his appearance as he thought.

No matter. He had more important things on his mind. He bowed curtly and then headed through the crowd to find Elsa.

He would have answers. And he would have them now.

Chapter Twenty

The evening was turning into a nightmare. Elsa had planned to eventually have a dinner party where Dante didn't wear his mask. She wanted him to be comfortable with the people she invited, to ease him into the idea. Instead, Rachel had ripped off his mask and thrown it on the floor, leaving him exposed for everyone to see.

And he hadn't minded a bit.

This was what she wanted, wasn't it? He was interacting with people without wearing his mask, and he seemed perfectly comfortable. Aside from a few rude gawkers, no one was paying attention to him.

Well, that wasn't entirely true. A few clusters of women had gathered at the edge of the dance floor, no doubt waiting for their chance to dance with him. They would all have to wait. He was completely absorbed by whatever Rachel was talking about as they danced.

The surge of jealousy that rose up within Elsa was like a tidal wave. It knocked the wind from her, made her dizzy. When Rachel stumbled into Dante's chest and he held her close, Elsa felt like she might be sick. The irony of her situation tore through her.

She had been clinging to her hope that Dante would choose her, even after meeting other women and learning that he had options. She thought maybe after dating some other people he would return to her.

Only now did she realize her mistake. What woman would let him go once they had him? What if Elsa had to stand aside as he fell in love with someone else?

She had a horrifying vision of standing in a church among other bridesmaids as a radiant Rachel glided down the aisle to Dante's waiting arms. Elsa's stomach churned again at the thought. She shook her head, trying to force the image away. It was too much.

She glanced back in their direction, but Dante didn't seem to be dancing anymore. He was striding through the crowd, stopping occasionally to either look down as if someone was speaking to him or to scan the crowd.

The bodies between them parted enough to give her a glimpse of women in sultry outfits circling him like piranha. Elsa could almost hear her heart shattering like Dante's mask. There was no one to help her pick up the pieces.

Desperate for space and air, she made her way to the exit. She sat on a bench seat in the foyer near the front door. When Dante was ready to leave, he would find her. She hoped he would be alone and not escorted by some woman looking to go home with him. Her stomach tightened with dread.

At least now he knew he didn't have to wear a mask to be accepted, to be desired.

Maybe it was time to tell him about reconstructive surgery. The thought of him going through a surgery she felt was unnecessary made her feel half sick. There were always risks. Garrett had been clear on that point. But it wasn't her decision to make.

If Dante wanted reconstructive surgery, she would support him however she could. Unfortunately, the most helpful thing she could do was obtain a legal identity for him. There would be paperwork to fill out and questions that would need to be answered. She still had no idea what to do about that.

Her thoughts were chasing their tails when a smooth voice brought them to a halt. "It's a sin for a beautiful woman to be alone."

A man in a cat mask sat down next to Elsa on the bench, leaning in close enough to make her uneasy, but not so close that she felt justified in doing something about it.

"If I see any I'll let them know."

"So modest."

The cat mask had a mane of dark hair attached with streaks of color running through it like a tomcat. The man's smile revealed two rows of perfect white teeth.

There was something about his eyes that gave Elsa a chill. They were cold blue. Emotionless, even when he smiled. She had longed for solitude when she left the party, but she suddenly found herself wishing there were more people nearby.

He leaned back against the window at an angle that put him even closer. "You're very reclusive, being out here all by yourself."

"I prefer to think of myself as selective."

"How interesting. You'd rather be a snob than a recluse."

"I didn't say—"

Before she could finish her argument, Dante stormed into the room. His eyebrows were lowered over his dark gaze, his hair in disarray, and his lips pulled down in a deep frown. Something else must have happened, and she had left him alone to deal with it. How could she have been so selfish?

Elsa leapt to her feet, guilt and relief warring within her as she ran away from the man on the bench.

"What's wrong? Are you all right?"

"I am fine, thank you." Dante's voice was cold and tense. He glared at the man sitting on the bench. "I do not mean to intrude."

"You didn't intrude," she said. "I was just waiting for you."

"Well, I am here."

"Are you ready to go home then?" She hoped so.

Before Dante could respond, the stranger from the bench stood and walked over to them. "Leaving so soon?

But we were only just getting to know each other."

"Perhaps another time." Elsa stepped closer to Dante, latching onto his arm as if he was a buoy on a stormy sea.

The stranger stared at her hands on Dante's arm, his gaze beyond cold. It almost seemed predatory. Dante must have picked up on it too. He put his arm around her waist and started leading her to the door.

"I'll take you up on that, Elsa." The stranger strolled back toward the rest of the gallery.

Elsa didn't remember giving him her name. Hearing him say it sent a chill down her spine. She couldn't keep herself from casting one last glance over her shoulder. Dante followed suit, pausing at the exit.

The man pointed to the right side of his face and said, "By the way, just because this is a masked ball doesn't mean you can crawl out from under your rock and pretend to be a normal person like the rest of us. Next time, stay home at the freak show." He stepped through the doorway, disappearing into the crowd.

At first, Elsa was so shocked that she simply stared after him. Then, fire flooded her veins.

She wasn't sure what she was going to do to that man. She did know that he wouldn't like it. She took two steps before Dante tightened his grip on her waist, pulling her back against his chest. He spun her around to face him.

"Let it go."

"Didn't you hear what he said?"

"Yes, I did. And it is a sentiment that I am quite familiar with. His words speak more of his character than mine."

"How can anyone be so callous?"

"He seems a man who is very accustomed to getting what he wants. I have met his sort before." Dante brushed a lock of hair behind Elsa's ear, then cupped her cheek and tilted her face toward him. "Think no more of it."

She wasn't sure she could manage that on her own. He must have sensed her need for distraction, because he stepped closer and slid his hand to the small of her back, all but pressing their bodies together. He let his fingertips trail along her skin as he shifted his other hand from her face to her shoulder.

The warm breeze from outside couldn't touch the heat that was rising within her. A hint of a smile lifted the corners of Dante's lips. His full, kissable lips.

She needed to do something quickly before this escalated any further. She looked away from him and pulled back a bit to break the spell of the moment.

"I'm sorry I left you alone. I just needed a minute to get some air." She could use even more of it now. Cold air. Or maybe a cold shower.

"I quite understand." He kissed her forehead so lightly she barely felt the brush of his lips on her skin. "Let us go home."

Chapter Twenty-One

The sky was inky black when they arrived at the manor, pinpricks of light scattered over the darkness above like diamonds. Concern had long since usurped Dante's anger. Elsa had hardly spoken to him after they left the gallery. During the drive home, she sat on the opposite side of the car, never once reaching for his hand.

In the foyer, she placed her feathered mask on a side table and stood with her back to him. Not knowing what else to do, Dante pulled the bundle from his pocket that held the remnants of his own mask and set it next to hers.

Hoping to draw her into conversation, he said, "Your friends are every bit as gracious as I would expect from knowing you."

"You really felt comfortable, even without your mask?"

"Very much so."

Elsa smiled at last, and the light he loved so dearly returned to her eyes for a moment. They were still pinched, as if she were in great pain, but did not wish him to know.

"I'm glad it was such a good experience. I hope that you understand things better now. Your options."

"Options?"

"You've seen that people will accept you as you are."

"You have already shown me that. I do not care what others think, only you."

She winced and her smile vanished. "I'm not the only person who accepts you. I wanted you to know that. You can have other relationships. Other friends."

"Friends." He let the word roll around on his tongue. He did not like the taste of it at all. Not when speaking of himself and Elsa.

"And more, if you'd like."

His gaze snapped back to hers, but she was staring very pointedly at the tile floor. She had gone quite pale. Dante's heart started thundering in his chest. It was a wonder she did not hear it, standing so close at his side.

"Rachel seemed fascinated by you." Elsa's voice was reedy. She cleared her throat before continuing. "So did the other women that approached you after your dance. I wanted you to know that you don't have to change to have relationships with other people."

"I am not certain that I understand."

"That's because I haven't told you about this yet."

Her features were pulled so tight, she looked as though she might shatter at any moment. Her eyes had become glassy, and she had to clear her throat again before continuing.

"I know that this has caused you grief throughout your

life." She reached up and gently stroked the right side of his face. Her fingers were as delicate as feathers. "I've heard other people say worse things to you than what that man at the dance tonight said. I know it affects you more than you show."

"Elsa—" Before he could say more, she silenced him, sliding her thumb across his lips with that same maddening touch. She stepped in closer, resting both of her hands on his shoulders.

"We've been focusing on the technological advancements that have occurred since your time, but there have been medical advances too. We haven't talked about them yet. But it's possible that you might be able to have reconstructive surgery to remove some of your scars. We still need to work out your identity issue, but if you want, we can talk to Garrett about whether you're a good candidate."

"Is this what you want for me, then? To change how I look?"

"Absolutely not!" The fierceness of her tone left no doubt she meant what she said. "I don't care what you look like. All I care about is who you are."

Dante stepped closer, leaving very little space between them. He dared to rest his hands on her waist. "I believe you."

"You just have to know that you have options." Her voice was barely above a whisper, yet he could feel the longing in each word.

"And what of you? Are you one of my options?"

She stiffened, but did not pull away. A flush spread across her chest, creeping up from the pale gold silk of her bodice.

Dante was done resisting. He leaned toward her and pressed his lips gently against hers.

Elsa trembled in his arms, her hands sliding up to clutch the back of his neck. He deepened the kiss, and her breath came out in a moan as she pulled him even closer.

Tangling her fingers in his hair to keep him captive, suddenly it was she who kissed him, and with a stunning ardor. Her lips were silken fire, starved for him. When she slid her tongue against his lips, he groaned in response to her invitation.

Elsa, his Elsa, warm and soft in his arms. This is what he had been longing for.

His tongue delved between her lips, a prelude of what was to come. He wrapped his arms around her, pressing their bodies together, desperate to be closer.

She gripped his shoulders and pushed him away, breaking off their kiss. Her chest rose and fell in quick breaths. The same desire he felt was mirrored in her eyes.

He could not form words to express what he was feeling. Hope, joy, expectation. All fell short of the immensity of his emotion.

Dante pulled her against his chest, burying his face in

her hair. He breathed her in, the scent of roses making him dizzy, the taste of her still sweet upon his lips.

"No." She shook her head and pushed him more firmly. His arms fell to his sides as she stepped away. "I can't do this."

He did not understand what had happened. She shook her head again, and held out one arm as if to ward him off.

"Elsa, I love you."

Of course. That one small word held everything that he felt for her within it.

"Are you sure?"

His blood was a deafening rush in his ears. He wondered if he had heard her correctly. "That I love you? I am certain of it."

She shook her head again, backing away as if she was afraid of him. His heart lurched in his chest. He had seen a similar look too many times before, but never from Elsa.

"You are my life."

"That's what I'm afraid of." She closed her eyes and pressed her hands to her chest as if to keep her heart from leaping out.

"Tell me." His throat was ready to collapse on itself from the weight of his emotion.

When she opened her eyes, they glistened with unshed tears. Her lip quivered for a moment, and she shook her head.

At first, he thought she was rejecting him, but then she

said, "How can you know you love me? How would you ever know for sure? I brought you here and gave you a home, a new life. How will we ever know if it's love or gratitude?"

"Elsa—" Dante took a small step toward her.

"No." She was building up her walls, brick by brick, word by word, putting distance between them. A panicky feeling fluttered up from his stomach. "I know you. You'd stay, even if you realized later that it wasn't love. You'd stay from a sense of honor. I don't want that. I never wanted that."

"What do you want?"

His question seemed to break her.

"I want you! I've always wanted you. For years!" Tears spilled down her cheeks as a torrent of words flew from her lips. "The first time I saw you, you were trying to save Heinrich. I could see the love and the pain and the fear in your eyes. And then I watched you with Mary, how kind you were to her, how encouraging. And I'm sorry that I watched you without you knowing. I never thought that we would meet."

"I have already forgiven that."

She continued as if she had not heard him. "All the torment others heaped on you, the pain you bore, and you never once complained to anyone. You never told anyone, but I saw how it tore at your soul, how it pushed you down to your knees. I know that pain, that weight. I've lived with it every day of my life. But I never knew anyone could be as strong as you."

He knew her powers made her feel isolated, that she felt she could not trust anyone with knowledge of her gift. He did not realize how very much that loneliness was costing her. He had no time to think on it, as she kept on, her voice rising.

"And now you're here and all I can think is that you're only interested in me because I'm the only woman you know who accepts you. I thought if you met someone else, maybe if things didn't work out between you, eventually we could…"

Her voice broke, and she covered her face with her hands. "I knew I had to let you go, but then I watched you dance with Rachel tonight and talk to those other women, and it hurt so much. So much more than I thought it would."

She shook her head as if trying to clear it of a nightmare. Dante could bear no more.

With two strides, he closed the distance between them, wrapping his arms around her again. He held her against his chest as she shuddered and cried.

She had not said that she loved him, but the intensity of her emotion left him with no doubt of how she felt. The depths of her pain were as great as her passion. He had to help her understand that his love was real.

"You are the strongest woman I have ever known.

There is no other woman I want to be with. Yes, you have given me much, and your generosity is part of why I love you, but it is so much more than that. I would know a feeling of obligation. I would know if it was gratitude. I am grateful, of course, but that is not the summation of what I feel for you."

He pulled her from him through an act of will, tilting her face up so he could look into her eyes. "Do you think that I have not watched you as well? How tenderly you care for Winston, how passionately you look after your friends? You are kind, intelligent, brave and beautiful. How could I not love you?"

"How can you be sure?" she whispered.

"I know my heart. And I believe I know yours. You defied time to bring me here with you. Let me be with you."

"Bringing you back was nothing compared to this." She backed away once more, shaking her head. "You're wrong about me. I'm not brave."

Without another word, she turned away, then walked up the stairs.

Dante did not know what to do. If Elsa would not trust him, how could they possibly have a life together?

He took the stairs slowly, following her path toward his own room. He paused before her door. For once, it was closed.

This was ludicrous. He loved her and he believed she

loved him, whether she would admit it to herself or not. They wanted each other, wanted to be together. Fear should not stand in their way. He would not let it.

He opened the door.

Elsa was curled on her side in bed, the lamp dim beside her. She sat up and stared at him.

He hesitated for a moment on the threshold, then crossed into her room and quietly closed the door behind him. "You are mistaken about me as well."

"About what?"

"You think I am overwhelmed with gratitude for all you have given me." He started to close the space between them.

She stood as he approached, as nervous as a bird trying to decide whether to take flight. He would not let it happen. He would not let her deny them the infinite possibilities of being together.

Dante stopped quite close to her. She had to crane her neck to look up at him. Errant locks of her golden hair spilled over her shoulder as she did. He slid his fingers along her skin, nudging her hair back so that he could see the gooseflesh that followed in the wake of his touch. He let the silence stretch on.

"How was I wrong?"

"I am grateful, yes. You have given me a home, companionship, friendship. But I am the most selfish being on this earth."

"No, you're not. How can you say that?"

"Because it is not enough. You have given me an entire world, and it's not enough. I want you."

Chapter Twenty-Two

Elsa could hardly breathe. The room seemed to disappear around her, until there was nothing left but the two of them. The focus, the purpose of Dante's gaze spread shivers over her entire body.

"I told you, I—"

Dante didn't let her finish her sentence. "You told me you want me. You told me that you have longed for me. I will not let you deny yourself this. Deny us this. All of your fears, all your doubts about us are unfounded, and I will spend the rest of my life proving that to you."

He slid one arm around her waist to the small of her back and placed the other on the side of her neck, lightly dusting her skin with his fingertips. The argument she had been ready to make vanished, the words scattering like sparks from a shorting power line as his touch overwhelmed her senses.

He pulled her closer and bent his head to hers. Just before their lips touched, he whispered, "Elsa…"

The thrill of his kiss was unlike anything she had ever experienced. She felt weightless. She wrapped her arms around his neck to keep herself from floating away. He was her anchor. The warmth of his body flowed into her. The softness of his lips was intoxicating.

His mouth moved on hers gently, tasting her, exploring her. He buried his fingers in her hair as his other hand pressed her to him. He deepened the kiss, his tongue coaxing her mouth open.

She didn't care about resisting him anymore. She wasn't strong enough. He was too warm, too real. How could she have ever thought she could let him go?

Elsa tightened her arms around his shoulders, parting her lips and inviting him in. He tasted like strawberries and champagne.

He trailed his kisses along her chin and neck. Sparks rained down through her body from wherever they touched.

"You are mine." His voice was a soft breath against her ear. "And I am yours. I will never let you forget that."

His words were as dizzying as his kisses. Elsa felt her heart lurch as he stepped back, every fiber of her being protesting the distance between them. But his gaze held hers without wavering.

He slid his jacket from his shoulders, then tossed it onto a nearby chair. Slowly, he removed more of his intricate outfit, never looking away from her. She watched him hungrily, imagining that she was the one removing each article of clothing.

When he was down to just the familiar white shirt and

black slacks, he stepped closer. He reached out with one hand, trailing his fingertips along the side of her neck, across her collarbones, and ever so lightly over the tops of her breasts.

He pulled her against him and kissed her deeply. His hands flew over the back and sides of her dress, finding the hooks and zippers and undoing them.

Elsa felt feverish. Every touch of air was like a cool breath as her dress slid over her skin.

Dante drew his hands along her hips, guiding the dress to the floor. He kept his gaze locked on hers, as if he was avoiding looking at her body while she stepped out of her dress, then he placed the golden fabric on the chair with his clothes.

He paused briefly before letting his gaze rove over her body. When he did, he let out an audible gasp.

Doubts sprang to life in Elsa's mind. She wasn't toned enough or thin enough or curvy enough. Her imagination produced a million ways he could be disappointed with her. She lifted her hands to her chest and took a step back, but he gently grasped her wrists and followed her as she retreated.

"Do not cover yourself." There was a rasp to his voice, as if speaking was a struggle. "You are so beautiful. Please let me look at you."

She felt herself blushing, but she lowered her hands. Dante released her and took a step back. His gaze was as intimate as a caress, lingering on her breasts, the antique gold lace of her panties. He ran a shaking hand through his hair, leaving it the tousled mass of soft waves she preferred.

Still staring at her, he pulled his shirt over his head, then threw it on the floor where it was quickly joined by the rest of his clothing.

Elsa couldn't keep herself from staring back. His body was all smooth lines of muscle, his chest tapering down to his narrow waist and hips. He was grace, lithe strength and pure masculine beauty. She tried not to stare at his erection, but it was hard to look away from it.

She knew that she would never be the same after this. She was about to ruin herself for other men, and she didn't care. Reaching up to undo her chignon, she stepped toward him. His lips parted as he watched her hair fall around her shoulders.

He smiled at her, running the backs of his fingers along her stomach, sliding them over her ribs, and finally cupping her breasts. He bent down to kiss her again, deeply, as his hands worked magic on her.

Lowering himself on one knee, he kissed her stomach while sliding her panties down her legs. For a brief moment, Elsa saw a possibility play out. A possibility that she knew would haunt her.

Dante on one knee, proposing with his mother's ring. A life, a future together. Truly together. It was an awful dream that held everything she wanted and everything that terrified her.

He stood and lifted her from the ground. She pushed all thoughts, all dreams, all hope and panic away. Instead, she focused on the feeling of his arms around her, his chest against hers as he lowered them both to her bed.

Everywhere, skin was touching skin, and it still wasn't enough. She wanted more contact. Needed more. As he kissed her, she tentatively slid her leg up his thigh. Dante groaned against Elsa's mouth, rolling her onto her back and pressing her into the bed. She could feel him between her legs, so close.

His whole body shook as he took a deep, shuddering breath and held perfectly still. "I know that I should take my time, but—"

"I don't want you to."

She was desperate to know him in this way. Her body was already begging for him. She slid her arms under his so she could run her hands down his back and over the firm muscles of his backside.

That was all it took.

She gasped as he buried himself in the soft flesh of her core, her back arching from the intensity of him filling her. He slid his hands under her back, holding her shoulders as he nuzzled her neck, pushing himself deeper. He was still trembling.

"Impossible," he whispered against her ear.

She had to agree. The moment was perfect, each sensation a miracle. Dante was here, joined with her. It was bliss.

Slowly, he started to move again, every thrust bringing Elsa closer to a precipice she was wholly prepared to cast herself from. She wrapped her legs around his thighs, urging him on. His pace increased, just like the sparks arcing out through her body from where they were joined.

As she felt the explosion start to cascade within her, Dante let out a deep groan and increased his pace to a near frenzy. She cried out his name, forever branding it on her soul.

He collapsed on top of her, his strength seeming to have left him. He nuzzled her neck, placing gentle kisses along the soft, sensitive skin. His touch echoed all over her body.

"Dear God," he said. "I never imagined…"

Elsa was still basking in the glow of things. Her mind slowly processed his words. What had he never imagined? She felt a heavy dread deep in her stomach.

"That wasn't…" She almost hated to finish the sentence. She wasn't sure she wanted to know. But she had to. "That wasn't your first time, was it?"

He managed to lift himself up on his elbows, smiling down at her and kissing her gently before saying, "I hope it was not too obvious."

The dread transformed to crushing guilt. Elsa knew that she was being weak by giving in to her desire for Dante.

She was being selfish, not waiting until he'd had a chance to date other women in her time. But knowing that she'd been his first, and that would mean that if he really did love her, she'd be his only...

"Did I do something wrong?"

"No. I did." She rolled out from underneath him. Sitting up on the side of the bed, she pulled the sheets around her.

He rose to his knees, his hands on her shoulders as he pulled her back against his chest. "What is it? Tell me what is wrong."

She covered her eyes with one hand, trying to figure out how to put her thoughts into words. She knew he was already upset by her reaction and didn't want to make him feel worse. Especially not after something that was supposed to be so special.

"I just... I didn't know that was your first time."

"I am gratified to know I performed so well." He brushed her hair from the side of her neck, then pressed a gentle kiss on her shoulder and wrapped his arms around her. "Was there something you would have done differently had you known?"

Not allowed herself to be so weak? She shook her head.

"Next time, I believe I will be better able to take my time. I want to savor you. I could spend days learning your body."

He pressed another kiss against her neck and she closed her eyes, willing herself not to cry. It was bad enough he had already seen that once this evening.

"I don't think there should be a next time."

His arms loosened around her, and she felt him sitting back, pulling away from her. That was good. They needed more distance between them.

"Did you not enjoy it?"

"I did. It was probably the most amazing thing I've ever experienced."

"I do not understand."

Elsa stood up, pulling the sheets with her so that she could wrap them around herself. She turned back to face him, trying to steel her resolve.

"I told you I was worried that you only think you want me because you don't think you have other options." She kept the focus on their physical attraction. She couldn't talk about love without breaking down. "I assumed at the very least you'd had relationships in your own time. I shouldn't have given in. If I had known it was your first —"

Dante rose from the bed, following as she backed away. Her resolve was already weakening. A sheen of sweat from their lovemaking clung to his skin, highlighting the dips and valleys of his muscles. There was a flash of something in his eyes. Intensity, determination.

"I wanted you." His voice was low and level. "And you wanted me. That is all there is to it."

"It doesn't matter what I want. This is supposed to be a

new life for you. What I want shouldn't matter."

"What you want will always matter to me. Always."

She shook her head. "No. This isn't right. What you're feeling isn't—"

"Do not dare tell me what I feel. You do not know what I think and you do not know what is in my heart. Only I know these things."

He stalked up to her. Even without touching her, his towering presence was overwhelming. She could feel the heat from him, catch his scent everywhere. She felt as enveloped in his essence as she had when he had been filling her, holding her as close as he could.

"You say that you want me to make a life of my choosing," he said. "I am. And you are part of that, whether you like it or not. There is no other woman I want. I have never desired a woman as I desire you."

"You'd never met a woman from my time before."

"And now I have met several. What does it matter?" He let out an exasperated sigh. "Has it not occurred to you that I have never wanted a woman as I want you, never loved a woman, because I had not met *you*? Do you think I would want you any less if we had met in my time?"

"I…don't know."

He didn't give her time to consider the idea.

"I do know. You say you do not care how I look, that what you care about is me. Do you not think I feel the same about you? I do not care that you are the one who brought me here, only that you are here with me now."

What could she say to that? But still, how could she let herself believe that everything she ever wanted was right in front of her?

Again, he didn't give her time to think. He gripped her shoulders and pulled her against him, crushing his lips against hers. He released her only long enough to tear the sheet away, then wrapped his arms around her, lifting her off her feet.

Elsa grabbed on to his neck as he stood up to his full height. She instinctively wrapped her legs around his waist, gasping as she felt his shaft nudge against her again. Never releasing her lips, Dante stumbled to the wall, pressing her back against it, as he drove himself into her core.

He shifted one of his arms to cradle her bottom, the other grabbing her thigh and using his grip to push himself even deeper. Elsa had never experienced such intensity. Their passion was consuming her and she didn't care. He was the flame, and she was the candle.

He broke off the kiss, his gaze boring into her. "I traveled across time to be with you. I want no other and will have no other. There is only you."

She clung more tightly to his neck, wanting to believe him, wanting to let go and cast herself into his love. But she was so afraid.

They had crossed the line. There was no turning back.

She pushed away the fear and doubt, again focusing on the union of their bodies. She gave him everything she could, everything except her heart.

Dante trailed his kisses down her neck, suckling the skin beneath her ear. She felt herself building toward another climax, this one looming on the horizon even larger than the first.

He plunged himself deeper into her, faster, pinning her against the smooth wood of the wall with his body. He released his grip on her leg, bringing his hand to her cheek and reclaiming her mouth. His tongue was just as hungry, delving into her mouth relentlessly.

Her climax hit her like an earthquake. Every part of her body seemed alive, singing with sensation. The aftershocks kept going as he threw his head back, crying out from his own release. She could feel him pumping his seed within her, the shockwaves of his pleasure reverberating through her body.

When he finally stopped, his body was pressing her against the wall firmly enough that he didn't even need his hands to support her. He caressed her cheek with his thumb, kissing her again, but gently.

The strange intensity was still in his gaze as he pulled back to look at her. He wasn't smiling, his lips instead set in a grim, determined line. Without saying anything, he carried her to the bed and set her down on it, crawling in behind her.

Even though she still wanted to argue, to run away, the look in his eyes said that he would not be dissuaded. He wrapped his arms around her, pulling her tight against his chest, as if he would never let her go. Elsa knew deep in her heart she never wanted him to.

Chapter Twenty-Three

"Those eggs are done cooking," Winston said. "I can smell them from here."

"I am aware of their state. Now please relax and rest, as your doctor has ordered."

Dante emptied the pan of eggs and diced peppers onto two plates that already held buttered toast with jam. When he picked up the plates and turned toward the table, Elsa was standing in the doorway to the kitchen.

His chest felt full at the sight of her. Her hair framed her face in a mane of chaotic gold and her lips were still swollen from his kisses. She stared at him with unfocused eyes and the deep teal top she wore was on backward.

It had been a delightfully long night.

"Good morning." A crimson flush spread up from her chest.

Dante turned back to the stove to hide his broad smile. He set down the plates and rearranged the toast. "Good morning."

"Oh, there you are," Winston said. "I was wondering if you were ever going to get up."

"I guess Jazz's party wore me out." Her chair squeaked

across the floor as she sat at the table with Winston.

Dante picked up the plates again, carrying them to the table. He let Winston know where the food was on his plate using the placement of time on a clock face. "Your eggs are at six o'clock, toast at twelve. The coffee will only be a moment."

Winston nodded at Dante, but was not quite done with Elsa. "Are you feeling all right? It's not like you to sleep in so late."

"I'm fine, Winston, really. But how are you? Are you still feeling better?"

"Fit as a fiddle. I've been trying to tell you both. Coddling me like I'm some kind of baby."

"Winston, we care about you," Elsa said. "We're just trying to make sure you're okay."

Dante did not try to hide his scowl. "But we are aware that you are no longer reliant upon us, and shall proceed accordingly out of respect."

Winston's brow knit and a curious smile lit his features. He laughed and shook his head, then began to eat.

The firm set to Elsa's lips as she frowned at Dante told him that she perceived his point, whether she agreed with it or not. He would simply have to show her the truth of his words.

Dante walked back to the counter and prepared coffee for the pair. He carried the mugs to the table and set them near their plates.

"Aren't you joining us?" Elsa asked.

"I have made other arrangements."

"What kind of arrangements?"

"Rachel will be arriving shortly to take me to the city for the day. I will be back by this evening." He placed the skillet in the sink and began to wash the dishes from preparing breakfast. "I apologize for the short notice, but the opportunity only arose this morning."

Elsa scooted toward the edge of her chair. "Are you sure that's a good idea?"

Winston laughed. "Listen to this one, Dante. That Rachel will wear your feet down to the ankles."

Dante crossed back to the table, then placed his hands on Winston's shoulders and squeezed them gently. "I assure you, everything will be fine."

Winston laughed again, reaching up to pat one of Dante's hands.

Elsa's frown remained. "I hope you two have fun."

"It will certainly be an adventure." Dante could see the lines of strain around Elsa's eyes. She still had so little faith in him—in them. He would prove to her that they could have a future together.

To help her along that path, he said, "Have you made any progress with your book?"

Elsa leaned back, the line between her brows deepening. "Not really."

"If it is not too bold of me to request, perhaps you

could give it some thought today. I very much look forward to discovering how it ends."

"Me too."

A horn sounded outside, and Dante said, "I am summoned."

He leaned down as he walked past Elsa, resting his hand on her shoulder. Her eyes widened slightly as he bent his head to hers and kissed her soundly. He lifted his hand to her cheek, then trailed his fingers along her jaw and chin.

"I am still hoping for a happy ending to that story." He did not wait for a response, eager to get underway.

As he walked through the foyer, he reached into his pocket and pulled out Garrett's mask. With the day Dante had planned, he preferred to keep his face covered. He wanted no distractions. The fit was snug as he pulled the mask in place, but not uncomfortable.

Upon reaching the front drive, Dante waved at Rachel, who was sitting in a green automobile that lacked a roof. Dark glasses covered her eyes, and she wore a kerchief over her hair. She returned his wave, smiling broadly.

He hastened to the side of the house, where he had placed several of his paintings earlier. They were already wrapped, prepared for the journey to Jazz's gallery.

Once the canvases were stowed in the back seat of Rachel's car, Dante climbed into the passenger seat. "Shall we?"

"We are going to have so much fun today." Rachel pressed her foot on the gas pedal.

He watched everything she did with keen interest, comparing what he had read with the reality of driving a car. He had only ridden in the back of an automobile, where he could not see their functioning.

"Jazz told me I'm supposed to be your personal assistant today," Rachel said. "So just let me know what you want to do."

"I hope that you are as full of energy as I have been led to believe, for there is quite a list." He was a bit nervous to be venturing out on his own, but the rewards awaiting him overcame his fears.

"Oh, I almost forgot!" Rachel stopped the car at the end of the long drive that led to Elsa's home and handed Dante a plain envelope. "Jazz told me to give you this. Also, before we run your errands, we need to go to the Shady Palms building. It has all these great newly renovated lofts. Do you know why she wants us to go there?"

"I am uncertain." Dante opened the envelope and pulled out a note scrawled on a small piece of paper.

"What does it say?"

"'A little something to start you off'," Dante read. Behind the note was a stack of bills that looked quite unfamiliar.

"Holy crap, Dante! That's a lot of money!"

"Is it? Well, we shall have to hope that it is enough."

"Enough for what?"

"To begin with, several outfits. Jazz and I agree I need to *update my look*, as she put it."

"Oh. My. God. I get to help you buy a new wardrobe?"

"If you are up to the task."

Rachel grinned, turned back to the road, then pressed her foot on the accelerator hard enough that the tires made a horrible screeching sound. Dante clutched his seat as inertia pushed him against the padded surface.

"You might want to fasten your seatbelt," Rachel said. "Because this is going to be the best day ever."

He did as she instructed, though the day ahead could hardly compare at all to the previous night. Gooseflesh rose along his arms just at the thought, his skin alive with the memory of Elsa in his embrace, his mind echoing with her cries of pleasure.

"Are you okay?" Rachel asked.

"Fine." He cleared his throat.

"You looked kind of far away there for a moment."

"Perhaps it would be best if you focused your attention on what lies before us."

She shrugged and looked back to the road. It was advice he himself needed to follow. He did not like being away from Elsa. He already found himself missing her and not only because of the night before.

He missed seeing her smile. He missed watching her at her writing desk, the sunlight casting a soft glow upon her hair. He missed their stimulating conversation, her gentle touch, and, most of all, her laughter.

They could not reach town and complete their tasks quickly enough. His only regret was that he could not both share these experiences with Elsa and also surprise her with his accomplishments.

It was probably for the best. He needed to show her that he was able to stand on his own, to support her just as much as she had been supporting him.

In the meantime, he enjoyed the feel of the wind in his hair and the bright blue of the sky. The land was exceedingly flat, and it gave the feeling of the sky being right upon them. The thin fabric of his shirt did little to shield him from the sun, but he did not care.

The drive did not take as long as he remembered, whether because he could actually see the operations of the vehicle, asking Rachel as many questions as he liked, or that she seemed to be driving at an extraordinary speed. In either case, the town formed around them, emerging from the dense palms and evergreens.

Rachel navigated several streets, then pulled up to the sidewalk before Jazz's gallery. "I thought we should drop off your canvases first."

"A wise plan." He opened his door and stepped out onto the shaded concrete.

She was too quick for him to help her from the car, appearing at his elbow and picking up one of the parcels.

Dante carried the rest as they entered the gallery.

Various people bustled about, cleaning up from the dance. Jazz stood in the center, pointing as she gave directions for moving sculpture displays back onto the main floor. She smiled brightly when she saw Dante and Rachel.

"There you are! I was hoping you'd stop by." She hugged Dante, kissing his left cheek, then stepped back. She looked him up and down and shook her head. "You cannot leave your house like this if you want to change your image."

"Rachel shall be helping me with that today," Dante said.

"Good. And thank you." Jazz smiled at Rachel, then pointed to a side room. "You'll be in there, Dante. Let's see what you've brought me so we can start to plan where to place things."

Once they had set down their burdens, he scanned the room, envisioning his paintings on the walls.

"There is another painting I am currently working on which I should like to be the focus. It is a bit larger than the others, but I think it would go well on the wall opposite the door."

"Is it another landscape?" Jazz was already busily removing the brown paper covering his canvases.

"It is a portrait."

She paused long enough to give him a cryptic smile.

"Okay. That'll be good to break up the rest. Also, that reminds me…"

She gripped his arms with surprising strength and swung him around so that his back was to one of the blank walls. She then pulled out a small rectangular object from a holster on her belt and pointed it at his face. He was unsure what to expect, but she merely tapped it, then put it back in place.

"What was that?"

"I just needed a picture," she said.

"That tiny device is a camera?" Dante's voice was louder than he anticipated. He had not read about cameras as of yet. The level of advancement was quite amazing.

Rachel had been standing in the doorway, glancing from one wall to another, but she fixed her attention on him. "They don't have camera phones where you come from?"

It was a phone as well? He wanted to ask so many questions, but he knew he had already piqued people's interest in a dangerous arena once more.

Instead, he cleared his throat and tried to sound more modern. "Where I'm from, the people were much more old-fashioned. This sort of thing wasn't ubiquitous."

Jazz let out a brief laugh. "They *were* old-fashioned? What, did a meteor blow up your home town?"

Scrambling for an explanation, he said, "I merely meant —"

"Relax. I'm just teasing you." Jazz smirked. "I'll be sure to add getting you a phone to my to-do list."

"Thank you. I would like that very much."

They spent the better part of an hour planning which paintings to place on each wall. Rachel had a keen eye for aesthetics, but listened attentively to all of Jazz's advice. When they were done, Jazz pulled a key out of her pocket.

"By the way, this is for you." She tossed the key toward Dante. He plucked it from the air and turned it over in his hand. The number 3B was inscribed upon it. Jazz said, "Hurry up with your business so you can get back to the easel."

"Of course. And Jazz..." He found himself a bit overcome at her generosity. Recalling her penchant for being direct, he simply said, "Thank you."

Jazz smirked at him again and nodded. She headed back to the main room of the gallery, giving out more orders.

He was prepared to leave, but Rachel gripped his hand tightly and pulled him toward a room with a rope stretched across its entryway.

"Before we go, you have to see Michael's exhibit! It hasn't opened yet, but I'm sure he won't mind." She unhooked the rope so that they could enter, then reattached it behind them.

Dante truly wished she had left the exit open. He wanted to leave the instant he saw Michael's paintings—

portraits of women in dark reds and grays. They were nudes, though most at least had sheets draped over parts of their bodies. But those bodies…

Each was elongated, hunched, curving in ways that were barely human, yet somehow bespoke of a despair and horror that resonated within him. The women were either covering their faces with their hands or looking away, as if hiding some shameful secret.

Dante had the strangest urge to try to reach into the paintings and pull the subjects out, to save them from having to endure an eternity on such bleak canvases.

"They're powerful, aren't they?" Rachel's voice had taken on a serious cast that Dante had not heard from her before. In the darkness of that room, it was fitting.

"Indeed." He was uncertain what else to say. She had not let go of his hand, and was staring at the paintings with something of a stunned expression. He remembered his concerns from the masked ball. "Rachel, are you all right?"

She shook her head and smiled. "Of course I am. Why wouldn't I be?"

He could think of several reasons, first among them that she was involved with the man who had created such monstrous works. In any case, Rachel did not give Dante a chance to respond.

"Come on! We have a lot to do today." Squeezing his hand, she led him from the room. He followed her quite gladly.

They left the gallery and crossed the street on foot rather than taking Rachel's car. Apparently, their destination was not far. Trees lined the streets, thick leaves casting shadows over the sidewalks.

She paused in front of a whitewashed building with large glass windows set on each story above them. "This is it. Do you have an apartment here?"

He held up the key, sunlight gleaming along its serrated edge. "We shall see."

He opened the door to the building and stood aside so she could enter first, then stepped into what was presumably his new home.

The floor was covered in gray slate tile, just rough enough to give traction. The white walls of the foyer rose three stories above them. Opposite the building's entrance, a staircase climbed the wall, pausing at landings that led deeper into the building. Windows set in the top two floors allowed natural light to pour in from three directions.

Beneath the staircase, stones had been cleverly set together to form a waterfall that ended in a small pool where fish swam among water lilies and other plants. A frog leapt from the side of the pond into the water as Dante watched.

"Mr. Lucerne?"

He turned at the sound of his name. A man approached them, wearing a tailored suit with the name of the building tastefully embroidered on his lapel. Apparently, Jazz hadn't chosen to change Dante's name after all.

"I am Dante Lucerne."

"Ms. Zhou told me that you might be stopping by today." The man extended his hand, and Dante shook it. "I'm Charles Brenner. I run the front desk during the day."

He pointed over his shoulder at a semi-circular desk with a top that perfectly matched the floor. The man continued to shake Dante's hand for a few moments before releasing it. Though his gaze strayed to Dante's mask a few times, he did not make any mention to it or seem uncomfortable.

"I wanted to introduce myself so you know where to come if you have any questions or problems." He handed Dante a large envelope. "Here's a welcome packet for the building. Laundry room, gym and elevator locations are marked on a map inside. Again, please don't hesitate to contact me with any questions. My number is inside."

"Thank you," Dante said.

He was already feeling a bit overwhelmed, so he refrained from opening the envelope immediately. It was just as well, because Rachel grabbed his elbow and started pulling him toward the staircase.

"Come on, Dante! Let's check it out!"

"It was a pleasure meeting you," Dante called over his shoulder.

She practically ran up the stairs. He had to walk briskly

to keep up with her. When they reached a door marked as 3B, she smiled and placed the key Jazz had given him in the lock.

Rachel paused, then released her hold on the key. She shifted out of the way. "You should do it. It's your place, after all."

"Indeed."

He took a deep breath, then turned the key. The lock clicked, and he exhaled strongly. Part of him had wondered if it would work. Apparently, this truly was his new home. He would need even more help from Rachel than he had anticipated.

Dante opened the door and stepped inside.

Chapter Twenty-Four

Elsa was miserable. She tried to write, but her thoughts kept circling back to where Dante might be and what he was doing. She tried reading, but that was just as useless. She couldn't even focus on watching TV. She wandered through her house and ended up in the studio.

A large canvas was sitting next to Dante's easel, covered by a tarp. She was curious, but respected that he wanted to wait until it was done to show it to her.

She opened the doors to the patio, imagining him standing in the sun with a fresh canvas, ready to capture another familiar view that she hadn't truly appreciated until seeing it through his eyes.

Now, he was out seeing the world with Rachel. He had left Elsa behind, and she was the one who told him to.

"You miss him."

She nearly jumped at Winston's voice. He was hovering in the hallway just outside the door. The studio and Elsa's bedroom were the two places in the house he wouldn't enter, never knowing what projects were underway and potentially underfoot.

"How…"

Winston laughed. "I can hear you moping all the way in the kitchen. And it's about bloody time."

"For what?"

"You know what," Winston said. "I'm blind and I can see it clear as day. You two are together, aren't you?"

"I…don't know."

"You listen to me. Dante's not the type to take liberties. If he started something with you, he's serious. You don't need to worry about that."

"That's not what I'm worried about."

"Then what's the problem?"

That was the question. And the only answer she could come up with was, "Me."

Winston made a *pfft* noise and waved his hand at her. "I never met anyone wound as tight as you. You work so hard to control everything and everyone, most of all yourself. But life can't be controlled. Not really. You can grab hold of it as tight as you can till you suffocate, or let go and enjoy the ride."

Maybe he was right. Maybe that was what had gone wrong with Elsa's parents. All their fighting was their way of trying to control each other.

"I'm not that great at letting go."

"Oh, my love. You can do anything you set your mind to." Winston smiled. "Just have a little faith."

Some of the fear gripping her heart eased as warmth suffused her. Winston was one of the dearest people in her life. He and Jazz were the closest thing Elsa had to family.

"I'll try."

"Good. Now go outside and quit your moping. Get some sun and relax!" Winston shuffled off down the hallway, leaving her alone with her thoughts.

Going outside wasn't a bad idea. Only a few bright clouds broke up the darkening blue of the sky. She stepped onto the patio, enjoying the fresh air and the breeze. She settled in the lounge chair under the shade of the table's umbrella and watched the flowers in the garden sway with the wind.

What seemed a moment later, she jolted awake. The sun was beginning to set, shadows stretching across the stone of the patio. She wasn't sure what had woken her, but her skin was crawling. Someone pressed down on the back of her lounge chair.

Elsa leapt up from her seat, then spun around to find Michael staring at her.

In a soft voice he said, "You look so peaceful when you sleep."

"What are you doing here?" Her heart was thundering in her chest.

"I keep telling you, Elsa, I want us to be friends." He circled the lounge chair. "We have a chance to get to know each other better with Rachel off carousing with Dante." He sneered as he said Dante's name.

His voice, his mannerisms, and those cold blue eyes…

Elsa wondered that she hadn't recognized him earlier. A rush of anger flooded through her.

"You were the one in the cat mask last night, weren't you?"

"See? We're understanding each other better already." He slinked toward the flowers, but didn't take his eyes off of her. "Not even Rachel recognized me."

"Why go to all that trouble?"

"Rachel is so clingy. I wanted a night off." Michael turned back to Elsa and took a few steps toward her. His lips curled up from his teeth for a brief moment. "Is that too much to ask for?"

Elsa eased back to keep the distance between them. With each zigzagging path Michael cut across the patio, he was getting closer.

"You could have just talked to her."

His face resumed its semblance of calm. With a smug laugh, he said, "You underestimate my effect on Rachel. She's so weak. Not like you, Elsa. You're strong."

"Saying bad things about my friends is not the way to get on my good side."

"See? So protective. When I trashed you, Rachel ate it up." He narrowed his eyes as he spoke, grinning.

"I want you to leave. Now."

"You should be nicer to me. We're bound to become close, with how serious things are with Rachel and me. Speaking of..."

Elsa didn't want to take her eyes off of Michael, but she heard footsteps behind her. She glanced over her shoulder to see Rachel and Dante walking down the path that stretched around the side of the house.

"Michael? What are you doing here?" Rachel looked from Elsa to Michael and back again.

"Waiting for you, of course." Michael crossed the patio to meet Rachel. Without a prelude, he wrapped his arms around her and started kissing her passionately.

Elsa actually took a step toward them, wanting to pull them apart, to get Michael away from her friend. Dante must have noticed, because he came to her side and placed his hand on her shoulder.

He leaned close and whispered, "Are you all right?"

Elsa shook her head briefly, then tucked herself under Dante's arm.

Michael finally ended his kiss, then turned to face them. His arm was around the back of Rachel's neck, holding her close. "I was in the neighborhood and thought I would pay Elsa a visit since we didn't get to talk much last night at the party."

"You were at the party?" Rachel asked, her brow furrowing. Michael ignored her.

Dante stiffened next to Elsa. "Your costume was quite an effective disguise."

"At least I can take mine off." Michael laughed, then looked down at Rachel. "Guess you won that bet, didn't you?"

Rachel glanced at Dante, her face pained. "Dante, I—"

Michael talked over Rachel. "You don't need to explain anything." His features softened when he turned to her, as did his voice. "What happened was an accident. You have nothing to feel guilty about."

Rachel was still staring at Dante, as if she wanted to apologize, but Michael placed his hand on her cheek, turning her to face him. His other arm was still around Rachel's neck. It looked more like a choke-hold to Elsa than an affectionate gesture.

He ran his hand over Rachel's hair, then twined a lock around his finger and tugged on it. "Except that you left me alone for the entire day."

"I'm sorry," Rachel said.

Elsa's stomach churned. How many times had her mother apologized just like that to Elsa's father, or one of the many boyfriends that moved in after Elsa's father left?

At least Elsa didn't see any bruises or cuts on Rachel. Or Michael, for that matter. Yet.

"I was lonely," Michael said. "I thought Elsa might be lonely too, so I stopped by to see how she was doing."

"That's so thoughtful." Rachel was eating up his story. Elsa knew better.

"That reminds me." Michael turned back to Elsa and Dante. "How's that butler of yours? I hear he took a tumble."

"Winston is quite well. Thank you for asking," Dante said.

For the briefest instant, a look of disgust flashed across Michael's features. Elsa couldn't believe that this was Rachel's boyfriend. She had to do something.

"Why don't we go inside and have some coffee?" Maybe Elsa could talk some sense into Rachel if they could get a moment alone.

"That's a lovely idea," Michael said. "Unfortunately, we'll have to take a rain check. I haven't been able to look at Rachel all day, and now that I have her to myself again, I don't really feel like sharing."

Rachel smiled, then actually sighed as Michael ran his fingers along her cheekbone. Her expression was rapt.

"I get it." Elsa had to figure out a way to separate them. She opted for the direct approach. "Only there's something that I wanted to talk to Rachel about. Girl-talk stuff."

Michael looked at Elsa keenly, but he smiled and nodded. "I suppose I could let Rachel go for another few minutes. For you. Since we're on our way to becoming such good friends."

Elsa had always wondered how her parents managed to fall in love and get married. Watching Rachel and Michael was almost like traveling back in time. History was repeating itself. Elsa had to try to help Rachel avoid that fate.

They headed into the studio, leaving the men outside.

Elsa didn't like the idea of Dante being alone with Michael, but she kept them both in sight through the window.

"What did you want to talk to me about?" Rachel still had a dreamy look in her eyes and kept gazing out toward the patio.

"How long have you been dating this guy?"

"It's been a couple of months now. Can you believe it? That's like forever. I've never had a relationship last this long. He says I'm his muse."

"How well do you know him, though?"

"Well enough to know I love him."

"Rachel, come on. What do you really know about him?"

Rachel let out a huff of breath. "Not all of us like everything laid out in a neat little line. I don't ever want to be with someone who doesn't have mystery. I'm not like you. I'm not ready to settle down."

"Who said I was—"

"I'm not just some dumb blonde. I notice things."

"I have never said that you're a dumb blonde." Elsa was disturbed Rachel would even think that. Rachel could be absentminded, but she was a brilliant designer and had offered Elsa insight any number of times.

"But you've thought it."

"Rachel, I never thought such a thing. I'm just worried about you. Michael is scaring me."

"I'm not the one dating a guy who's pretending to be the villain from a bunch of horror stories."

"What?" Elsa gasped.

"This is exactly why Michael didn't want you to know about him. About us. He was right."

"What are you talking about?"

"You always do this with my boyfriends. You say they're too reckless and unsettled, or too old and experienced. And with Michael, you think I don't know enough about him?" Rachel shook her head. "This is my life. Stop trying to control it."

"I'm not trying to control your life."

"Of course you are. It's what you do. Normally, I don't care. It's cute, even. But not this time. This is off-limits."

"Rachel, please, I'm worried about you."

"I can take care of myself."

"I know that, but I just think—"

Rachel cut Elsa off before she could finish her statement. Elsa had never seen Rachel so angry.

"You want to know what I think, Elsa? I think you keep yourself busy meddling in other people's lives to avoid living your own."

"I'm just looking out for you."

"Who asked you to?" Rachel snapped.

"Rachel, please."

Before Elsa could say more, Rachel turned around and stalked out the door. Elsa followed, but couldn't speak freely with Michael present. She didn't want to set him off and have Rachel pay the price later.

As Rachel passed Dante, she said, "I had a lot of fun today, Dante. Call me if you need another break."

Is that what Dante's day out had been? Was Elsa driving away the people she cared about by trying to protect them?

"Rachel—" Dante began, but Rachel was well down the path to the front of the house. Michael followed.

Before he strolled out of sight, he turned and waved. "It was lovely to see you, Elsa. We'll pick this up again very soon."

Elsa's mind churned, but she couldn't think of anything she could do to help. She hadn't felt so helpless since she was a child, watching her parents' marriage self-destruct, their violence escalating. Were all relationships doomed?

There was nothing she could do about Rachel and Michael, but Elsa could do something about her relationship with Dante. She would make sure that they didn't fight. She would stop trying to control him. If she did, maybe they stood a chance.

Dante put his hands on Elsa's shoulders. "Are you all right?"

"Yes." She forced herself to smile, her heart constricting with every breath. "Everything is fine."

Chapter Twenty-Five

When they were alone at last, Dante and Elsa stood silently on the patio. She had said that she was fine, but he did not believe her. Something was very wrong. He could feel her trembling, could sense her fear.

"I am sorry I was not here for you."

She slid her arms around his waist and pressed herself against his chest. He had not quite expected this, though he welcomed her seeking comfort from him.

He wrapped his arms around her shoulders, then rested his cheek on the top of her head. "I should never have left you alone. It was selfish of me."

"No, it wasn't." He felt her tense, and she stumbled over her words as she continued. "I mean, you should be able to go out and have fun with your friends. You don't have to stay with me twenty-four hours a day."

"It would hardly be a chore," he said, chuckling.

He had expected a lighthearted retort, but instead, her arms tightened around him. He had never known her to be frightened like this, and his anger toward Michael grew.

Dante did not have time to ask her more of what had passed between the two, as Winston appeared in the doorway on the far side of the studio.

"Dinner's ready. In case anybody cares." At least Winston was his normal self.

When Elsa did not respond, Dante spoke in her stead. "We do, and we appreciate your efforts. We shall join you shortly."

Winston shrugged, then shuffled down the hall. Dante took Elsa's hand and led her inside. He made sure the doors were locked behind them.

In the brighter lights of the indoors, he could see a strange haunted quality to her wide eyes. He wondered what ghosts lingered in her mind and how he could possibly banish them.

"Did you eat?" Elsa asked.

"Some time ago. I waited to dine with you and Winston. I missed having my meals with you."

She gave him a subdued smile as they walked to the kitchen. She had always been so strong, but now she seemed to be made of glass. He was afraid if he said the wrong thing that she might shatter. It did not improve as they sat around the table for their supper.

"Did you have a good day out?" Winston asked.

Dante was grateful that someone was talking. Elsa was methodically eating her food, barely even making eye contact. Perhaps she was disturbed that he was wearing his new mask. He had not yet had a chance to remove it.

"Yes, it was both enlightening and productive."

"What did you do?" Winston asked.

Dante glanced at Elsa, who showed a bit of interest in the conversation for the first time. She opened her mouth as if to say something, but quickly closed it again. Then she folded her hands in her lap and stared at her plate.

"Errands, I would say." He wished that she would speak her mind, would confide in him about whatever had happened.

"You've got to be careful with that Rachel." Winston laughed. "She'll run you ragged. I can't tell you how many times Elsa came back from a day like that and just collapsed in bed, groaning about how much her feet hurt."

"I assure you, my feet are quite fine."

The rest of the meal passed in a mix of silence and subdued conversation between Dante and Winston. Elsa barely spoke, and then only when spoken to. Dante missed the confident woman who had brought him to this time. And yet, his heart went out to the vulnerable Elsa sitting next to him.

After dinner was done and the dishes put away, Dante and Elsa sat at the table sipping tea. Winston had retired for the evening and, aside from Leonardo sitting on the counter, watching them through slitted eyes and twitching his tail, they had the room to themselves.

The silence stretched on for as long as Dante could bear it. "Are you going to tell me?"

"Tell you what?" Her voice was so small he could

barely hear her.

"What is troubling you."

She shook her head. "There's nothing troubling me."

"That is twice this evening that you have told me something I do not believe to be true. Have we not always been forthright with each other?"

"Like the way you're being open with me about your day?" She gasped, her eyes widening as she sat up straighter. "I'm sorry. I didn't mean that."

"There is no need to apologize. And I certainly think you meant it."

Her shoulders hunched, her brow knitting together so fiercely that his own head began to ache in sympathy.

"I have reasons for keeping my agenda from you," Dante said. "Can you say the same of whatever is troubling you?"

"Yes."

"Then I shall trust that your reasons are sound." He reached across the table and took her hand in his. "And hope that you will share them with me when you are ready."

She smiled faintly, which he found encouraging. Not knowing what else to do, he carried their empty mugs to the sink, then returned to the table.

"Shall we retire?"

He offered Elsa his hand, but as she rose, she wrapped her arm around his waist instead. He would certainly not complain. He smiled at her, putting his own arm around her shoulders and relishing her warmth as she nestled against his body.

They went upstairs and paused before the door to Elsa's room. She turned to him and grasped his shirt. "Will you stay?"

"Will you tell me what that man did to you?"

"Nothing." She would not meet Dante's gaze. "He just scared me, that's all."

"I am sorry I was not here to protect you as I promised." Dante placed his fingers gently beneath her chin, tilting her face back toward him. "But I promise you, I shall not leave your side again."

"That's not practical." Again, her eyes widened as if she was panicked. "I mean—"

Before she could say more, he leaned down and pressed a tender kiss to her lips. He had meant for it to be no more than that, but her taste was too sweet. The scent of roses blossomed around him.

He slid his hands to her waist, pulling her against him. Elsa wrapped her arms around his neck, her kiss carrying all the passion he had missed. She held on to him as if he was the sole thing that kept her anchored in this world.

Her need left him breathless.

Dante lifted her up, carrying her into the room and closing the door behind them. As soon as he set her on her feet, she grabbed his neck and pulled him down to her.

At least here the odd timidity that shrouded her at dinner was gone. She devoured his lips, running her hands through his hair as she pressed herself against him.

He panted for breath when she finally released him. They paused only long enough for her to pull his shirt over his head. His lips found hers again, his hands sliding beneath her shirt as he explored the smooth skin of her sides.

Elsa pulled back once more, tearing off her own shirt and throwing it aside. The golden skin of her breasts bared before him, Dante bent his head to trail kisses over each in turn as he held their soft fullness in his hands.

Her chest rose and fell with quick breaths, her fingers buried in his hair. She started to lift his mask from his face, but then went suddenly still.

He smiled at her as he straightened. "Do you prefer me not to wear it?"

Elsa nodded haltingly. "I don't want anything between us."

The irony was not lost on him, for he knew there was something keeping her from him—an emotional wall he did not know how to surmount.

"Nor do I." Dante pulled off his mask and tossed it onto a stack of books near her bed.

There were still times when he could barely believe any of this was real, but perhaps the most miraculous thing of all was that she preferred him without his mask. She accepted him as he was, entirely. If only he could make her understand he felt the same about her.

He placed his hand over her heart, feeling the staccato of its beating against his fingertips, like the wings of a bird striving for the sky. He bent his lips to Elsa's once more, vowing that he would find a way to free her from her fears.

The next day greeted Dante with all the hope of a cloudless sky. Sunlight streamed in through the windows, clear and bright, but Elsa was not beside him.

"Elsa?" When she didn't answer, he sat up and glanced around the room. He was alone.

He quickly rose and pulled on his pants, then headed off to find her.

Winston was in the kitchen by himself, sitting with an untouched cup of tea, his brow knit with worry. As Dante entered, Winston sat a bit straighter.

"Is that you, Dante?"

"Yes."

Winston stood up, adjusted his shirt, and then took two steps to the center of the room. "You and me, we're going to have those words now."

"I beg your pardon?"

"What have you done to Elsa?"

Dante felt a flush spread across his face, memories of

the previous night playing through his mind. He thought that this time had different sensibilities about a man and woman sharing a bed, but perhaps he was wrong.

"I assure you, my intentions are honorable."

"I don't give a crap about intentions. I want to know what you've done to Elsa that's got her cowed."

He was not sure what to say. That Winston had also noticed the change in Elsa both reassured and distressed Dante. But he could not think of anything he might have done to bring about such a change.

When he did not respond, Winston said, "Don't play like you don't know. Last night at dinner, she hardly said two words. And this morning was the same. It's not like her." His voice rasped into a whisper at the end, as if it was breaking.

"Winston, I assure you, I am as disturbed by this change in her persona as you are. And I am equally mystified."

"You two didn't have a fight?"

"No. I believe she was upset by Rachel's boyfriend visiting unannounced again, but Elsa will not tell me what transpired."

"Then maybe he's the one we should be trouncing. Where does he live?"

"I do not know, nor am I certain that a trouncing is in order." Dante was not a violent man by nature, though circumstances were beginning to tempt him.

"It'd make me feel better to trounce someone." Winston had a dejected look about him.

Dante was just as lost. He sat, then leaned his elbows on the table and rested his head in his hands. "Winston, I do not know what to do."

"Neither do I. But I have an idea who might."

Dante found Elsa in the studio. She was bent over a tall table, so focused on her project that she did not notice his arrival.

It was good to see her working on something. Perhaps this was a sign that things had improved. He would certainly rather that than resort to using the advice Jazz had given him when he and Winston called her moments ago.

"Good morning," he said.

Elsa started at the sound of Dante's voice, bouncing inches off her stool before landing again, eyes wide as she stared at him. Apparently, things had not improved so very much.

"I did not mean to frighten you," Dante said.

"You didn't. I mean, it's fine."

He crossed over to her and set his hands upon her shoulders, then ran them down her arms. She did not pull away, for which he was grateful. At least he could reach her physically, if not emotionally. She had become even more affectionate since her strange fearfulness had manifested.

He glanced at the table, curious about her project. A chill swept over him as he saw the mask he had worn to the ball. She had pieced most of it back together. An open container of glue sat at her elbow.

"What is this?" Dante stepped closer to the table.

"It's your mask. Well, not your mask. It's the one Jazz sent you. I'm fixing it."

"But why? I thought you preferred me to not wear a mask."

"You still wear them sometimes. Now you'll have two options."

The remaining fragments lay on the table like a disjointed puzzle. She picked up one of the pieces and applied glue to the edge, then held it in place against the main body of the mask she had already repaired.

"Always you speak to me of options," he said. "And yet you do not listen when I tell you I have already made my choices."

He brushed her hair back over her shoulder, tucking it behind her ear. The only response he received was a tightening of her lips. She did not even turn to look at him.

"Why will you not talk to me?"

"What do you want me to say?" Her voice was flat when she spoke. Emotionless.

"I want you to say whatever is on your mind, as you

have always done."

After a brief pause, she said, "I'm thinking about fixing your mask. How I can make the cracks less apparent when it's done."

"Elsa, please. Talk to me!" He put his hands on her legs, spinning her around on her stool so that she faced him. Her eyes widened again, her breath quickening.

"I don't understand," she said. "I am talking to you."

"Words. These are only words. What is on your mind? What is in your heart?" He leaned forward and kissed her, leaving his forehead resting against hers when he pulled back, his hands on the sides of her neck.

Lightly brushing his thumbs across her cheeks, he said, "I can touch you. I can kiss you. And yet, I feel that you are miles from me. I am bereft of your presence, and it is killing me. Please."

"I don't know what you want." Her voice was tight and thin. "I'm sorry."

Dante closed his eyes, remembering his conversation with Jazz a few moments ago. Apparently, this had happened before between the two friends. When Elsa had been dispirited and distant in the past, Jazz would harangue Elsa using topics she was quite passionate about until she finally fought back. In that way, they had emotionally reengaged.

Jazz's advice was simply to *rattle Elsa's cage.*

It went against everything Dante felt was right, and yet,

Jazz was Elsa's oldest friend. He had no other insight with which to work.

"There is no need to apologize." He stepped away from Elsa, forcing his voice to be cold. "I believe I more fully understand the reality of our situation."

"What reality?"

"Your true desires are all too clear. You used your ability to bring the Phantom of the Opera to your time as your companion. Here I am."

He spread his arms wide in a theatrical gesture. That there might once have been some truth to his words pained him, and he let his displeasure show.

"That's not true," Elsa said, but then she snapped her mouth shut. At least she did not try to immediately withdraw her words or apologize.

"The irony is not lost upon me. All my life, I have been so concerned that people would look at me and only see my face. As if somehow the mask could not hide what lay beneath and I would be cursed to forever be reviled for my appearance. Yet with you, I fear that all you can see is the mask."

Her eyes were wide, her lips parted. He could practically see the words she longed to say fighting for their freedom. He pressed on.

"Tell me. When you look at me, do you see Dante, the man holding his heart out to you, or do you see this?" He gestured toward the mask in her hand. "A phantom?"

"You know I don't care about—"

"Don't you? Are you certain?"

He remembered his fear that she saw him as nothing more than research and his relief when he determined her password was his name. She had proven herself to him. He wanted to do the same for her, but she was not giving him a chance.

"If you care so little for the legend, why fix the mask? I have the modern one Garrett provided me. I can make others of new design and with better materials. Yet you fix this mask. Why is that?"

"This is what you're used to. I want you to be comfortable."

"Have you listened to anything I have said these past days? I want this world. I want this time. I do not care about familiarity. Relics from the past have no place with me, and yet you cling to them. You refuse to let go, of your fears, of your doubts, of this!"

He reached for the mask, but she jerked away. The piece she had been newly attaching came loose, and she lost her grip. He tried to catch the mask, but it bounced from his hand and fell, shattering against the floor.

Dante had not intended for the mask to break, though he could not say that he was sorry. Perhaps this time, she would let it go.

"Elsa, I—"

His voice caught in his throat when he saw the look in

her eyes. They were wide as a startled dove's, her mouth hanging open and her delicate brows drawn so sharply together they nearly touched. Her chest rose and fell like a bellows.

"Are you hurt?" He reached for her so he could carry her over the debris on the floor.

Elsa ducked beneath his arm, stumbling in her eagerness to get away. Away from him.

"It was an accident."

She let out a mirthless laugh, then spat out, "Right. It's always an accident."

"I don't understand."

He took another step toward her, but she shrank back from him. She was frightened of him. He was trying to push her, yes, but he had never intended to frighten her.

Dante felt his heart shatter, the shards falling through his body, leaving his soul in tatters. He wished he could go back, could take it back, but it was too late for that. He could see it in her eyes. He had somehow gone too far.

"I'm sorry." He kept his voice as gentle as he could while trying to puzzle out what had affected her so greatly.

He knew that he had been expressing his frustration openly, but no more so than he had done in the past. He did not understand the severity of her reaction. She seemed frozen, staring at him with those terrified eyes.

He just wanted to fix it. If only he could fix it.

"Elsa, please. Say something. Do something."

Without a word, she bolted from the room.

It took him a few moments to recover, but when he did, he followed her. He could not let her slip away. He had to make her understand how sorry he was for his mistake. And once he did, he and Jazz were going to have a very long talk.

Chapter Twenty-Six

The last few moments replayed in Elsa's mind over and over again. Dante knocking the mask from her hand—everything seeming to slow down as it fell—the horrible crash as it hit the floor.

The instant the mask had left her grasp, she felt a small part of herself break. It was too familiar.

Once the courting was done, the *real* masks came off. The invisible ones that everyone wore until they had what they wanted. She was a fool to have thought it would be any different with Dante.

And now she was back in her usual hiding place—huddled on the floor in her bathroom, knees pulled to her chest, chewing on a towel to muffle her sobs so that no one would hear her. So that no one would find her.

She had never seen that side of him before. Was this the man that he was? The man he so desperately wanted her to see? If so, she wanted nothing to do with him. Nothing.

He'd never acted like this before, though. He'd been kind and gentle. He'd never made her feel afraid. Not like today. How could she have been so wrong? Maybe this was just what love did to people.

When she heard his soft rap on the door, her heart started beating frantically. Thank God she had remembered to lock it.

"Elsa? Are you all right?" His voice was deceptively gentle. The doorknob jiggled, and she scooted closer to the bathtub, pressing herself against it and hugging the towel to her chest. "I am so sorry. Please, this is all a terrible misunderstanding."

How many times had she heard her parents say that to each other? How many times had they talked their way back into the other's good graces, only to fly off the handle again at some imperceptible slight?

"I did not mean to frighten you." His voice sounded strange, constricted. "Please, let me explain. Winston and I were worried about you. You have been so withdrawn. We didn't know what to do, so we called Jazz. She said we needed to push you until you pushed back. I should have just talked to you, but I have been trying so hard to do things on my own, to show you that I do not need you."

Elsa heard Dante groan, then he said, "That came out wrong. It is not that I do not need you. I do. But not in the way you think I do."

She slowly stood, staring at the door. She could hear soft thumping, as if he was tapping on it or knocking his head against it. Every tap sounded like a threat. They echoed in her mind, taking her back to the child she had been, reminding her that she was trapped. Again.

"I love you," Dante said. "I am afraid I love you somewhat desperately, and that has led me down this errant path. Please forgive me. Please tell me how to fix this. I will do anything…"

And then he tried the doorknob again.

Elsa covered her ears to stop the sound of its rattling, and shrieked, "Go away!"

There was a long pause. She slowly lowered her hands from her ears, wondering if he had done as she asked and left. Strangely, the thought didn't comfort her. In fact, it threw her into a near panic.

She didn't want him to go away. She wanted him to be with her, the way he had been before. Laughing with her, sitting in the sun, spending time together in the studio.

But hadn't she changed first? He was right about her being withdrawn. She had purposefully shut herself away from him, trying to avoid the very situation they were in now.

"I will not trouble you further." There was a rough quality to his voice and it broke over the words, as if he could barely manage to speak them.

If he moved away from the door afterwards, she didn't hear him. Moments ticked away, counting down with her heartbeat. If he actually left, she imagined her heart would just stop. If he left, she'd be alone. Truly alone. She'd never get over it, never move beyond where she was.

It wasn't just Dante that Elsa was keeping out. She

didn't let anyone in. Ever. And now, she had yet another excuse to keep everyone at arm's length, to keep them all at a distance. To keep herself safe. And alone.

If she had told Dante about her parents, he never would have listened to Jazz's advice. He would have understood what was bothering Elsa in the first place and helped her through it. She was certain of it.

But she hadn't even told Jazz, her oldest friend. Not even in college, when Elsa went to identify her mother's body after she wrapped her car around a tree during another drinking binge. Elsa told Jazz she was away on family business and refused to answer any questions until Jazz finally gave up.

Elsa kept everyone out. She thought she was leaving her past behind by never mentioning it, but she was stuck there, making herself repeat it. Hiding in a bathroom again.

The result was a crushing loneliness that made her gasp for breath, that made her so desperate for companionship that she had traveled over one hundred years into the past to find a kindred soul. And even still, she couldn't—no, wouldn't—let Dante in.

This wasn't fair to either of them. She wouldn't let things go on this way. Elsa had allowed her fear to keep her isolated for long enough. She wouldn't remain trapped in her past.

Dante was her future, her present moment. Everything

she wanted was right in front of her. All she had to do was have the courage to embrace it. And to do that, she had to let go of what she was holding on to.

She took a deep breath and opened the door.

Chapter Twenty-Seven

Panicked, Dante paced in his room, running his fingers through his hair and tugging on the strands as if he could pull ideas from his mind on how to fix the situation. No solutions came.

Elsa wanted him away from her. The very thought made his chest constrict painfully. He had terrified her, and he still did not understand how, what he had done that was so terribly wrong. How could he possibly fix a problem when he had no idea as to its cause?

He slumped down onto his bed, burying his face in his hands. If she wanted him to leave, he would, though it would devastate him.

He did not understand how she could have reacted so viscerally. The raw emotion on her face replayed in his mind, an image he did not think he would ever forget.

Elsa had been afraid of him. Terrified. It was his worst nightmare come true.

Despair was encroaching on his mind as he heard the door to his room swing open. Looking up, he was astonished to see Elsa standing in the doorway.

Dante did not dare move, afraid that she would flee

again. So he sat where he was, waiting, praying, for her to come to him.

She lingered in the doorway, as if she was uncertain what she wanted to do. Finally, she took a tentative step over the threshold, and then another. When she was in the room, she turned and closed the door behind her.

Resting her forehead against the wood of the door, she said, "I know you didn't mean to scare me."

Dante longed to agree, but kept himself silent. He could tell she remained at the edge of flight by the tense way that she stood, how her shoulders were bunched so that they nearly brushed her ears.

"When the mask left my grasp, why did you reach for it?" she asked.

Her question baffled him, yet he could sense the importance of his answer. "Whatever your reasons, you had worked diligently to repair it. I was trying to catch it before it fell. I am sorry I failed to do so."

Her body trembled as she let out a huge breath. "That isn't what I thought happened. I'm glad I was wrong."

Eventually, she turned to face him, though her haunted gaze passed through him as if he was a ghost. She slowly crossed the room and sat on the farthest corner from him on the bed.

She looked even more hopeless than he had felt just a few moments ago. Dante wanted to wrap his arms around her, to tell her that everything would be all right, but he fought the impulse.

"My father left when I was ten," Elsa said, her voice having that same dull, emotionless quality as earlier in the studio. "I never talked about it. Not even with my mother when it happened. I'm not sure why he left."

She stared blankly at the floor for some time. Dante held his breath, willing her to continue. She cleared her throat and obliged.

"I was glad, really. That he left." She glanced briefly at him, perhaps to gauge his reaction. He tried to temper his surprise.

Her gaze dropped back to the floor. "When he was around, he and my mom fought. Constantly. Violently. They didn't send each other to the hospital often, but it did happen a few times. Mostly when they threw things."

She wrapped her arms around herself and shivered at some unseen memory. "When I was five, I ran between them, trying to get them to stop. I don't remember what it was that hit me, but they had to go to the hospital then. They grounded me for a month." She let out a sharp burst of air, a hollow specter of a laugh. "They grounded me for not ducking fast enough."

Dante felt his heart grow cold toward these callous people. To treat a child in such a manner was reprehensible. That his Elsa had suffered it made his heart break.

"After my dad left, my mom became an alcoholic.

That's why I don't drink. I would go straight to the library or museum after school, stay there till they closed, and then go home and find something in the fridge and go to bed. On good days, she was passed out on the couch. On bad days, she was awake..."

Elsa's voice trailed off again. He waited patiently for her to go on.

"She would get sober every once in a while. Usually when she went back to church. It gave me just enough hope to think that maybe she would change, that she was finally ready to be a real mom." She turned to him and gave him a sad smile. "It's hard to give up on your parents. I think that's why I made my mistake."

Her gaze moved to the wall, as if she could see images, memories playing out across its surface. Dante waited as long as he could, but she seemed so forlorn, he could not bear to let her reverie continue.

As gently as he could, he said, "Your mistake?"

Elsa nodded, still staring at the wall, her eyes wide and unblinking. "I came home one day and she was on the couch, lying so still I thought she was dead. But her eyes were open and moving, as if she was watching something. It took me a while to figure out, but then I realized that she was traveling, like I do. I don't know what would trigger her. There was no art in the room, but I'm sure she was traveling."

"She shared your ability?" His astonishment overcame

his caution for a moment, but Elsa seemed not to take note of his outburst.

"I'm pretty sure. I was so excited. She'd been sober for a long time then. I waited for her to come back to herself, and then I told her about what I could do."

Elsa's gaze changed, her eyes glazing over as she seemed to shrink into herself, her arms tightening around her middle.

"How did she respond?" Dante asked.

"Riding the Devil," Elsa said. "That's what she kept saying while she beat me."

His chest swelled with air as he sucked in a breath. He wanted to yell, to rail against the injustice Elsa had suffered, but that would certainly frighten her. At least now he understood the origin of her fear.

His arms twitched with the urge to hold her, to protect her, even from the memory. But he was uncertain if even that would overwhelm her in the face of such raw emotions.

"How could she?" The words slipped out before he could catch them, barely more than a whisper. When Elsa glanced at him, he said, "How could she when she shared your power?"

"Not that she ever admitted." Elsa shrugged, the deadened expression returned, along with that even monotone. She was shutting down, removing herself from emotions too strong to experience. "From then on, when she was sober, I was some kind of demon. When she was drunk, I was just a freak."

Rage built within him. His own experiences fed into his sympathy for her. He knew what it was like to be reviled in such a way. But that her own mother had done so, and for a trait that they shared… He found himself hating the woman.

"That was the worst part," Elsa said. "I thought it would help her to know she wasn't alone. I guess she really hated herself. And when I told her I was like her, she hated me too."

"I am so sorry."

Elsa shrugged again and her hands dropped to her lap. "When I turned sixteen, I became legally emancipated. I changed my name, I applied for early enrollment in college and worked hard to get all the scholarships I needed to get far away."

"Have you not spoken to her since?"

Elsa cleared her throat. When she went on, her voice was raspy. "I got a call from the police during my second year of college telling me that she had died. She was driving under the influence and she hit a tree." Elsa's breath became ragged. "At least she didn't hurt anyone else."

But Elsa had been hurt. All the walls that Dante faced, that he worked to overcome, finally made sense.

If her parents had presented violence masquerading as

love, Elsa must have been terrified when Dante began to court her. And he had no idea how much courage she had demonstrated by sharing her secret with him. That her mother had *beaten* her when she did the same…

No wonder Elsa had found it so difficult to trust anyone. Such an early betrayal, and from the one person in the world who was supposed to love her unconditionally, as Dante's mother had loved him.

His heart bled for her.

Elsa had been dealing with so much—alone. He could scarcely believe she kept functioning.

A tear rolled down her cheek, and she quickly wiped it away. She was piecing herself back together from the shattered remnants of her childhood, just as she had pieced together Dante's mask—as she attempted to fix everything for those she cared about.

"I never looked back," she said. "At least, I didn't think so. Not until today. Today, I realized that I never really left." She turned to him, placing one hand on the bed between them. "Dante, I don't want to be there anymore."

He closed the distance between them at last, wrapping his arms around her and pulling her against his chest. "Then let it go. You need not remain in your past. All of this is done. You are here with me now."

She shuddered, then wrapped her arms around him, holding him tight. He kissed the top of her head.

"I don't know how to let go of this. It's clouded

everything in my life."

"You have told me that I am free to build a life of my choosing. You have that same freedom. Release yourself from these memories. Put them behind you and do not dwell on them."

"You make it sound easy."

"I know that it is not. But if we want something, we must work toward it. Do you think that you can try?"

She was quiet for a moment, then said, "Yes. But it's going to take time."

"Said the time traveler to the man from the 1800s." He was gratified when she laughed, however briefly.

"I've never told anyone any of that."

"I will keep your secrets, if you wish. But I hope that you will consider sharing at least some of this with your friends. They are all good people. Supportive and caring. You do not need to go through this alone, and more than I will help you."

Elsa looked up at him and smiled. "I think I can actually believe that."

He smiled back at her, brushing stray locks of hair from her forehead and tucking them behind her ear. They sat together in silence for some time, holding each other close. His relief that he had not lost her was so great that he felt almost giddy.

"Sharing that was kind of a big deal," Elsa said. "I'm not sure what to do next."

"Whatever you want. Let us do something to make the present moment fill your mind. We could return to the studio, go for a walk in the garden—"

She lifted her lips to his, melting against him as she pushed him back onto the bed. Dante was delighted by her choice.

There was no pause as her tongue slid into his mouth, her hungry strokes fueling his desire. He tried to roll her over onto the bed, but she straddled him, putting her hands on his shoulders and holding him in place.

She had never taken such initiative, and he was eager to see what she had in mind.

Her hands slid down his chest, over his stomach. She deftly unfastened his pants, then leaned forward to kiss him as she ran her hand along his length. He gasped as waves of pleasure crashed through his body from her touch.

He had thought that she had given herself to him physically before, but this... This was different. There were no reservations as her hands roved his body, and each exploration of her lips, her fingertips, inflamed him more than they ever had before.

Dante finally rolled on top of her, grinding his hips against the warmth of her center, aching to feel her body clench around him. Her groans urged him on.

He sat back on his knees and pulled his shirt over his head, then tossed it aside. Elsa followed him up, raining heated kisses over his chest. She pulled off her own shirt and threw it after his.

Her breasts bared before him, he took a moment to drink in their beauty with his eyes before bending his head to them and covering each with loving kisses. As his lips latched onto one of the dusky buds, she gasped, burying her fingers in his hair and clutching him to her. She breathed his name on a whisper, conjuring streaks of lightning that arced through his body.

Reclaiming her lips, he pressed her back against the pillows. He reached down to rid her of her pajama bottoms with her assistance. She gave him no chance to linger, grabbing his wrist and pushing on his arm as if she thought to roll him onto his back once more. He indulged her, smiling as she straddled him again.

It took every effort of his will, but this was the first time that she had taken the lead in their lovemaking and he was not about to discourage her. He closed his eyes and focused on the sensations flooding his body.

Her kisses moved down his cheek and jaw, along his neck and collarbones. The hunger was still there, apparent in every nip of her teeth on his chest, the strength of her grip on his arms. He opened his eyes as she moved to rid him of his pants. Then she rose to her knees and simply looked at him.

Dante had learned not to be abashed by her gaze. In fact, he was starting to love it, as he loved everything about her. This amazing woman, whose gaze traveled over all of him—even his face—not just without wincing, but with reverence. He had worshipped her body as a temple, and now it seemed she was doing the same for him.

She ran her fingers down his chest again, through the dark trail of hair that led toward his manhood. Without his pants in the way, she gripped him in her hand, languidly stroking him as he gasped from the intensity of her touch. All the while, she kept her chestnut eyes locked on his, watching his reaction, gauging what gave him the greatest pleasure.

She leaned forward to press a kiss against his navel, her mouth moving in a slow line farther down. He was not sure of her intentions until she looked up at him, her tongue running quickly over her kiss-swollen lips. His mouth went dry at the sight.

He managed to swallow and was about to say something, when Elsa dipped her mouth to his shaft, running her tongue over the tip. He nearly came right then. His breath left him in a rush, incredible sensations sparking through his body at this, most intimate kiss. She continued to wet his crown, then wrapped her lips around his shaft, taking him into her mouth.

He pressed his head back against the pillow, trying desperately not to release. He groaned from the effort, which only spurred her on. Her hand kept moving, even as she swirled her tongue around him and sucked him deep within her mouth. It was taking him too close to the edge.

Finally finding his voice, he said, "Elsa," in an urgent, hoarse whisper. He moved his fingers through her hair, tilting her face up so that he could look at her. And still, she did not stop. "Please."

She lifted her head from him, her sultry smile promising pleasures he could scarcely imagine.

"Are you asking me to stop or continue?"

Dante swallowed hard. "I fear that if you continue, I shall not last long."

She simply shrugged. "That's fine. We have all night. And tomorrow. And the next night."

She dipped her head to him once more, running her tongue along the entire length of his shaft. Another groan escaped him before he could stop it, but as much as he was intrigued by the idea of letting her continue her stimulating ministrations, he wanted even more to feel himself inside of her, buried deep. He wanted to know this ravishing Elsa completely.

He had experienced her body, but not her heart. Until now.

Elsa was giving him everything. At last, nothing stood between them.

He reached out for her, then pulled her against his chest and rolled her onto her back so he could lie on top of her. She smiled up at him, eyes crinkling at the corners. The sight of her so joyful took his breath away.

His heart was pounding, along with other parts of his anatomy. This was a true union. He could barely wait to begin, yet knew he was still too aroused to last long if he hurried. He wanted to savor every nuance.

He settled between her legs, letting his shaft rest just at her entrance, but not pressing further, no matter how much he wished to. He kissed her, but kept his kisses slow, his tongue languidly thrusting inside her mouth. He could feel her writhing, trying to pull him closer, deeper, but he kept himself only barely parting the warm flesh of her quim.

Finally, when she seemed to be growing more frustrated than tantalized, he thrust himself deep.

She cried out as he filled her, her fingers digging into his back. He took a deep, shuddering breath as he regained his control once more. She had brought him so close to the edge. It was his turn to do the same for her.

Slowly, he rocked his hips, feeling her clench around him as if her body was reluctant to let him go even a little. He relished the feeling as he moved within her, his lips trailing down her neck, where he suckled her skin till he left his mark on her.

He could feel her passion growing, mirroring his own. Pressure built within him, spurring him on to thrust faster, deeper, until she finally shouted his name, her legs wrapping around his as she pulled him as deep as she could within her.

His body answered hers as if a nova had gone off

within him, every atom thrumming as waves of heat rippled out from where they were joined. Spent, he collapsed on top of her, their breaths mingling as they panted from the intensity of their union.

On a gasping breath, she said, "Dante…"

He lifted himself on his elbows, smoothing her hair away from her face. He kissed her, then said, "Yes, Elsa?"

She smiled at him, but the mischievous edge was gone. She simply looked happy.

And then she said, "I love you."

Chapter Twenty-Eight

"Are you ever going to tell me what you and Jazz are up to?"

Elsa was lying with her head on Dante's chest. They had spent more time in bed than out of it over the last few days, and she was still in a bit of a stupor from their most recent activities.

"Whatever are you referring to?" His voice echoed in her ear like the low rumble of thunder.

"Yesterday's visit. I know she wasn't just here to visit Winston."

"No, she was also visiting you."

"And you."

Elsa knew they were planning something, but she actually didn't care too much what it was. She was curious, but she trusted them. She was still getting used to the feeling.

"There is something I wish to show you." Dante stroked her hair away from her shoulder, the strands tickling her back.

She raised an eyebrow. "You know, at some point, we really are going to need to sleep."

"That is not what I meant. Although, now that you mention it…"

He rolled her onto her back, kissing her slowly, as if savoring every touch. He paused, then lifted himself on his elbows. "I thought we might go into town later."

A spike of nervousness shot through her at the thought, but she knew they couldn't hide in their home forever. She wasn't sure when she had started thinking of her home as *theirs*, but realizing it made her happy. It was their home, for as long as he wanted to live there.

She pushed away the doubts that still chewed at the corners of her mind. All she had was this moment, and she was going to enjoy it. "Okay."

"I do suppose our trip could wait a little while longer." Dante nuzzled the side of her neck.

"Only a little?"

Elsa hadn't been able to distract Dante for too long. The afternoon sun beat down on them as she drove her convertible toward town. He seemed to be enjoying the trip. He wasn't even bothering to wear the mask Garrett had given him.

The sight of Dante smiling, his eyes closed and his face tilted up toward the sun, was one of the most beautiful things she had ever seen. His linen shirt was open to the wind, his long legs stretched out before him.

He looked so relaxed. It was all she could do to keep her concentration on the road, but she managed, focusing more intently when they crossed into the city limits.

She had a feeling they were headed for the gallery, and he didn't correct her as she drove in that direction. Elsa found a parking spot as close as she could manage. By the time she stepped onto the street, Dante was there, offering his arm.

He didn't lead her toward the gallery. Instead, they walked across the street, then down a few blocks. She wanted to ask him where they were going, but took a deep breath and used the opportunity to practice giving up control. Hopefully, someday it would be easier.

They headed up the walkway to an apartment building that gleamed brightly in the afternoon sun. White walls, glass and chrome gave it a modern look.

Dante smiled broadly as he opened the door for her and followed her into the lobby. She had never seen him so excited.

"Good afternoon, Mr. Lucerne." A dark-haired man in a suit approached them from across the large open space. He blinked when he saw Dante's face, his smile seeming to stumble for a moment, but it passed quickly. When he reached them, he shook Dante's hand. "Ms. Montgomery has been very busy. I hope you're pleased with the results."

"I'm certain we will be delighted," Dante said. If he

had noticed the man's reaction, he wasn't calling attention to it. Gesturing to Elsa, Dante said, "This is Miss Sinclair."

"Ah, yes. Miss Sinclair." The man bowed slightly, then shook her hand. He pulled a key out of his pocket and gave it to her. "Ms. Montgomery let me know to expect you."

She stared at the key, her curiosity reaching a breaking point. Dante covered her hand with his, curling her fingers over the key. He slid his arm around her waist and guided her toward the stairs.

"Thank you, Charles," Dante said.

When they had climbed to the third floor, passing a gorgeous waterfall built into the wall, Elsa said, "Charles?"

"I was able to accomplish a great deal on the day I ran errands with Rachel," Dante said. He led Elsa down a corridor deeper into the building. "As you will soon see."

Her stomach was doing flip-flops. She hadn't decided yet if they were the good kind or the bad. But Dante was still smiling, his expression a mix of pride and happiness. She forced herself to smile back at him.

She kept telling herself everything was going to be fine. Whatever this mysterious surprise was, it was going to be good.

"Are you all right?" he asked.

"Yes. I'm just a little nervous, I guess." That was another thing she was getting used to. Actually telling someone how she felt instead of pushing her emotions aside.

"Please trust me a little longer. I promise, I won't disappoint you."

"You could never disappoint me."

Dante traced his fingertips over her cheek and along her neck. He bent down to kiss her briefly, then smiled as he stepped behind her. She was left staring at the door to an apartment marked 3B.

"Open it," he said.

Her heart was racing as she unlocked the door and opened it. Dante gestured for her to go inside.

"After you."

Elsa stepped into a loft with floors of honey-gold hardwood and bright white walls. All the fixtures were chrome, and the wall facing her was made of windows that climbed two stories. There were no curtains, light streaming in and reflecting off every surface, almost blinding her.

An island counter separated the kitchen area from the rest of the great room she stood within, and a spiral staircase led to a second level that covered half the loft.

"I shall return presently," Dante said. "If you will give me but a few moments."

"Okay…"

He walked up the staircase, leaving Elsa alone. She crossed to the windows, impressed by the spectacular view. Restless, she turned back to the great room and noticed an easel in one corner. There were shelves built into the wall behind it filled with paints, brushes and blank canvases.

A few abstract paintings hung on the walls. Aside from the art, splashes of color were added by a few bright cushions on the white couch. Some dyed glass vases filled with exotic flowers softened what otherwise might have seemed too starkly modern. There were more cushions in hanging mesh chairs suspended from the raised level above.

"Hammock chairs," she murmured.

"Thank you for waiting."

Elsa glanced back to the stairs. As Dante trotted down the spiraling metal, her breath caught in her chest.

Dark brown loafers had replaced his polished shoes, and he wore formfitting jeans that showed off his strong, long legs. His backside looked so good, she couldn't imagine anyone not drooling over the sight. The linen shirt she was so used to was replaced by a comfortable-looking T-shirt, tucked in at the waist and accenting his perfect V-figure.

His hair was still mussed from their ride in the convertible, and he had spent so much time in the sun that it had lightened to a tawny brown. It hung around his face in flowing waves. Elsa wanted nothing more than to bury her fingers in it.

She stammered a bit, then said, "This is yours, isn't it?" She looked around the loft again, tearing her gaze away from him for the briefest of moments.

He smiled as he approached, then leaned down and kissed her, leisurely exploring her, as if they had all the time in the world. Ending the kiss at last, he said, "I prefer to think of it as ours." He paused, some of the enthusiasm leaving his voice. "Do you like it?"

"Dante, this…"

It was completely antithetical to the room that she had made for him in her manor. She had strived to recreate the home that she thought would comfort him, but she'd just been perpetuating a life he'd already decided to leave behind.

"If you do not like it, we can make changes," he said. "I truly want this to be your home as well. I want you to feel welcome here—comfortable, as you made me feel when you opened your home to me."

"I don't understand how you did this."

A sudden thought struck her, as she remembered Jazz and Dante's quiet conversations that ended abruptly when Elsa approached. She glanced at his fingers, searching for what she already knew wouldn't be there.

"Where is your mother's ring?"

He took her hands in his and kissed each of them. "That ring has bound many lives together. My parents, and Mary and Edgar. Now, for us, in its way. Do not be distressed that it has been freed to continue its journey."

Elsa's heart tightened, but she nodded. She had already visited every moment she could connect to through the ring. They were both letting go of the past. This was Dante's choice to make. Still, she would miss having it close.

He drew her into an embrace, kissing the top of her head. "You never answered my question. Do you like it?"

"I love it." She laughed, wiping the back of her hand across her tear-filled eyes. "I knew it was your place as soon as I saw the hammocks."

"They add a certain modern sensibility, don't you think?" He said it deadpan, but then grinned.

She laughed again, and let him lead her farther into the loft. A few feet from his painting area, there was a writing desk with a cushioned chair. The wood was deep chestnut brown and the upholstery a rich gold. The design of the set was a perfect mix of classic and contemporary style.

"I thought perhaps this could be your writing desk," Dante said.

Elsa felt tears on her cheeks. For once, she didn't care. He had built a new life for himself, but had made sure there was a place for her in it, right at his side.

"Do you not like it?" he asked

"I love it." She threw her arms around his neck and pulled him down for a deep kiss.

When she finally released him, he laughed. "Well, I

believe you have made your sentiment quite clear."

"Maybe we should go upstairs so I can show you what I really think of the place."

"As appealing as that sounds, there is one more stop on our trip, and I am afraid if I take you upstairs now, we will not leave this place for quite some time."

"True." She grabbed his arm and pulled him toward the door. "Let's go."

"You seem to be in quite a hurry."

She stopped, leaning in and running her hands up his chest, finally burying her fingers in his hair as she pulled him closer and kissed him again. She nibbled her way to his ear, tantalizing the sensitive skin until his hands were clutching the back of her shirt.

"The sooner we go," she whispered in his ear, "the sooner we can come back."

Dante groaned, dropping his forehead to her shoulder. "I am so tempted to stay."

She stepped away from him, then grinned as she took his arm once more. Leading him toward the door, she asked, "Where is this mysterious second stop?"

"The gallery, of course."

"Of course."

They laughed the entire way back to the gallery, though she couldn't remember exactly why. She was just so happy. She had never been so happy in her entire life.

Dante grew quieter when they entered the gallery, but

he was still smiling as he led her into one of the back rooms. It was roped off, not ready for public viewing yet.

"If Jazz catches us back here, she's going to be really mad," Elsa said.

"Ah, but new exhibits are only off-limits to the public. They aren't off-limits to the artist." He stood in the center of the room, that same gentle smile on his face.

The artist? Her heart soared as she slowly spun around, taking in all of the paintings hanging on the walls. Dante's landscapes. She was surrounded by his vision of the world.

Elsa had always thought his paintings were inspired, but seeing so many of them at once, seeing them all on display, they were breathtaking.

"Dante, this is—"

"Wait, this is not all of them."

He put his hands on her arms, turning her around and guiding her toward the wall opposite the door. A large canvas covered with a sheet filled her view.

"I waited to let anyone see it until I had your approval," he said. "I wanted to be certain that you are comfortable with it first."

"Comfortable with what?" She looked at the nameplate as he worked the sheet loose. *Portrait of my love.*

Dante whisked the sheet away, revealing a portrait of Elsa sitting at her writing desk and staring off into the distance. There was a softness around her eyes in the painting that made her look vulnerable, a hopefulness in her parted lips, and a glow about her that made her heart catch in her throat.

"Do you like it?" he asked, stepping behind her and sliding his arms around her waist.

His secret painting. It was a portrait of Elsa.

"Is this how you see me?" She could barely speak, her throat was so tight with emotion.

He pressed a kiss to the top of her head and pulled her closer against his chest. "Yes. It is how I have always seen you. But you haven't answered my question."

"I love it."

Dante let out a breath, hugging her more tightly. "I am so glad. But are you comfortable with me displaying it? I rather think it completes the exhibit."

"I'm honored."

She was more than honored. She could feel herself surrounded by Dante's love, and for once, when she felt her soul stirring from the incredibly moving pieces of art around her, she was absolutely content to stay just where she was. She didn't want to disappear. There was nowhere else she would rather be in the world—in the universe, in all of time—than right here in his arms.

He had managed to make a life for himself without her help, a life he wanted to share with her. He'd known her fears about him being dependent on her, and he had proven them baseless. She turned around, staring up at him.

"How did you do all of this?"

"I did not do it alone. Your friends have been incredibly supportive. Rachel took care of decorating our loft, and Jazz has been..." He shook his head, and said, "Amazing."

"I still don't understand—"

Dante leaned down and kissed Elsa before she could say anything else. He kissed her deeply, passionately, until her head spun from lack of oxygen. Or maybe it was just his arms around her, his closeness, the love and trust that was still so new to her.

"You're doing that on purpose, aren't you?" she asked when he let her come up for air.

"Only when necessary."

He kissed her again, this time, presumably without ulterior motive. She let her fingers burrow through his hair, clutching him against her as if she would never let him go. But she would have to for just a little while, until they could get back to their loft.

They walked out of Dante's exhibit room, arms around each other's waists. Nothing stood in their way now. They could have the life together that she had always dreamed of. An even better one, because it was one they were going to create together.

They had almost exited the gallery when a loud crash, followed by swearing, caught their attention. From the stream of Mandarin that followed, Elsa knew Jazz was in her very rare freak-out mode.

Dante took Elsa's hands and led her toward their friend.

"We should find out if she needs assistance," he said. Elsa nodded.

They found Jazz kneeling in the middle of another roped-off room. A display stand was on its side on the floor, brochures surrounding it. Jazz was on her knees, gathering them together.

"Let us help you," Elsa said.

She knelt next to Jazz and started gathering brochures. Dante righted the stand, then set it down slightly off to the side so it wasn't in their way.

Jazz said something else in Mandarin that had to be a curse-word. "Thanks. I'm running so far behind, and Rachel hasn't shown up yet. The new exhibits open tonight, and—" Jazz looked up, as if seeing Dante and Elsa for the first time. "Oh, Dante. I'm glad you're here. Is your exhibit ready? I want to open it tonight along with this one. Can you be here?"

"The exhibit is ready to show, however, I believe Elsa may have other plans for me this evening." He gave Elsa a mischievous grin, running his hand down her back as he knelt beside her to help pick up brochures.

"Let me have him for one night." Jazz turned to Elsa, waving brochures. "Honestly, I'm trying to start his career here."

"I'm sure we can work something out," Elsa said. "But you really need to calm down."

"Calm down? Rachel decides to miss work for the first

time ever on the opening night of not one, but two brand-new exhibits. And you want me to calm down?"

"She didn't call?"

"No. And she's not answering her phone, either."

Elsa felt a heavy weight in the pit of her stomach. "That's not like her."

"Who knows what she's like anymore. Ever since she started dating this guy." Jazz gestured around the room. Only then did Elsa notice the art hanging on the walls.

A dozen portraits of women surrounded her. There was a brutality in the brush strokes, dark paints and shadows dominating each scene. All of the subjects were hiding their faces, cowering from view.

She stood up slowly, the fine hairs on her body standing on end. The brochures dropped to the floor from her suddenly numb fingers as she turned in a circle.

As expansive and filled with light and hope as Dante's paintings were, these were the exact opposite. Elsa felt the weight of them crushing her. She collapsed into a ball, trying to make herself smaller, to get away from the feeling, but it was everywhere.

Snakes crawling on her skin. Ants in her veins. Sheer, naked terror.

There was no hope in this room. Only despair.

And then she traveled.

It wasn't like any of the times she'd traveled before. She felt herself leave her body, but she moved straight up into the air and could look down and see the city beneath her. It was like she was flying, but she couldn't control where she was going.

She felt herself being pulled away from the city, to an area sparsely housed and overgrown with palms and patches of Evergreen. She plummeted toward the earth so quickly that she screamed, though she knew no one could hear her.

When she landed, it took her a moment to realize that she had stopped. There was no light. She was so disoriented, it seemed she could feel the world spinning.

She heard a faint rattling noise. Chains. And then she heard a whimper. Someone was in the room with her.

A door opened and a light came on, casting the room in a harsh fluorescent glare. Elsa was in a garage completely filled with workbenches and shelves. Mason jars containing nails, broken glass and other bits and pieces sat in meticulous lines on every shelf.

The center of the floor held an easel, with a huge canvas visible above the tops of the workbenches. Two vaguely feminine forms had been outlined in what she thought at first was heavy graphite, but there was a weird reddish cast to it. One of the figures was just starting to be filled in with dark paints.

Michael stepped into the room, his hair tied back and a crimson smear on the front of his white shirt. His lips were pulled in a tight smile. He was wiping something bright and red from his hands with a towel.

"That was really stupid, you know." He rubbed the towel over his shirt. "Now I need to take more."

Elsa followed at a distance as he navigated the labyrinthine room. Chains were bolted to the far wall, ending in manacles around a woman's wrists. She had her arms over her head and her blonde hair was matted and tangled. Her wrists were covered in rough cuts, blood coating the metal. She looked up at Michael, and Elsa felt as if lightning had struck her.

Oh God, she thought. *Rachel.*

"It's a big night for me, Rachel," Michael said. "You're so selfish. This is my night. Mine!"

Rachel flinched as he yelled, hunching closer to the wall. Michael went to a cupboard and took out a mason jar and a length of plastic tubing attached to a needle. He carried them over to Rachel, then set them on the workbench nearest her.

As he bent toward Rachel, Elsa tried to get between them, to shove him away. Her hands passed through him.

"It's okay," he said, smoothing Rachel's hair. "You all think you're so much better than me, but I know the truth. I'm the one that's going to make you immortal. What does that make me, Rachel? Think about what that makes me."

Rachel let out a whimper as Michael stood. "I have to get ready for my opening. I'll be leaving for the gallery soon. Just remember next time you want to throw a fit that

I can always take more. And I will take more. Till there's nothing left."

Michael walked away, and Rachel collapsed against the wall, sobbing.

Before Elsa could do anything else, she felt as if a tether connected to her middle had suddenly been pulled taut. She found herself hurtling back over town toward the gallery. With a jarring jolt, she snapped back into her body, arms lashing out at whoever was holding her.

"Elsa! Are you all right?"

Glancing around, Elsa saw that she was in a different room in the gallery. Dante was on the floor next to her, holding her against his chest. Jazz hovered just behind him, one hand holding her phone and the other clasped over her mouth. Dante looked stricken, a deep furrow between his brow and his eyes wide with fear.

"Dante?" Elsa said.

"Thank God. I thought I'd lost you." His arms tightened around her.

"No." Elsa pushed him away, trying to get to her feet.

She didn't have time to be comforted by Dante. Rachel was out there—scared, alone, hurt. Michael said he was going to the gallery, so she might be safe for a while, but what if he went back?

Elsa had to get to Rachel. To save her.

"What the hell, Elsa?" Jazz slid her phone back into its holder at her waist. "Was that some kind of seizure?"

As Dante helped Elsa to her feet, she realized she couldn't save Rachel alone. And no secret was worth Rachel's life.

"You need to call the police and paramedics, right now."

Jazz pulled her phone back out, then paused. "Police?"

Elsa nodded. "Send them to Michael's house."

"What are you talking about?"

"Michael has kidnapped Rachel. He's hurting her." Elsa shook her head, the horror of what she had seen returning. "I think he's going to kill her."

"What are you talking about?" Jazz said. "Michael's a little off, but—"

"Jazz, I'm telling you, I know this. I just saw him."

"You saw him? How?"

Elsa reached down and found Dante's hand, gripping it tightly, as if it was a lifeline. It was time to trust Jazz, to tell her.

"I can't explain everything now, but that wasn't a seizure. It was more like a vision."

Jazz snorted. "What, you're psychic now?"

"No. I mean, yes." Elsa shook her head. "I honestly don't know what I am. I've always been too afraid to research it."

"Research what?"

"I can use art to leave my body and travel to other places and times."

"This is really lame," Jazz said. "You know I'm a believer."

"Then believe me. Michael has Rachel. If you don't want to call the police, fine. But at least tell me where Michael lives so I can go and help her."

Jazz was still scowling. She crossed her arms and glared at Elsa.

She had no idea what to say. She'd spent so much time trying to hide what she could do, she never thought about people not believing her. Elsa had to convince Jazz to help.

"Please, Jazz. He's hurting her."

Chapter Twenty-Nine

Dante's stomach clenched as he thought through the implications of what Elsa had told them. He had sensed that Rachel needed help, but had no idea how far things had gone.

"I know this must be a shock for you, Jazz, but you must believe Elsa."

Whatever Elsa had seen, it terrified her. He and Jazz had watched as Elsa's expression changed from fear to horror, as her body started to convulse, her limbs flailing wildly.

The only thing he could think to do was to get Elsa away from the art in Michael's room. Dante was terrified himself—that it was not the proper course of action, that he might lose her forever.

"You're in on this too?" Jazz said. "I bet this is Rachel's idea. I don't have time for jokes, and this one sure as hell isn't funny."

"Rachel's the one who doesn't have time!" Elsa said. "I can't believe all these years I was so afraid to tell you about what I can do, and you don't even believe me."

"Maybe because it's you. You're the most grounded

person I've ever met. We've known each other for a decade. There's no way that you could be into this stuff without me knowing."

"I've been hiding it," Elsa said. "I use art to travel through time to research my books. That's why I had you find all those pieces for me over the years. That's why I always insisted on a private viewing alone in a locked room the first time I saw them. I didn't want anyone else to know."

Jazz remained unmoved. "This is bullshit."

"I'll prove it to you. When I went into that room and saw Michael's paintings, I traveled to his house. Normally, I go to different times, but I traveled over the city instead."

Elsa closed her eyes, her brow furrowed in concentration. Dante wrapped his arms around her to anchor her where she was. He didn't want her to leave again. Not to go to such a horrible place.

"He lives several miles south of town," Elsa said. "Away from the suburbs, in a forested area near swampland."

"You could've looked that up." Some of the harshness left Jazz's features, pensiveness taking its place.

"But I didn't. Rachel is in danger. I'm begging you to help me."

"So all this time, you've been using astral projection for your research?"

"Astral what?"

"Astral projection. The ability of the soul to travel outside the body, unbound by the limits of space or time."

"That is quite an accurate description." Dante wished he could ask Jazz more questions. She seemed to know more about Elsa's ability than anyone.

"Let me guess," Jazz said. "You're a time traveler too."

He could hardly refute it, but now was not the time to open himself up to a line of inquiry regarding his origins. He simply said, "I am Dante Lucerne."

"Yeah, I know." Her forehead creased and her mouth fell open as she stared at him. Her arms dropped to her sides. "Wait a minute—"

"We don't have a minute!" Elsa said. "I swear to you, I will answer all your questions after we've saved Rachel."

Jazz nodded. "Have your phone handy. I'll send you his address, then call the cops. When this is done, we're going to have a long talk."

Elsa grabbed Jazz and hugged her briefly, then practically ran for the door. Dante muttered a hasty, "Thank you," and followed.

The car's engine was already humming when he jumped into the passenger's seat. Elsa accelerated away from the curb so quickly her tires screeched in protest.

"We must be alive in order to help Rachel," he said.

Elsa nodded and slowed down a bit, but did not turn to look at him. Her gaze was intent upon the road, her focus palpable. He wondered if she had been this intense when trying to save him.

One thing he knew for certain. She would do whatever it took to save Rachel. And so would he.

Moments later, he was relaying Michael's address to Elsa from the text message Jazz sent to Elsa's phone.

When they reached Michael's home, Elsa didn't bother trying to be furtive. She drove right down the driveway and stopped close to the house. Dante looked around them, but did not see any other cars. Perhaps they were fortunate and Michael had indeed gone to the gallery as Elsa thought.

The gravel of the drive crunched beneath her feet as she leapt from the car. She ran to the trunk and opened it. Dante wasn't certain what she had in mind until she pulled out a large metal cross. From his research on cars, he knew that it was one of the tools used to change tires. This one had a flattened end that could be used as a crowbar.

He followed her to the house. "Should we not wait for the police?"

"I don't know if we have enough time for that."

She tested the door, but it was locked. With barely a pause, she smashed the glass window that ran alongside it with the tool, then knocked out all the loose shards. She reached in to unlock the door and let them in.

They passed through a small foyer. She led him toward the right side of the house, where the garage was situated. A door with a heavy padlock blocked their way. She struck at the lock with her tool to no avail.

"Allow me." He took the tool and placed the flat end between the door and the metal that held the lock in place. Prying the mounting loose took much less force than trying to break the lock itself.

Elsa pushed open the door when he was done, then turned on a light as she stepped into the garage. She did not even have to look at the switch to find it.

The room was completely filled with neat rows of shelves and workbenches. There were narrow aisles between them, but it was impossible to see the entire area at once. The shelves were metal and filled with jars. Some held screws and nails, some pencils or bits of broken glass. Some held liquid with things floating in them that Dante refused to examine too closely.

One of the jars contained fragments of porcelain. Dante halted for a moment, drawn to the familiar material, the shape of the larger pieces... A chill swept over him as he realized it had once been his original mask.

Michael had been the one who broke into their home. The very idea made Dante's skin crawl. They must leave as quickly as possible.

Elsa ignored the shelves and ran along the rows of workbenches toward the far wall. She disappeared from view as she dropped to the floor. Dante heard her say, "Rachel? Rachel, it's Elsa."

He ran to assist them, but froze in horror when the

women came into view. Rachel was chained to the wall, her arms outstretched like a butterfly pinned in a collector's case. She was deathly pale, dark circles standing out under her eyes like welts. The hopelessness and despair on her face was worse than any he had ever seen.

"Elsa?" Rachel's voice was thin and gritty. She was still blinking repeatedly, her eyes adjusting to the bright light overhead. "Oh no. Did he get you too?"

"No, sweetie. We're here to rescue you."

"Oh thank God," Rachel sobbed, leaning against Elsa. "How are you going to get me loose?"

The chains rattled as she moved, even with the little amount of slack in them. Her bloodied manacles were pulled tight against the wall, threaded through the first of several grommets that trailed up to the ceiling. Dante followed the lengths of chain to where more grommets suspended the taut metal above them before the chains trailed back down to a winch firmly anchored on the floor.

He stepped forward, determined to free Rachel. "Do not be afraid. I will have you free presently."

Rachel turned her haunted eyes toward him. "Dante?"

"Did you not recognize me with my new look?" He was trying to distract her, to give her some respite from her terrifying circumstance. He kept his tone light, belying the turmoil within him at what had been done to her.

The skin of her wrists would be scarred. Every time she

saw those scars, she would remember this event. The horror of it. After escaping her bonds, she would still have to free herself from the cage of fear Michael had created for her.

But Rachel was surrounded by friends. She would not be alone in this.

Dante managed to work the winch, slowly letting out all of the slack in Rachel's chains. Once that was done, he began to use the tool to try to pry the anchor of the chains free from the floor. It was much safer than trying to break the manacles.

Rachel let out a low moan. "That will take forever. Dante, you have to get Elsa out of here."

Elsa smoothed Rachel's hair away from her face, making shushing noises and holding her close. "It's okay, Rachel. I'm not leaving without you."

"You don't understand. He wants you too."

"Well, he can't have me," Elsa said. "And he can't have you, either."

Rachel clung to Elsa, sobbing against her as Dante kept trying to get the chains free. Rachel would be able to move about now, but she was still trapped in the garage. If only they could find the key to her manacles.

"Dante..." Elsa said.

"I know," he said. "I am hurrying."

A chill swept over Dante's neck, and he turned back toward the door. He saw a flicker of movement through the shelves.

"Elsa, run!"

He turned back to her, but his words were drowned out by a loud pop. The sound of shattering glass accompanied it, along with a searing pain that ripped across the side of his face.

His vision clouded with red. Dante fell to his knees. He lifted his hand to his cheek, but his fingers flinched away faster than he could command them to—pricked by sharp objects embedded in his flesh. Elsa screamed, possibly his name, but it was hard to hear over the rushing sound of blood in his ears.

She appeared at his side, but he waved her away, back between the workbenches. She had to stay out of the aisle he was kneeling in, out of Michael's sight.

She looked stricken, but nodded. She grabbed the tool from where it had landed nearby, then disappeared around the side of the workbench.

That was not what he had intended. He wanted to keep her safe. Instead, knowing her, she was planning to sneak up on Michael to attack him.

The best that Dante could do was provide a distraction. He managed to rise to his feet, using the workbench to steady himself, though the movement sent threads of agony worming through his brain.

The pain clouded his thoughts. Blood was flowing freely down his neck, coating his chest beneath his T-shirt and making it stick to his skin. His only thought was that he had to help Elsa, to protect her and Rachel.

"Whatever it takes," he whispered.

Chapter Thirty

"This is more than I hoped for." Michael emerged in the space between the shelves. He kept his gun pointed at Dante. "I get Elsa hand-delivered, and the freak thrown in for free." He laughed, then said, "I think I've made an improvement on your face."

Elsa had never hated anyone more in her life. She ducked back out of sight, praying that Rachel was staying hidden now that she could at least move within a few rows of the workbenches.

Elsa clutched the tire iron in her hand tightly as she crept up behind Michael. His attention was on Dante. If she could sneak up behind Michael, she could clock him. It was the best plan she could come up with.

"I can't believe that Jazz wanted me to share the opening with you," Michael said. "I'm a true artist. Not like you, with your boring little landscapes. How much are you willing to sacrifice for your art?"

"Art is about creation, not sacrifice," Dante said.

"There is no creation without sacrifice. I'm willing to give up what I love most. Over and over again. I imbue the canvas with their essence. It's how I immortalize them."

Elsa could see the backs of Michael's legs. He had stepped closer to Dante, giving her more room to work. She slowly stood, brandishing her weapon, though her hands shook.

"And how many women have you immortalized?" Dante asked.

"How many paintings have I done?"

She thought of all those canvases in Michael's exhibit, each one representing a lost life. All of her hesitation vanished.

She brought the tire iron down on the back of Michael's head as hard as she could, hearing a sickening crunch. He crumpled to the ground, and his gun skittered underneath the workbenches, toward the far wall.

Dante's knees gave out just then. Elsa tried to run to him, but Michael's hand snaked out, grabbing her ankle.

She fell to the floor hard, hitting her chin with enough force that she saw stars. Dante was dragging himself toward her, but Michael pulled her back, out of Dante's reach. Michael's hands locked around her throat, cutting off her air.

"You think you can make a fool out of me?" he shouted. "You're mine! You belong on my canvas. All of you!"

She struck at Michael's arms, but his grip never loosened. When she clawed at his face, he put even more of his weight on her throat. He straightened his arms to get away from her nails.

The lights seemed to be dimming when another loud pop echoed through the garage.

Michael's grip went slack. He looked down at the rich crimson circle spreading out from the center of his chest, then past her, before falling forward like a puppet whose strings had been cut. His eyes remained open and staring.

Elsa hacked and retched, rolling onto her side as she gasped for air. When she recovered enough to look back toward Dante, she saw Rachel standing behind him, holding Michael's gun. Rachel was still pointing it at Michael's body, as if she expected him to move again.

Elsa wasn't sure he wouldn't. Though his eyes stared sightlessly at her, she wondered if at any moment he might lunge at her again.

Apparently, Rachel wasn't willing to risk it. As Elsa scooted away from Michael, Rachel walked toward him, her chains clattering with each step. She fired round after round into his body and kept pulling the trigger even when the gun merely clicked.

Michael wouldn't be getting up again.

Elsa struggled to her feet and cautiously made her way to Rachel. When Elsa was close enough, she put her arms around Rachel and reached down to take the gun. Rachel's gaze remained fixed on Michael's body.

Desperate to check on Dante, Elsa led Rachel to where he had fallen. Elsa set the gun on the workbench closest to him, then knelt at his side.

There was so much blood. She didn't even know how she could apply pressure to stop the bleeding.

Bits of glass and other shrapnel stuck out from his right cheek and temple. She couldn't keep herself from crying as she looked at him, carefully smoothing back his hair.

"You've never cried when you looked at my face before." He actually chuckled.

Elsa lowered her forehead to his for a moment, then pressed a kiss against his left temple where the skin was still intact. "I'm so sorry this happened to you," she whispered.

"Is Rachel safe?"

"She's okay. She'll be okay. We all will," Elsa said, though there was a part of her that was wondering, doubting. She pushed that part away.

Dante would be fine. He had to be.

Footsteps sounded behind them. She glanced over her shoulder, relieved beyond belief to see Jazz and Garrett standing in the doorway. Elsa heard the sound of sirens approaching.

"Oh my God, Elsa," Jazz said. "Are you okay?"

"No." Elsa's voice broke on a sob. "Dante's hurt."

Jazz went to Rachel and Garrett ran to Elsa's side, his eyes briefly darkening as he took in the bruises that must already be forming on Elsa's throat. She shook her head, then looked at Dante. Garrett's focus needed to be there.

Garrett's expression was grim as he examined Dante, asking questions. At least Dante was able to answer them all. That must be a good sign.

The police and paramedics arrived at the same time. Jazz quickly took charge of answering the officers' questions while the paramedics worked with Garrett on Dante.

After Rachel was freed from her manacles, she and Dante were loaded onto gurneys. It took all of Elsa's strength to move away from him. She didn't want to let go of his hand.

As they were wheeling Dante from the room, he grabbed Garrett's arm, pulling him close. Whatever Dante said, Garrett nodded.

Jazz came to stand beside Elsa. "I'm sorry I didn't believe you."

"But you trusted me enough to help anyway. That's all that matters."

Jazz wiped away an errant tear and nodded. "Dante will need this." She handed Elsa a plain leather wallet.

"What is it?" She opened the wallet, shocked to see a driver's license with Dante's picture, along with a library card, credit card—everything he'd need to answer any questions that came up at the hospital. "How did you—"

"Don't ask." Jazz smiled and shook her head. "Come on. We can ride along in the ambulances."

Elsa saved her questions for later. She held on to her

faith that everything would be okay. For the moment, she was grateful for the chance to be back at Dante's side. It was where she belonged.

Chapter Thirty-One

Summer Park, Florida—2016

The sun was shining brightly as Elsa sat at one of the tables in the hospital's outdoor eating area. Dante had refused to let her be in the room while he met with his doctors for his final post-op discussion.

He had spent most of the last few months with his face in bandages, needing several surgeries to recover. Apparently, he wanted a chance to deal with the aftermath on his own before letting her see the final results.

She respected his decision to not have her present when the bandages were removed, even though she hated not being at his side. At the first meeting Elsa had been present for, his reconstructive surgeon told them there might be further permanent damage, maybe even partial paralysis.

She had been preparing herself for the worst ever since, imagining what his face might look like in vivid detail so that she wouldn't wince or flinch in the slightest when she saw him. Already, his face had changed in her mind's eye —new scars added upon the old, his expressions muted from a loss of muscle control.

It killed her to think of him having to endure that. The least she could do was make sure he knew it didn't affect how she felt about him in the least.

All that mattered was that Dante was out of danger. Whatever resulted from the surgeries, they would handle it together. She was so grateful he was still with her.

To keep her mind off her nerves, she reviewed the latest copy of their manuscript. She and Dante had finished the first draft while he was recovering, and they were planning to celebrate as soon as this was behind them.

She imagined all the various ways they might go about that, smiling as her face probably flushed more from her wayward thoughts than the sun.

"Hello."

Elsa glanced at the stranger who stood next to her table. She'd been so engrossed in her thoughts she didn't notice him approach.

"Good afternoon." She turned back to the manuscript in the hopes that he'd get the hint and leave.

"May I?" Without waiting for an answer, he sat in the chair next to her.

Elsa sighed and said, "I'm not sure what this is about, but you should know, I'm not available."

When he didn't leave, she finally gave him her full attention. A slow smile spread across the man's face.

She had to admit it was a nice smile. A nice smile in a very nice face. A strangely familiar face.

The man's brown hair was highlighted from time in the sun and framed his face in gentle waves. He was handsome enough that he probably wasn't used to women rebuffing him.

Elsa stared at the man openly, a nagging doubt in the back of her mind. His eyes were bright turquoise against the pale blue sky, his jaw was strong, and his nose straight. There was a playfulness in his gaze that drew her in and made her like him.

"Have we met?" she asked.

His smile turned into something of a wicked grin, his full lips parting over straight, white teeth. Elsa knew that smile.

"I should certainly think so," he said, his rumbling voice oh so familiar.

"Dante?" Elsa gasped.

His smile broadened, the skin around his eyes crinkling from it. The skin around *both* eyes.

Elsa reached out and cradled his face in her hands, gingerly running her fingertips over his right temple and down along his cheek. She couldn't see any new damage at all, and more than that, his older scars were all but gone. The skin was a bit pinker than the rest of his face, a few white lines crossing the surface.

They'd addressed his scars while performing the reconstructive surgery.

"Before you say anything," Dante said, "I know you

were opposed to the idea of me undergoing what you considered unnecessary surgery. However, I had already consulted with Garrett shortly after the dance, and since surgery had become somewhat more necessary in the intervening time, we decided to take care of the matters all at once."

She didn't know what to say. She could tell that her mouth was hanging open, but she didn't have it in her to do anything about it. She just stared. This was Dante?

He scooted a little closer in his chair. "I know it is quite a change, and you would have preferred that we discuss the matter before I made such an important decision, but it was my last decision to make as a single man. So, as Jazz would say…" His grin became downright mischievous. "Deal with it."

Elsa couldn't find any words. She just stared at him. She was so used to how he looked before, it was almost unsettling to see him like this.

"What are you thinking?" Dante asked. His voice was a bit thin, as if he was worried about her reaction.

"I think you've been talking to Jazz too much."

Elsa leapt on him, kissing him probably more passionately than was advisable. But it had been so long since she'd been able to kiss him without worrying about sutures and bandages.

And he seemed *fine*. He didn't show any signs of pain as he smiled or narrowed his eyes, and from what she could see he hadn't lost any of his expressiveness.

She sat on his lap, finally coming up for air.

"I trust that means you like it," Dante said.

"I like that you're well and I can finally kiss you again. I can kiss you again, can't I?"

"I certainly hope so. Otherwise, I'm very confused about what we were just doing."

"You know what I mean. Did your doctor say everything's okay?"

"I am in perfect health, and the procedures went better than expected. We have no need to worry about lingering side effects, aside from the need to adjust to my new appearance."

"I think I'll live. As long as I can keep doing this."

And then she kissed him again, deeply and thoroughly. She didn't stop until something he said earlier rose up in her mind.

"Wait a minute. What do you mean, 'your last decision as a single man'?"

Dante rested his hands on her hips, guiding her first to stand and then sit in the chair opposite him. He knelt on one knee and produced a small black velvet box from his pocket. Elsa could feel her heart beat in her throat.

"Elsa Sinclair, you have given me a new world and a new life. I cannot imagine spending that life without you." The sunlight gleamed off the box's contents as he opened it. "Would you do me the incomparable honor of becoming my wife?"

"A lifetime with you? Absolutely. Yes!"

He paused, feigning a puzzled expression. "It occurs to me, perhaps I should have asked for more than one lifetime, given that you are a time traveler."

"I will gladly spend every lifetime with you."

With a gentle smile, he lifted her left hand in his and slid the ring in place. It was only then that she calmed enough to actually look at it.

"The ring... Your mother's ring. I thought you sold it."

"As did I. Jazz was to broker the exchange, but told me that she held it as collateral instead. She has been able to recoup the money she lent to me and more from selling my paintings and returned the ring when I told her I planned to propose."

"I can't believe you're all still making secret plans around me, and this time I didn't even notice."

"I should warn you that Rachel insists on designing the dress, and Jazz is already making plans for the event. I know you prefer to be in control of such things, but—"

"Are you kidding?" Elsa laughed. "I get to spend every day with you. I don't care about anything else."

"Don't forget the nights," he said, his smile softening.

"For the rest of our lives."

Dante leaned in to kiss her again. They had found the ending to their book, and Elsa knew in her heart that their story was only beginning.

Epilogue

Garrett leaned against a counter in the doctor's lounge, chugging another cup of coffee to stay on his feet. He didn't trust himself not to fall asleep if he dared to sit down. A dull ache filled his chest.

The bruises on Elsa's throat were mostly superficial. Damn, she had done a good job fighting off that psychopath. She was resting, sedated, so Garrett would need to wait to tell her Dante was out of surgery and doing well.

He wished he had more good news to share.

Last he saw, Jazz was sitting next to Elsa's bed, watching her like a hawk, dark eyes following anybody who dared come into the room. The nurses said it was sweet, but he knew better. Jazz was guarding Elsa, not just watching over her. If anyone dared to make a mistake in Elsa's treatment, Jazz would crush them, any way she could.

And she would come for him soon, full of questions. She would want to see Rachel, and Garrett would have to explain why that wasn't possible.

Rachel was on the fifth floor. The psych ward.

His hands were still shaking. The memory of Rachel being held down, strapped to a bed as she thrashed and screamed, begging Garrett for help, to make *the voices* stop... His stomach churned, the coffee rising into the back of his mouth with an acid finish.

After what Rachel had been through, he'd expected something, but not a full-blown psychotic break. It was killing him that he couldn't help her. And he had a feeling there was more going on with her than she was telling anyone.

As if being abducted and tortured, and then killing a man wasn't enough.

He turned around and punched the cabinet, hard. He'd feel it for days and he didn't care. The pain was a balm, took his mind off the terror of it all for a few seconds. Long enough to remember that Finn had left a voicemail hours ago, when Garrett's world was still bright and his friends all safe and whole. Garrett hadn't been able to listen to it yet.

He pulled out his phone, then hit *play* as he lifted it to his ear.

"Hey, man. I know you told me to stop digging into Dante Lucerne, but you're going to be glad I didn't. He isn't conning Elsa. That *Dante Lucerne* I told you about from the 1800s? It's the same guy! I don't know how she did it, but Elsa brought him here straight from that theatre fire that supposedly killed him. This is so fucking unbelievable!"

There was a pause where the only sound was Finn's quick footsteps. What the hell was Finn talking about? When he spoke again, his voice was quieter, but still thrummed with excitement.

"She didn't call the cops after the break-in because she's terrified of anyone finding out. After how cool you were when I showed you what I can do, I know you'll help her and not freak. And you need to know. I picked up another trail. Someone else is following her."

Garrett's stomach roiled again. Had the voicemail come in time for him to do something, to prevent what happened to his friends? Why hadn't he checked it sooner?

"I have a really bad feeling, Garrett. And you know what it means when I say that. Keep Elsa close, but be careful, man. I'm going to see what else I can dig up."

Garrett kept the phone to his ear, too stunned to move. If Finn said Dante was from the 1800s, Garrett believed it. Finn's word was beyond doubt. And as Garrett thought about it, pieces clicked together in his mind. It made sense.

How insane had his world become that time travel was the most rational explanation for a host of mysteries?

How insane…

His thoughts went back to Rachel on the fifth floor. Sweet, smart, sensitive Rachel, who had saved her friends but not herself.

Garrett wouldn't let her slip away, he wouldn't let this break her. If Elsa could travel through time to save Dante, Garrett sure as hell could help Rachel put the pieces of her life back together.

He would find a way.

—

I've always wanted to see the Phantom of the Opera get his "Happy Ever After". *Wandering Soul* is my vision for how that might unfold. This is only the beginning for the Summer Park Psychics! Rachel and Garrett face down their demons in the next book, *Whispering Hearts*. Then Jazz must confront her past to protect those she loves in *Lingering Touch*. This close-knit group of friends aren't out of danger yet! Read on for a sneak peek at *Whispering Hearts!*

Whispering Hearts

The Summer Park Psychics
Book Two

Prologue

Rachel hung from the chains that held her to the wall, her arms splayed like a dismal butterfly. Her wrists were searing points of agony, her knees throbbing from the cold cement beneath her. Holding still helped keep the pain at bay.

Nothing could help with the voices.

"The exhibit is opening tonight."

The peculiar echo that accompanied the voices of the dead sent a chill down Rachel's spine that had little to do with her circumstance. This one she recognized as Veronica. Her voice was higher than the others'. Gentler.

"They won't know. All those people looking at our portraits, and they won't even know what they're seeing."

"He'll kill her afterwards."

Pragmatic, forceful. That would be Anna. Rachel wondered if any others were present. From the conversations she had overheard, half a dozen spirits haunted Michael's garage.

"I can't watch him kill another one." Veronica's voice rose in volume, the echo growing with her distress. She let out a long, high wail.

Keening was the worst sound Rachel had ever heard. She couldn't stop the shuddering sob that wracked her body. She only hoped the ghosts didn't figure out it was more from their conversation than anything else. They couldn't figure out that Rachel heard them. She hadn't given up hope yet. If she made it out of this alive, she didn't want the dead to know that she was clairsentient.

Nicole joined the conversation, her deep voice distinct from the other two. *"At least she won't suffer as long as we did."*

"We should be here to help her in case she doesn't cross over," Anna said.

"There's nothing we can do to help her."

No one had a rejoinder for Nicole's statement. Finally, a moment of blessed silence.

Except for the thoughts churning through Rachel's mind. Garrett was always at the forefront—with his easy smile and gorgeous blue eyes. Garrett who always showed up whenever and wherever she needed him. This time, she was afraid he'd be too late.

She might never see him again. The idea tore at her heart, but at the same time, she wondered if he would be better off. No more need to rescue Rachel from her poor decisions or step in as her emergency date. No more mixed messages.

She did wish that she had kissed him. But she knew it wouldn't have ended there. If she had ever opened that door, he would've walked right through to meet her and been doomed to a lifetime of this—living with the dead. Knowing they were everywhere. Wondering every time her attention strayed if they were truly alone.

Keeping Garrett at arm's length had been a good choice. She only wished her judgment had been as sound with Michael.

There had been so many things she had explained away. The way he kept scaring Elsa by showing up at her house uninvited. The way he had talked about her friend, Dante.

Rachel had finally ended their relationship. Michael had seemed to take it well. When he'd asked her to sit for a portrait, she'd been too flattered to resist. That vanity might cost her everything.

She had ignored the voices, tuned out the whispers when she walked into Michael's house—even though she could tell there were so many of them. How could she have been so stupid?

Oh, right. Years of practice.

"I'm going to the gallery."

Rachel jerked her arms, startled by Nicole's voice close by. Her wrists sent lightning strikes of pain along her arms, punishing her for her loss of control. She feared the consequences of her lapse would be greater than that momentary increase in suffering.

Several moments of tense silence followed.

"Did you see that?" Veronica's voice. Right next to Rachel's ear. *"You don't think she can hear us, do you?"*

Rachel closed her eyes and focused on the pain. It was an easy distraction, with her nerves clamoring for attention. If the ghosts decided to test her, to shout at her or try to startle her, she could ignore them. When their attempts failed to get a response, they would decide she couldn't hear them.

Please let them decide she couldn't hear.

Light struck her retinas, burning through her eyelids. That was new. Rachel flinched away. She couldn't help herself. It was so bright.

"Rachel? Rachel, it's Elsa."

The voice was solid—no unearthly echo. And it was accompanied by touch. Soft, but firm.

Rachel opened her eyes. The bright lights made them burn, and she blinked several times, trying to bring the room into focus. The shelves and workbenches crowded into the garage filled her view. She turned her head and saw a small blonde woman next to her.

"Elsa?"

Elsa was kneeling on the floor at Rachel's side. How was that possible? Only one theory presented itself.

"Oh no. Did he get you too?" Michael had talked about Elsa after chaining Rachel to the wall. He had told her Elsa was his next "model".

"No, sweetie. We're here to rescue you."

"Oh thank God." Rachel trembled as another sob escaped. She leaned against Elsa and looked around the room, her eyes finally adjusting. No one else was in view. "How are you going to get me loose?"

Dante's face appeared above the workbenches. The

fluorescent lights washed out the red scars covering his right cheek and arcing across his forehead. "Do not be afraid. I will have you free presently."

"Dante?"

"Did you not recognize me with my new look?" His tone was playful, but Rachel could see the strain around his eyes, the tightness to his smile. He was wearing one of the new outfits that Rachel had bought for him. Dante's exhibit was opening tonight as well.

Rachel's heart seemed to freeze in her chest. Dante and Elsa were supposed to be starting a new life together—a life Rachel had helped him create. She had walked blithely into this nightmare, and now her friends were being dragged into it as well.

Metal clanked and rattled as Dante worked the winch that controlled her chains. Elsa helped support Rachel's arms as enough slack was let out for them to drop to her sides.

The winch was lined up so that Rachel could see Dante work. He was using the crowbar arm of a tire iron to try to pry loose the moorings that attached her chains to the floor. Michael always had a sick smile on his face when he let out slack or pulled them tighter, delighting in watching her suffer.

There was no way Dante could get her loose with that tool. Michael wore the key on his necklace. Rachel had asked about it when they'd just started dating. He'd said it was the key to his success. She shivered at the memory.

A pins-and-needles sensation in her arms let her know her circulation was returning. The burning would be nothing next to her wrists when more feeling returned there.

Rachel didn't care.

How many times was she going to let other people save her? How much longer could she play the fool before someone she loved was hurt trying to help?

She didn't know how they had found her, but Rachel couldn't let Elsa and Dante continue to endanger themselves. They needed to leave and call the police.

Rachel moaned. "That will take forever. Dante, you have to get Elsa out of here."

Elsa pulled Rachel closer, stroking her hair. "It's okay, Rachel. I'm not leaving without you."

"You don't understand. He wants you too."

"Well, he can't have me. And he can't have you, either."

Rachel had said such awful things to Elsa the last time they spoke. Yet here Elsa was, risking her life for Rachel. She gripped Elsa's arms, more sobs shaking her, listening to the rattle of the chains as Dante worked to get her free.

Elsa hugged Rachel tighter. "Dante…"

"I know. I am hurrying."

The voices began to whisper something, the echoes distorting their words, but not their urgency.

"Run."

"Run."

"Run!"

There was a brief pause, then Dante shouted, "Elsa, run!"

A sharp pop and the sound of breaking glass joined the sudden keening of the ghosts. Blood sprayed the shelves as Dante jerked back, then fell to his knees behind the workbenches, out of Rachel's sight. Elsa scrambled toward Dante as Michael stepped into view.

Rachel saw his gun first, then that horrible smile. Michael had them caught. He knew it. And he was enjoying every moment of their pain.

A hand appeared on top of one of the workbenches. Dante pulled himself up to stand, leaning on the heavy table. Rachel couldn't see his face. She knew that was a mercy. She could see the trail of blood still running down his neck, staining his shirt red.

Michael leveled the gun at Dante, stepping further into the garage. "This is more than I hoped for. I get Elsa hand-delivered, and the freak thrown in for free."

When he laughed, Rachel heard a faint echo from the ghosts—a grieving moan.

"I think I've made an improvement on your face," Michael said. "I can't believe that Jazz wanted me to share the opening with you. I'm a true artist. Not like you, with your boring little landscapes. How much are you willing to sacrifice for your art?"

Dante's voice was strained. "Art is about creation, not sacrifice."

"There is no creation without sacrifice. I'm willing to give up what I love most. Over and over again. I imbue the canvas with their essence. It's how I immortalize them."

"No, no, no..." A loud screech pierced Rachel's ears. She shook her head, but couldn't block out the sounds, no matter how hard she tried. Echoes, moans, sobs, prayers.

"And how many women have you immortalized?" Dante asked.

"How many paintings have I done?"

"Don't kill him!" the voices shrieked.

Rachel heard a thud, then something skittered toward her beneath the workbenches. The light glinted off of Michael's gun. Another thud brought her attention back to where Michael had been.

Without thinking, Rachel picked up the gun as she stood. She walked between the benches, ignoring the pain searing through her wrists as the chains rattled along behind her.

Dante was on the ground again, pulling himself toward Elsa. Michael was on top of her, his hands around her throat.

"No, please no. Don't kill him!" The voices were so distorted that Rachel couldn't tell who was speaking.

"She's going to free him!"

Michael was strangling Elsa, screaming at her as he did. "You think you can make a fool out of me? You're mine! You belong on my canvas. All of you!"

Elsa was fighting, but Michael was too strong.

"Don't kill him!"

"She'll set him free!"

Michael straightened his arms to avoid Elsa's fingernails as she clawed at his face, giving Rachel the opening she needed. She lifted the gun and pulled the trigger.

Red bloomed on his chest, spreading in a circle from the bullet hole. He looked down at the spot, then up to Rachel. His eyes were wide, full of surprise. Then he fell to the floor.

Rachel kept the gun trained on Michael's body. She wasn't sure if he was dead. Even with his eyes staring blankly at the room, it didn't feel as if he was dead.

"Run! Run! Run!"

The voices blurred together, growing fainter. Michael's presence remained strong.

Elsa was coughing, but that meant she could breathe. She rolled away from Michael's body as Rachel approached.

He needed to die. Why wouldn't he die? Rachel pulled the trigger again. And again and again. She kept pulling it even when all the rounds were spent.

She still felt him in the room.

Elsa stood and staggered toward Rachel. That wasn't right. Dante should be Elsa's main concern. But Elsa hugged Rachel instead, one hand sliding down her arm to the gun.

She let Elsa take it. Rachel didn't care. There was nothing more it could do to help them.

She wondered if it had really helped them at all.

—

You can get *Whispering Hearts* now! I'd love to keep in touch. Join my newsletter to get sneak peeks and behind-the-scenes insight into my many worlds, and check out other ways to join my community on my website at cassandra-chandler.com/community. I really want to know what *you* think. If you enjoyed this book, please consider leaving a review at your favorite book review site. I'd really appreciate it—reviews help readers and authors alike!

Thank you for reading *Wandering Soul!*

Cassandra Chandler

About the Author

USA Today Bestselling author Cassandra Chandler uses her vivid imagination to make the world more interesting, spawning the ideas she turns into her captivating Science Fiction Romances and enthralling Paranormal and Urban Fantasy Romances. Fast-paced and funny, lighthearted or filled with suspense, her stories will introduce you to characters you'll fall in love with and worlds you long to explore.

www.ingramcontent.com/pod-product-compliance
Lightning Source LLC
Chambersburg PA
CBHW070307040726
47501CB00018B/381